BOOKS BY

KATHLEEN NORRIS

THE FOOLISH VIRGIN
WHAT PRICE PEACE?
BEAUTY AND THE BEAST
THE FUN OF BEING A MOTHER
MY BEST GIRL
BARBERRY BUSH
THE SEA GULL
HILDEGARDE
THE BLACK FLEMINGS
LITTLE SHIPS
NOON
ROSE OF THE WORLD
THE CALLAHANS AND THE MURPHYS
BUTTERFLY
CERTAIN PEOPLE OF IMPORTANCE
LUCRETIA LOMBARD
THE BELOVED WOMAN
HARRIET AND THE PIPER
SISTERS
JOSSELYN'S WIFE
UNDERTOW
MARTIE, THE UNCONQUERED
THE HEART OF RACHAEL
THE STORY OF JULIA PAGE
THE TREASURE
SATURDAY'S CHILD
POOR, DEAR MARGARET KIRBY
THE RICH MRS. BURGOYNE
MOTHER

THE FOOLISH VIRGIN

THE
FOOLISH VIRGIN

BY
KATHLEEN NORRIS

THE BLAKISTON COMPANY
PHILADELPHIA

This Triangle Edition is published
By arrangement with Doubleday, Doran and Company, Inc.

REPRINTED DECEMBER 1944
REPRINTED MARCH 1945

Decorations by Howard Willard

Because of the acute shortage of regular book cloth
under war-time rationing, this book is bound in a
sturdy paper fabric especially designed for this purpose.

TRIANGLE BOOKS is a series published by
The Blakiston Company, 1012 Walnut St., Philadelphia 5, Pa.

PRINTED AND BOUND IN THE UNITED STATES OF AMERICA
BY THE AMERICAN BOOK—STRATFORD PRESS, INC., N. Y. C.

TO ROSEMARY

Niece, daughter, confidante, companion-cook,
    Counsellor, comrade, dearest of the dear,
    When all I have is yours, why make it clear
That doubly yours is one especial book?
Is it perhaps to see your grave surprise
    When first you read these lines; perhaps to see
    A certain slow, reproachful smile for me
Caught by your eyes from unforgotten eyes?

THE FOOLISH VIRGIN

CHAPTER I

FOG. It came creeping in over the blue Pacific like an army with banners, advancing steadily, irresistibly, across the burned, flat meadows beside the sea, rolling over the low line of the coast hills, and burying all sleeping Carterbridge, and a score of smaller, tributary villages and towns, under a blanket of creamy and impenetrable mist.

Carterbridge had looked up at a velvet summer sky spangled with a million stars, on Thursday night. This was Friday morning—the most important Friday morning of the whole year, the festal Friday of Rodeo Week. The town had long awaited this day; it was decked from one end of its brief business district to another with flags and bunting and lanterns.

But there was no town when the citizen who chanced

to be earliest astir looked forth into the dull yellow opaque glimmer that did duty for dawn. There was no real dawn this morning. There was only the ghost of a fence or a garage wall, here and there, dimly sketched in yellow-gray upon the gently undulating, pulsing, changing layers of the fog. Street corners were lost, telegraph poles disappeared into a sky of warm, closely pressing mist, and postmen and milkmen loomed suddenly, ominously, like giants, close at hand, without sign or sound of their familiar approach.

Carterbridge, lying in one of the brown California valleys that go down past scattered ranches to the rolling open sea, knew her fog. She knew that for the hundred mornings of every summer that ever came, scarfs and streamers of mist would drape the town at breakfast time, to be dissipated into golden sunshine long before noon. But a fog like this—one of the real old-fashioned kind—had not been anticipated by even the most pessimistic director of the Rodeo. This, opined Carterbridge gloomily, awakening on the first of the two great Rodeo days, this would "cost the town good money!"

Roads were unsafe this morning, early motor cars were accompanied along the highways by the constant cautious honking of horns. Heavy dews dripped from the dejected plumes of the towering eucalyptus trees and pearled the drooping green whips of the willows. Peppers and eucalyptus and Spanish willows, in a heavy fog, on a mid-July morning—there was all California in a phrase. Not one's idea of summer. "But then," said one of the town's mildest little residents philosophically, "when you think of blizzards an' thunderstorms an' all the things folks have in the East, Mr. Silver, it doesn't seem like we ought to complain!"

Mr. Silver was a postman. He said cordially: "That's right, ain't it?"

"An' tornadoes and hurricanes," Mrs. Raleigh added.

"That's right," said the postman again, departing. "Children well?" he asked, jerking his heavy bag to his shoulder.

"They're both real well, thank you."

"They'll be out at the Rodeo to-day, I s'pose?"

"Oh, I suppose so. They just don't have anything *but* good times," the woman said, sighing contentedly.

He was gone, and she stood at the side door for a minute, watching the warm fog sinking and swelling softly among the near-by colourless shadows that were rose bushes and tall shrubs, watching fingers of it spread themselves like spilled cream over the shabby side wall that was buried in black ivy.

Then she turned back into the dilapidated old house, crossed a hall scented with plaster and dust and food and rotting fabrics, and mounted the stairway to an upper front bedroom, with windows opening into the mist-dimmed upper branches of tall pear and enormous oak trees.

She went to the bedside, touched a sleeper there gently—then more vigorously.

"Pam, are you awake?"

There was no movement under the humped blankets, but beneath Pamela Raleigh's tumbled mop of tawny hair an eye opened intelligently, and the girl's voice said affectionately:

"No. But come in, M'ma. Hello, darling, how are you, and what kind of a day is it for the Rodeo?"

She tossed the covers from her shoulders, rolled over, and stretched a long arm to jerk another pillow under her head. So propped, she lay regarding her mother with a sleepy but welcoming smile.

"It's terrible. There's the most awful fog we've ever had," Mrs. Raleigh said in a mildly complaining little voice, as she sat down close to the bed. "I s'pose they'll have the Rodeo," she went on, "but it seems as if you could hardly see the horses!"

"Don't tell me," Pam said, in a low, shocked voice, "that that horrible clock is right?"

"Yes, it is—it's half-past eleven," her mother said, with a sort of aggrieved triumph.

"And I've got to be at Sue Rose's for lunch at half-past twelve sharp!"

But Pam made no effort toward arising, none the less; the panic was merely in her voice. Physically she remained inert, her face flushed from deep sleep, her hands locked behind her tousled head, and her long slim figure stretched straight beneath the blankets.

"Have you been out, or are you going out, M'ma?"

"I was goin' down to Judge Beaver's," the older woman said in an absent-minded voice. Her thoughts were evidently elsewhere. "Pamela——" she began with an effort.

"Go ahead, dear!" the daughter said, almost encouragingly.

"Pam," Mrs. Raleigh began again painfully, "I really—I really *cannot* stand it any longer!"

The girl settled herself. Her voice was patient.

"What now?"

"How late"—the older woman made the plunge—"how late were you-all out last night?"

"About three," Pamela answered unhesitatingly.

"About three! Yo' grandmother," said Mrs. Raleigh bitterly, "would turn in her grave!"

"It might be a wonderful thing for her if she did," the girl remarked cheerfully. "Nothing like a change!"

"Yo' brother," the other woman continued reproachfully, "was home an' asleep befo' you came in!"

"But that only means"—Pamela was still affectionate and undisturbed—"that only means that I was having a good time, M'ma, and that Carter wasn't!"

"I really do not know what the mothers of this town are goin' to *do*," Mrs. Raleigh resumed, on a desperate note. "Young girls yo' age an' Maisie's age—runnin' round until three o'clock in the mornin', with no chaperon——"

"But, darling, chaperons went out with puffed sleeves!"

"No chaperons," the loving little voice continued disconsolately. "Drivin' about with boys in speed cars, smokin'—when I just kissed you now all I could smell on yo' hair was smoke—drinkin'—I tell you, Pam, it's dangerous an' it's bad, an' the time's comin' when you're goin' to see it like I do——"

"M'ma dearest," the girl said, amused and penitent and wholly charming, as she raised herself on her elbow, and stretched out her smooth young hand to pat her mother's hand placatingly, "things are just as they always have been! We're no worse than the girls were when you were young; we just do things differently, that's all. Men used to sow their wild oats, and girls used to flirt—you told me yourself that your Aunt Katie was engaged to two men at once, and everyone thought that was all right. We just—we just have our fashions in shocking our elders, and you get scared because they're different!"

"We had good times, we used to have spider-web parties, an' play ping-pong, an' dance barn dances, an'

I don't know what all," Mrs. Raleigh protested. "But we never allowed boys to kiss us, an' as for goin' off alone with men at night—well, any girl that did that was called fast, that's what *she* was called!"

"But, listen, darling," Pam said, bunching her finger tips close to her face, and studying her nails attentively. "Listen, darling. When it comes to girls like Patricia Miller, we *do* draw the line——"

"Well, my gracious, I hope so!" the older woman said, scandalized.

"Not that I wouldn't bow to Pat, and all that, if I met her," Pamela resumed musingly. "But she never was a Cinderella Club girl, M'ma, you must remember that! And lots and lots of girls aren't in the Cinderella, simply because they aren't nice. Doris Runyon, for instance. Doris would give her eyes to get in. We do have an awfully good time, I'll admit that, and we're not prudes——"

"Prudes!" Mrs. Raleigh echoed in nervous scorn. "No, if there's one thing you girls aren't, it's that!"

"But now, seriously, what's the harm, M'ma? There's no real harm in cigarettes—I don't smoke half as much as some of the girls, anyway. There's no real harm in an occasional taste of something stronger than ginger ale—why, some of the finest men in the world have been drinkers. There's no harm in having a boy kiss you; old ladies kiss each other, and everyone kisses children and——"

"Pam, you're talkin' absolute nonsense!" Mrs. Raleigh said sharply, becoming irritated. "An occasional dance or drive, or maybe even a kiss, might be all right. But there is something about a girl smokin' an' drinkin' that fairly makes my flesh creep."

"But that's just your prejudice, M'ma! Men have

smoked for generations, and women have admired and loved them just the same. And as for liquid refreshments," the girl said, with her joyous laugh, "haven't you told me a thousand times that my grandfather Carter, right in this very house, *always* had claret and everything else on the table?"

"An' that's a very different thing from the way you youngsters do it now," Mrs. Raleigh said, with a sort of vexed dignity. "Runnin' down to the Arms pretty nearly every afternoon of yo' lives, lettin' this one an' that one carry you off for dances at places decent people wouldn't go to—I tell you, Pam, it's dangerous. A girl has to remember that she could lose mo' than her life, takin' chances with all sorts of men."

"If a girl has any sense she doesn't have to take chances!"

Pamela had got out of bed before this, and had gone to the window, standing, a tall girl in faded blue pajamas, to stare down at the jungle of trees and shrubs and overgrown garden flowers below, all shrouded and dripping this morning in the warm, creamy folds of the summer fog. Now she was wandering about the rooms, opening closet door and bureau drawers, and assembling on the bed her costume for all-important Rodeo Day.

"When I came in here this mornin'," said her mother, "yo' good dress was lyin' right in the middle of the flo', yo' slippers looked like you had been dancin' in mud . . ."

The dissatisfied little anxious voice continued on and on. Pam went about quite undisturbed.

"This isn't disrespect, M'ma," the girl called, from the bathroom, when a great splashing presently testified to the vigour of her ablutions, "but I am in the world's greatest rush!" she pleaded, reappearing, breathless and sweet, clad only in a brief peach-coloured garment, energetically towelling her beautiful mop of lustreless, tawny hair.

"I wish there was somep'n I could say that'd make you see just what silly risks you're takin'," her mother said discontentedly.

The girl, seated on the side of her bed, was running an exploratory hand into a transparent silk stocking. Now she drew a pair of these up on her slender legs and stepped into a small pair of white buckskin pumps.

"Florrie," said she then anxiously, "did you remember to put an iron on?"

"Yes, I did," Mrs. Raleigh answered, baffled in her righteous attempt to deliver a sermon, and speaking, for her, quite crossly.

"Oh, you angel! You're what I call a good mother," Pam said gratefully, tying herself into a limp kimono, catching up several garments, and balancing a small felt hat on her fingers as she went downstairs.

Her mother followed her through the damp, dark magnificence of the shabby old house. Brass rails were loosened on the imposing curved stairway, and the splendid Moquettes that had been laid on the floors of hall, drawing room, and dining room fifty years ago were worn down to the ugly brown webbing.

Most of the high old windows were curtained in rotting rep. Behind their dusty panes the fog showed, pressing urgently against the house, making the garden and yard only places of vague shapes and gently undulating opaque veils of mist.

Pamela led the way briskly to the kitchen, where, as always, the coffee pot was kept hot on a small gas stove for her, and a small fat cream-coated bottle, half full, awaited on the table, with rolls and butter.

The last regular servant had left the Carter house in Pamela's babyhood; the girl could remember in her place only occasional intervals of slatternly Mexican women from Carterbridge's poorest quarter, or Japanese houseboys from orchard ranches, who were sometimes procurable in winter, but never to be had when there was fruit to pick. The Raleighs could afford little service now, and that little was of the cheapest.

She poured herself a cup of coffee, produced an ironing board, and while she breakfasted was busy pressing a slim little shapeless dress of white silk, a scarf striped with all the colours of the rainbow, and a beaded evening dress of pink satin.

"If I don't do this now, I'll never have time for it!" she murmured, spreading crushed tulle with nervous, clever finger, and holding the iron close to her peachy cheek to test it. "Don't do the dishes until later, M'ma," she pleaded. "Sit down and talk! What'd you do last night?"

"What I want to know is what you did?" Mrs. Raleigh persisted. But she obediently and idly seated herself, and her tone was mollified.

"It was the Cinderella Club's monthly dance at the Club, darling. We all went to Sue Rose's first——"

"An' had cocktails!" the mother said resentfully. "I declare I don't know what the mothers in this town are thinkin' of!" she muttered to herself.

"The boys did. But if they didn't get it there——"

"Pamela, I know *you* don't. But just *tell* me you don't!" begged her mother.

"I had about—that much!—of Harry's." Pam measured an infinitesimal space between thumb and finger.

Mrs. Raleigh, a small, faded, birdlike person, made a sound of utter exasperation, hooked her little feet on the chair rail under her, bit her lip, and looked at the ceiling, violently holding her peace.

"An' were all of you—the whole Cinderella Club—out of your homes until three o'clock?" she presently demanded darkly.

"Oh, no! Only a few of us. We went down to the Arms," Pam admitted blithely, "and danced. And then, about two, we went into 'Bob's' for coffee. The whole town is full of Rodeo boys, and there were a lot at Bob's. We had"—she pounded on the iron, regarded her work critically, and repeated the little phrase as contentedly as if she did not use it every day afresh—"we had the time of our lives!"

"You didn't dance with any of those cowboys?"

"Oh, didn't I? There's one darling called Goldie Dunton, and he and I—did we dance? I'll say that we danced. Why, M'ma, you told me once you thought I ought to ask Gregory Chard to a party, and what is he but a cowboy?"

Mrs. Raleigh, like all the women of her type, was never so serious as when touching upon the sacred subject of genealogical claims.

"Pam, he's no such thing! He may live down there with those Mexican hands of his, but his mother was a fine girl, came of one of the oldest Spanish families in this state, that boy has good blood in his veins! His father was an English gentleman, and *his* father—Gregory's grandfather—was what they call a younger son. He came here a pioneer, no money, but a fine family. He married a Mrs. Charteris, a widow," pursued

Mrs. Raleigh, absorbed in the subject. "She had a little boy——"

"Well, anyway, he wasn't there," the girl, half-listening, interrupted after a while, "and a lot of the others were, and we were all too tired to care much what we did. Oh, and, M'ma!"—enthusiasm rose in Pam's voice and her eyes danced—"I didn't tell you! Chester Hilliard's back. Perfectly stunning! They say old Porter Hilliard's going to take him into the bank in poor Jim's place. Anyway, he's staying at the Hilliards'—and he's a *sheik*. He and I and Sue Rose and the Beavers—about seven of us—went on to Bob's Coffee Parlour; the others went home. And it was then that we had the real *fun*."

"Doris Runyon wasn't there?" the older woman asked suspiciously.

"Well—yes, for a while," Pam admitted unwillingly. Her mother, deeply displeased, was silent.

"Maisie didn't go with you, I notice," she began again presently. "I guess Dr. Broome has too much good sense to let his daughter run 'round."

"Well, *he* may have," said Pam good-naturedly, "but Maisie hasn't. It makes her perfectly wild to have to go home at half-past ten o'clock, except on special occasions, and not to be allowed to smoke, and all the rest of it. She was about ready to cry last night."

"She'll be glad some day!" the older woman predicted warningly.

"But *why?* What's the harm?" the girl asked reasonably. "Mrs. Catherwood was giving Sue Rose a terrible scolding yesterday, it seems. Sue Rose was telling me about it. Mrs. Catherwood and Sue Rose's aunt and her grandmother were all calling her down, and they said, 'We want you to grow up pure and

sweet and innocent, dear, as your mother did. We
don't want you to smoke and drink and let boys kiss
you and pet'—well, maybe they didn't use that expression," Pam corrected herself, "but that was the meaning. They said, 'We want you to preserve your
sweetness and not to make yourself cheap and common
with boys.' And Sue Rose simply looked from one to
the other and said, 'Why?' Isn't it wonderful?" Pamela added, with a laugh of relish. "Do you know,
M'ma, not one of them could answer her!"

"Well, there's plenty of reason why!" Mrs. Raleigh
said rashly.

"But *what* reason? I'm not a fool," Pam argued.
"I'm not a mid-Victorian heroine, to have a disappointment in love, and be—'led astray'——"

"Pamela!"

"Well, I'm *not*, M'ma. We're just honest, that's all.
If we like a boy, we'd just as soon kiss him as kiss a
girl, or a baby, or an old uncle or grandfather——"

"You're talkin' perfect nonsense, Pam! There's such
a thing as—as fallin' in love."

"I know it. And I hope to do it. In the meanwhile,
I'm having all the fun I can. Why, look here, darling,"
the girl said comfortingly, "how many people are there
in this town? Sixty thousand? Sixty thousand. And we
have schools and libraries and banks and canneries
and trolley cars and radio stations, haven't we? And
isn't the Cinderella Club the smartest in this town?
Isn't it?"

"Well, yes, it is," Mrs. Raleigh admitted, softening.

"Aren't there plenty of girls—and girls' mothers,
too—who are breaking their necks to get into the Cinderella?"

"There surely are."

"Well, and aren't your own two beautiful children *prominent* in the Cinderella Club? Is there a girl in the club more popular than—— Look at me. Am I beautiful?"

Having pressed the actual garments she intended to wear, she had been dressing while she talked; slipping the little tube-like white dress over her head, as she threw the kimono aside, jerking its trim folds into place over her slim, boyish figure, pulling the small blue hat down over her tawny hair. Now she hung the gay scarf about her throat, catching it under the collar of a little white coat whose cuffs and collar were faced with blue, and pulled on immaculate loose white gloves.

"What the young gell will wear to the Rodeo!" she said gaily.

"You look lovely, Pam," her mother had to say.

"I look lovely, everything *considered*," the girl said, studying herself keenly in a small mirror beside the dining-room door. "Maisie spends hundreds on clothes, and Sue Rose practically can charge anything, and I have pretty near as many! I don't see how I do it. I must be smart, Florrie."

"You *are* smart, dearie," her mother said sadly.

Something in the gentle, discouraged voice touched the girl as no reproach or blame had done, and she came, belted and hatted and gloved, the picture of smart and exquisite girlhood, to sit childishly on the arm of her mother's rocker and embrace the small, withered form as she said reassuringly:

"It's not half as bad as you think, darling. Why, we Cinderellas are considered exclusive—we're proud of ourselves. And I *am* a Raleigh, you know," Pam went on whimsically, humouring the other's favourite fancy, "and my grandfather Carter *did* give the ground for the library and the race track, and we're—we're *the* people of Carterbridge! Aren't we, Florrie? So cheer up. I'll not disgrace you, and one of these days I'll give you a fine son-in-law, and about ten nice little grand-children."

"I wish you would!" her mother said lovingly, fervently, anxiously. "No, I don't mean the grandchildren," she went on, with a smile. "They can wait. But you're so fine," she went on, with a little emotion, "there's so many things you can do—so many better things than runnin' round with this crowd all night an' sleepin' all day long. You've not got any father to stand up for you, Pam, an' you and yo' brother 've got to make yo' own friends an' yo' own way. An' I guess that's what worries me, dearie—seein' you such a power among the young folks, an' so much admired, an' yet not feelin' happy about you!"

Pamela was serious now, looking down at the floor, while she balanced on the arm of the rocker, kept her arm closely about her mother, and gently rubbed the top of her mother's head with her soft cheek.

"But we all do it, darling. Everybody rouges and smokes and jazzes and pets, nowadays! I'm no worse than the rest."

"But you will be careful, dearie? It takes so little to have a girl talked about!"

Another laugh from Pam, at the door now.

"It used to, M'ma. But nowadays it's different!— Cart Raleigh, didn't you go to market for M'ma?" the girl said accusingly, as her twin, wrapped in his dressing gown, unshaven and dishevelled of hair, came smiling into the kitchen.

He gave his mother the serene, sleepy kiss of an adored baby, and kissed his sister, too.

"Gosh, you smell sweet, Pam!"

"Oh, Cart, I thought you were going out to market for M'ma!" Pam said, lovingly reproachful. "Did she have to go herself?"

"I didn't mind," the mother said hastily, feasting her eyes upon the slim, tall, tawny boy and the slim, tall, tawny girl—a lovely sight together, for as Pamela was the prettiest and most aristocratic-looking girl in Carterbridge, so her twin was certainly the handsomest boy. Their smooth young cheeks burned clear apricot colour, their gray eyes smiled in exactly the same sleepy, Oriental fashion, and the soft, rich, lustreless fair hair curled about their broad low foreheads in exactly the same lines and curves.

"I would have gone!" Pam said rebukingly.

"Yes, you would!" Carter countered good-naturedly, busy now with his own breakfast. "You were home later than I was!"

"Well, I was with the crowd."

"Say, that reminds me," the boy said animatedly, looking up. "How'd you like Chester Hilliard? Did you tell M'ma he's here again?"

"It must be ten years since that boy went East," Mrs. Raleigh mused. "Yes, it was, because you were nine when he was about sixteen, and he came with little Jim Hilliard to your birthday party."

"And he remembers that party, too, to this day," Pam said, a little self-consciously. "He told me last night what games we played, and what we had to eat, and everything."

"I hear you lifted him painlessly off Maisie Broome," her brother suggested.

"He doesn't belong to Maisie!"

"If you did, it was Dirty Trick Number One Thou-

sand Two Hundred and Eighteen," Carter commented, after a moment's shrewd scrutiny of his sister's fluctuating colour and an inexplicable deep laugh
over his cup.

"No, but isn't he a heart-breaker?" the girl asked.
"Scholarly, M'ma," she told the other woman enthusiastically, "slim and dark—oh, Eastern collegey, you
know. And with such a pleasant voice. Maisie knew
him when she was in Connecticut at school—that's all
the claim Maisie has on him!" she added, apparently
for her own satisfaction.

"I hear you annexed him, and that he was asking
everyone why the movies hadn't gotten you, and what
not," Carter drawled lazily.

Her happy colour flashed up again, and there was an
abashed laugh in her gray eyes.

"Who on earth told you any nonsense like that?"

"I s'pose he'll come in for poor Jim's share of that
fortune," Mrs. Raleigh was thinking aloud. She was
accustomed to Pam's meteoric affairs of the heart; she
paid small attention to them. The girl was too popular,
too busy, to take anything seriously—as witness this
morning's maternal scolding. "Jessy'll get a lot. But if
he goes into the bank with Mr. Porter Hilliard he's a
pretty lucky young man!"

She accompanied her daughter to the side door, and
they looked out together at the depressing weather.
Carter Avenue was lined with big trees, locusts and
maples and sycamores, planted fifty years before, and
in some of the gardens the natural oaks spread their
tremendous gnarled arms as well. Two blocks beyond
ran the town's main thoroughfare, the old Camino
Real of the Spanish padres, the Royal Highway of
the Cross, that had knitted San Diego and San Jose

together in the long-ago days of sheep herding and vine growing.

It was a flourishing business street in Carterbridge now, the Camino, lined with parked cars and theatres and banks and restaurants, with a trolley humming briskly along its tree-shaded length, and drug stores that flashed electric signs at night.

But just now something of its old frontier pictur-esqueness had returned, for the two great days of the Rodeo; visitors were pouring in from as far north as Sacramento and as far south as Santa Barbara, and there was hardly a man, woman, or child in town whose costume was not enriched by a gay handker-chief, carelessly knotted about the throat, a cowboy shirt in violent shades of green or yellow satin, or a belled sombrero worn in defiance of the gently enclos-ing and dimming fog.

All down the Camino lengths of red, white, and blue bunting hung limp in the mist; motor cars, blundering in from contributory highways, honked confusedly and moved cautiously to and fro, and frankfurter and pop-corn stands, gallantly holding their own against the general depression of the day, sent shrill whistles into the heavy, silencing air.

Up in the little Plaza, under towering eucalyptus and heavily fruited fig trees, a band played bravely at intervals. The crowds surged to and fro in the warm murky gloom: mothers of families in limp voile gowns, children impatient and interrogatory, cowboys magnifi-cently self-conscious, leading their dancing horses, or mounted upon them, and cowgirls, strangely simple, sweet creatures straight from mountain ranches, with hard faces, and heavily ringleted or clubbed hair fall-ing on their lean necks. Rouged, capped like jockeys,

awkward in tight trousers and stiff boots, clad in yellow satin blouses, these went proudly, absorbedly,
authoritatively upon their way, elbowing against mere
onlookers, elaborately unconscious of admiring eyes.

There would be no parade to-day, everyone told
everyone else, but of course there would be a show.
No parade to-day—no parade to-day—voices said, up
and down the fog-filled Camino, but of course the
show'll go right along. Tough luck, huh? No parade.
But the show would be all right. Why, what would be
the use of parading? You couldn't see half a block
away, much less the length of the Camino!

She was lifting a little, though. Sure, she was lifting.
But there wouldn't be any parade.

"No parade. But he says the show's goin' on justa
same, Señor!" said a tall, handsome Spanish boy, coming out to the corrals at about noon, down on the old
Rancho del Molino Solitario, on the very shores of the
Pacific.

The master of some four thousand spreading brown
acres of cattle pasture and sunburned beaches looked
up sharply from the concerned inspection of a horse's
hoof.

"Who said so?"

"She 'phone'," explained the boy.

"Who 'phoned?"

"The Jush."

"Judge Beaver, huh?" the other muttered, standing
up, drawing a long breath, and dusting together the
palms of big, hard, brown hands. "Oh, all right. We
don't have to hurry, then. Tell Bill this mare's all
O.K., and send some of the boys in to me. I'm going to
get my dinner."

He turned toward the fog-smothered outlines of an old hacienda, lying low and long under old trees and facing the sea. All about it were mighty barns, sheds, stables, and fences; an enormous windmill, with a smithy beneath it, rose four-square for some fifteen feet and was then lost in mist.

Everything was drooping, disguised, masked to-day. The very dogs—and there were a score of them, of various sizes and breeds—moved about bewildered and subdued. There were tiny beadings of water on the pale red berries of the pepper trees, and the old plaster-walled dining room, in which Gregory Chard presently seated himself for his *chili con carne* and red beans, was so darkened by the unfriendly weather that Maria, one of many slipshod Spanish and Mexican women who attended to his wants, had lighted two candles upon the littered table.

Lamps, books, writing materials, a leather whip and fringed gauntlets, a bottle of horse medicine, a hunting knife and a fishing creel, gun oil, a ball of string, with half a hundred other small miscellaneous articles, had been jumbled carelessly on one end of this table; the red cloth bunched into high folds as it was pushed aside to make room for Gregory's plate. He was sitting, a mighty, brown young man in corduroy riding breeches and a faded old shirt, his black hair tumbled, and his black eyes absent and contented, like a child's eyes, eating, when a group of two or three other young men entered the room and scattered to chairs.

"This is a hell of a nice day for the Rodeo," one of them said sourly. The others ruefully laughed.

"You fellers had your dinner?" Gregory asked over his fork.

The disconsolate cowboys nodded. They sighed,

shifted their fringed and spurred legs, and lighted cigarettes. Their shirts, all checked, were of the brightest shades of red, yellow, and green; they wore neckerchiefs of violently contrasted colours.

"Rotten day for the Rodeo, Mr. Chard," one of them muttered, for the tenth time.

"Well, all right. But what can you do about it?"

"It's a lousy break!" another man grumbled.

Chard said nothing. Eating *chili con carne* and sour Mexican bread, he looked on their discomfiture with a grin that shone dazzlingly white in the Indian brown of his handsome face. Younger than most of them, yet there was a certain easy and insolent poise about him, a certain Latin sureness and brevity that marked him obviously the master of them all. He was dressed more simply than the rest, his shirt white, his high laced boots old, his coat of well-worn leather, and he wore no handkerchief about his throat. But, as Mrs. Raleigh had pleaded in his defence, Gregory Chard had good American and English blood in his veins, as well as the simpler strain from Castile, and it showed in every gesture and every word.

"It don't matter what we do to-day, there won't nobody see us!" said a slim boy in angora chaps and a heavily embroidered hat. "I'll bet you can't see the tracks from the grand stand, day like this!"

"It's good for your complexion, Goldie," said Chard.

"That's all right, that's all right," the boy said surlily, in the general laugh.

"Goldie danced with Miss Pamela Raleigh at Coffee Bob's last night," one of the lazy, drawling, uncultivated voices volunteered significantly, "and he sees himself cuttin' up in front of that grand stand to-day like a moving-pitcher sheik!"

"Danced with *who?*" the master of the house, suddenly interested, demanded, scowling.

"I was sayin' that some of us went into that coffee place last night, after we'd done all the pitchers an' dance halls we could find," one of the original speakers explained, "an' there was some of the swells in there, an' Miss Raleigh, she was just havin' the time of her life, an' she sent word over to Goldie that she'd dance with him if he ast her."

"Who said she did?" Gregory asked harshly.

"We was *there*, Greg," a specially privileged old friend said mildly.

"When? Last night?"

"Yep. A lot of us went in there to get some coffee before we started home last night. 'Bout half-past one, maybe."

"There was a Cinderella Club dance at the Country Club last night, Al," Gregory Chard said. "You saw somebody else at Coffee Bob's."

"No, I guess they come in there later, Greg; it was her all right," the man persisted. "The little Catherwood girl was with 'em, an' the Beaver boys. An' Doris Runyon was there, too, with Billy Allerton."

"Is that so?" Chard asked, nodding indifferently. He was silent for a moment. "I didn't know they'd go into a joint like that," he said then. "It's all right, but it seems a little rough for girls. All right, Maria—I'm finished. You girls are going with Berto in the old car, are you? Got your tickets?—Hang on to 'em. Come on, fellers, let's go. Who's bringing up the horses?"

He went into the adjoining room, the only one, except for the kitchen and the general living room in which he had his meals, that was used in the enormous hacienda. Like the living room, his bedroom was disorderly and uncomfortable; there was a jumble of heavy covers on the flat wooden bed; there were no curtains on the small, square window openings, deepset, with whitewashed adobe sills; there was a tangle of old rug on the floor. A tin-encased shower bath had been set up in a corner; casual towels, garments, leather straps, spurs, books, open typewritten letters with business headings knives and guns, further furnished the room; a kerose.. lamp stood by the bed; the shutters were wide open, and the fog was making a silent, gently persistent entry.

There were no pictures in the room, but stuck into the frame of a wavy-lined mirror over the marbletopped walnut bureau was a halfsheet roughly trimmed from an illustrated Sunday newspaper. Underneath it was the caption:

MISS PAMELA FAIRFAX RALEIGH

One of the buds of the past season, prominent member of the Cinderella Club, unanimously elected Queen of the approaching Mardi Gras Ball.

Gregory poured water from an old ewer, washed his hands, and combed his thick, heavy black hair. He took a much-worn, stiff-brimmed sombrero from a wooden peg and pulled it over his eyes.

During this time he had studied the picture steadily. Now he took it from its place and stood looking at it even more intently.

"So you dance with cowpunchers, do you, Miss Pamela?" he asked, half aloud. "Is that *so?* You think that's funny, I guess. Go down to Coffee Bob's after midnight, and mix in with greasers and roughnecks and cowpunchers, that's the idea."

The girl smiled up at him confidently; he had seen her in evening dress once or twice, when he had made himself go to one of the less exclusive dances at the Club or at the Carterbridge Arms. He had seen her in just such a gown, a tall, slim, spangled creature, with her curly hair framing her exquisite, proud young face, just like that, and the slender, haughty cut of the chin and throat and beautiful shoulders accentuated by the long earrings.

"You're the handsomest girl in this town, or in any town," Gregory said to her, in a whisper, "and I guess you think a good deal of your folks, too—that little widowed mother of yours does, anyway. And you go down to Coffee Bob's the night before Rodeo Day, with the whole town full of crooks and rough-necks——"

He could hear an increasing racket outside now; champing feet and the clatter of decorated harness. The boys had brought the horses up; it was time to start for the Rodeo.

"Goldie Dunton!" Gregory said disgustedly. He crushed the newspaper clipping with one big brown hand, and going into the adjoining room he opened the top of an airtight stove that had been attached to the big black-mouthed fireplace there.

Gray wood ashes from last winter half filled the stove, and upon them the slovenly Mexican women who took care of the Señor had thrown other rubbish, crumpled envelopes, curls of string, cigarette ends.

Gregory Chard put the picture on the pyre and lighted it. He saw that it was burning before he clanked the top of the stove again into place, and

strode out into the fog-filled patio, and through it
again into the open corrals and cattle pens.

Here were the cowboys, with some twenty horses;
bays and roans, one magnificent thin, nervous black
mare, one buckskin, small and vicious, a dapple-gray
with a rouged, smiling woman astride, and Gregory's
own favourite pacer, a claybank with a black blaze between his wild white eyes, a black mane and tail, and
four black stockings. The pacer had taken a stance, and
stood braced, like a horse in a monument.

"Hello, Pepita," Gregory said unsmilingly to one of
the women. "Hello, Jenny. Fine racing weather, hey?
Say, who took the ponies down?"

"Pablo!" said half a dozen voices.

"All right, let's go." He was into his own saddle
and off in the lead. The gaily dressed men and women
galloped beside him. They crossed a wagon track
through oak-dotted fields, went through opened farm
gates, reached the Camino, and headed toward Carterbridge and the Rodeo.

CHAPTER II

THERE were eight seats in the Raleigh box—the very front box of the Rodeo—and fifteen persons in the hilarious young party of which Pamela was one. But nobody minded the discrepancy; all the surrounding boxes would be filled, or rather half filled, with relatives and friends; there was always plenty of room. Pamela Raleigh wouldn't have been stopped at the big entrance gates if she had had fifty persons with her instead of fourteen. Question the right of old Major Tom Carter's granddaughter to do anything she liked at a Rodeo? Not Carterbridge!

So Pam and Chester and the others walked through the crowded gates like royalty, and if the girl took it for granted in her own friendly, happy way, Chester did not. His stepfather's house in Boston was hospitable and cheerful, in an academic, middle-aged sort of way, and Chester, during his college years, had shared several pleasant enough expeditions and parties with men friends. But anything like the gracious, widespread, joyous hospitality of this Western town and these delightful persons, he thought he had never imagined, much less experienced.

The soul of it all, of course, was this superb, tall girl, in her loose white coat and little blue hat. Pamela

Raleigh—he rather thought he remembered her, even
as a child, as blonde and proud and imperious and
beautiful, with this clean-cut, high-held chin, and the
long, black-lashed gray eyes. What eyes they were!—
it seemed to him a sort of miracle that one girl could
encompass all this loveliness of texture and shape and
colour, and had the right to move those amazing eyes
so responsively to one's face, to show those shining
teeth in any casual laugh, to touch one's hand, quickly,
involuntarily, as she had indeed touched his, with such
warm, satin-smooth fingers.

She had touched his hand at luncheon, if that was
the correct name for the scrambled and interrupted
meal they had all shared at a candy-store counter. She
had touched him because at the moment he happened
to be leaning far forward, talking to Sue Rose, who
was some several high revolving seats away. And he
had come back, like a person bewitched, to turn upon
Pam the full battery of his bewildered eyes, and to say,
in a hushed voice, as if he were a little afraid to believe
his senses, "Was that for me?"

"Billy says we'd better get started. The roads are
jammed with a million cars on Rodeo Day!" she had
answered, laughing confusedly.

Bewildered and bewitched, they were both that.
Neither remembered yesterday or thought of to-
morrow; this one thrilling and glowing moment was
all life: the moment he held her little white coat for
her; the moment he gave her a piece of gum and she
raised her gray eyes with an absent-minded smile—
for she was busily talking at the moment to someone
else—to thank him; the moment when it was his privilege to buy her a red handkerchief with yellow horse-

shoes on it, and a Rodeo programme, and pay for her special chicken sandwich and cup of chocolate.

He sat beside her on the almost empty grand stand —for they were much too early—and they looked down at the race track immediately beneath them, not a dozen feet away, and the big bull ring beyond. The Fair Grounds were on level meadows, two miles out of town; the mountains toward the east, far away, were lost in warm fog to-day, and even the other side of the course's big oval was quite smothered and gone.

But toward the south, where the stables and sheds and pens and corrals were, the giddy group in the grand stand could dimly see the forms of men and horses getting in line, two abreast, for the slow march about the track, and they could hear the men's voices shouting and laughing, and the jingle of harness chains. Now and then a cowboy, magnificent in fringed buckskins, beaded vest, and broad-brimmed sombrero, galloped down the empty course, waving a gauntleted hand carelessly at the audience, which was filtering in steadily now, trailing down the slant of the seats, searching for numbers, quarrelling amiably over places.

"No, you here, Belle—I can see perfectly well. They're all good seats. Make Belle sit next to you, Joe. Not yet, lovey, we have to wait for them all to come in. Look up there, show her up there, Brother, where they're all getting ready. See the horses up there . . ."

And always, "Oh, isn't it! It does seem such a shame, we've been having such gorgeous weather! However, Henry says . . . Yes, so Henry was saying, it's clearer here than in town."

"Everybody—I mean the nicest people, used to ride

in the Rodeo," said Pamela, eating peanuts, her bright eyes missing nothing, seated beside Chester in the box. "My mother says she remembers—how do you do, Mrs. Bates!—my mother says she remembers coming down here with my grandfather—it was really just a sort of cattle show then. Look, that's the Three Bar Dot outfit—see the bars and dots on their sleeves? That's one of the Molino horses there—how do you do! Hello, Chuck."

This last was to a big cowpuncher who had galloped up to sit his horse comfortably, just below the box, and stretch a big hand to her. Chester noted the line of her lithe young body as she bent forward, noted the tones of her rich, laughing voice.

"Who's Chuck, if I may ask?" he questioned presently.

"He's one of the Molino cowboys, Mr. Hilliard. I went to school with him."

"How long," said Chester in an undertone, "must it be 'Mr. Hilliard'?"

She picked a peanut from its shell, shook free the encasing brown papery covering, put the kernel in her mouth, and looked up.

"How long would you say?" she asked dutifully, thoughtfully.

"I should say about five minutes more," he murmured, intoxicated. "What do you think?"

"Well?" she hesitated. She turned about, offered the peanuts to someone behind her, and turned back again. "I was going to say *four*," she suggested.

"And do I call you Pam?" he asked. "After all, I went to your ninth birthday party."

She was looking off toward the ring; the fog had perceptibly lifted; there were no distances, but the

Rodeo at least would be visible. Now she brought her gaze back to his, facing him with wide-open, slightly puzzled gray eyes. When she spoke it was with a woman's deliberate decision.

"Yes. If you like."

"I ask you"—pathetically reiterated the voice of Sam Billings just behind them—"I ask you if you'll try my little Hungarian place to-night. It's a sixty-cent table d'hôte—and it's *good*. The place is rough—I mean to say, girls, that it's no place for ladies. Cuspidors, and sawdust on the floors———"

"Sam, don't be disgusting!" Pam said.

"I'm not. But the place positively is," Sam ··
"Come on, girls, let's give it a chance."

"It sounds wonderful. I can go," said Sue Rose Catherwood, daughter of one of the town's most respectable families.

"It's down near Chinatown. You can get anything you like there," Sam assured them. "Cocktails, pink ink—they tell me people simple pass out! This guy told me that he saw a feller knocked for a row of ashcans———"

"It sounds wonderful!" Pam said enthusiastically, as Sue Rose had.

"Sh-sh!" Maisie Broome breathed warningly, with her back to the adjoining box, into which her mother and father had just made a rather imposing entrance. "My mother hates that part of town!"

"Here's what we could do," Pam said in an undertone, rapidly, "we could meet at the Arms, and give the impression that we were going to dine there, and then go on to this Hungarian place."

"You're a quick thinker," Chester Hilliard commented admiringly. "I'll say that for you!"

"Oh, that's nothing to what we get away with!" Pamela laughed. "Don't we, Doctor?" she added more audibly, leaning graciously over the side of the box and greeting the Broome family.

"Don't you what, Pamela?" Maisie's father, stout, bearded, handsome, said with a smile, nodding and greeting the others beyond her, as he shook hands. He disposed of his flock—a pretty woman, three small girls—before seating himself. "Don't you what?" he repeated.

Maisie, who was afraid of her father, drew an agonized breath. But Pamela laughed.

"Don't we get away with murder, nowadays?"

"Have we missed much, girls?" said Mrs. Broome, smiling through strong glasses, consulting the big purple cardboard programme, and looking intelligently at the ring.

Dr. Broome smiled annoyedly, as a dignified man who feels he is being chaffed smiles at a pretty girl.

"I don't know that you youngsters get away with quite as much as you think you do, Pamela," he laughed drily.

"Tuck your hair in, Maisie girl; Mother hates to see it standing out under your hat that way," Mrs. Broome said fondly. "Is your mother coming this afternoon, Pamela?—How do, Harry—I didn't see you.—No, I agree with the doctor. I'm afraid," she went on, with a rather acidulated smile, "from what I hear on all sides, you girls are much more criticized than you have any idea!"

"No, M'ma isn't coming until to-morrow, Mrs. Broome.—I loathe you," Pam said. The last three words were inaudible, however, and Mrs. Broome continued to smile sweetly and study the adjoining box through her glasses. "You've seen Mr. Hilliard—Chester Hilliard, since he came back?" the girl asked, with a little indication of Chester with her head.

"No, I haven't, and I want to!" Mrs. Broome answered, frankly interested. "That's right, give him your seat, Sam, and let me talk to this nice boy whose mother I knew so well," she continued smoothly as the boys changed places, and Chester, smiling, was seated close beside her. His face wore the expression Pam liked so much and thought so cultivated, a brightly responsive look, but as he passed her he pressed the girl's foot to the paining point. She felt an inner geyser of disrespectful mirth.

"My little big girl told me that you were here, and I had rather hoped to see you to-day," Mrs. Broome continued, in her best manner. And again the respectfully cordial and sympathetic Chester pressed Pam's foot.

Maisie's mother was like that; it was "Daughtsie," and "Maisie-girl," and "my little big punkinny girl, there"—the Broome household was full of endearments of the sort. There were four girls in the family: Maisie, whose real name was Yolanda Joan, but who chanced to have been born and nicknamed in the month of May; Angela, sometimes called "Spratsy"; Florence, or "Flopsy-wopsie"; and the much younger baby, Elinor, often shortened to "Bootsy."

"And where is that dear mother now, Chester?" Mrs. Broome asked. "I never see her, and we don't write—both too busy. But no news is good news, and old friendships——"

"She and Professor Thompson live in Cambridge, Mrs. Broome. He's doing some work at Harvard this summer."

"And isn't there a wee half-sister—or *real* sister, I'm going to say, because I know you must make a real pet of her!"

"Jane, yes. But she's not a baby any longer. She's eight, and she's a regular bruiser," Chester said.

"Eight! Sure enough, she's older than my Bootsy here. Bootsy, pull your little skirt down, sweetheart; Mummy can see that little leg!—Pam," Mrs. Broome resumed, as Pamela turned back from the fascinating study of an especially cross and lively bull, "what was this you were saying about getting away with murder?"

"Oh, that was just nonsense, Mrs. Broome. That was—generalizing!" Pamela said, with her angelic, gray-eyed smile.

"Nonsense, indeed," Mrs. Broome said smartly. "I tell them," she explained to Chester, "that a good deal of this pulling the wool over the grown-ups' eyes isn't *quite* as successful as these clever youngsters imagine! I'm one of the old-fashioned mothers whose daughters tell them everything," the lady continued simply. And now it was Chester's turn to feel Pamela's foot gently but unmistakably pressing his. "And my Maisie-girl there sometimes surprises me!"

"I should think she might," Chester said soberly, his eye never wavering, but his foot busy.

"Your cousin Jessy—dear little Mrs. Stokes—was speaking to me about it only a few days ago," said Mrs. Broome. "She has a baby girl."

"Yes, I know she has. I saw her yesterday," Chester said.

"Jessy's one of the loveliest women in this town," Mrs. Broome said severely, almost challengingly. "She's president of the Cinderellas, and she said to me

—let Daddy alone, dear, and enjoy the wonderful Rodeo!—she said to me yesterday, 'Truly, I do not know what to do about the girls nowadays'—what is the absurd creature doing, butting at that scarecrow?" Mrs. Broome interrupted herself, displeased, as the entire grand stand half rose to its feet, paying the involuntary tribute of a shout of terror to the cowboy in the ring.

Pamela Raleigh clutched the nearest arm—Maisie noted, and Sue Rose noted, that it was Chester Hilliard's arm—everybody gasped; then there was a general laugh. The danger passed, as danger usually does, and everyone could sit down again.

On each side of the bull ring, just the other side of the racing track that stretched before the grand stand, there were wooden chutes, painted white, behind which the bulls and horses who were to figure on the long programme churned restlessly, and were prodded and steered from paddock to paddock by a score of galloping cowboys. At intervals a revolver shot was fired at one chute or another, a wooden gate went up on ropes, and a furious bull, with a reeling, shouting, hat-flapping cowpuncher astride him, bolted madly into the ring.

The fences and bars were black with clustered boys and young men, who waved their hats, screamed, and not infrequently dared a few flying steps into the field, further to enrage the bull. In the ring two ragged scarecrows had been fastened to poles, and when a bull, having charged the fences and menaced the crowds with his heavy, swinging horns, made for the scarecrows and demolished them with viciously dancing hoofs, the excitement in the grand stand arose like a rising wind.

Sometimes the rider, clinging precariously to the belt that encircled the brute's great body just back of the shoulders, was immediately unseated and stumbled to earth in a cloud of dust, the frantically plunging bull either turning to terrify him and the nearby onlookers with a sullen onset, or swinging off down the field, angry, bewildered, refusing to be baited further. Sometimes a cowboy, a long leg dangling on either side the animal's big bulk, hat waved triumphantly, kept his seat for the hundred yards that usually tired his mount.

Whichever way it was, the audience applauded generously; the old ranchers, sitting sombreroed and bronzed in the seats, would identify this bull or that: Ojeda's "Captain," or one of Chard's polled Herefords from Molino.

"Who is it?" Chester said to Pam inaudibly, his head bent with hers over the purple programme. His shrug indicated his neighbour.

"Maisie's mother—Dr. and Mrs. Broome."

"And is she always like that?"

"Always. You can imagine how much fun Maisie has!"

"Help!" said Chester. And suddenly he was shaking violently with laughter, and Pamela, to her horror, was infected, too. They continued to bend their heads over the programme; tears streamed from their eyes. "Behave yourself, Pam!" Chester said, in a quavering tone held stern above convulsion. It was the first time he had called her by her name, and the thrill went through her veins like wine.

"Those remarks about the Cinderella Club were directed at me, of course," she said, drying her eyes, quite herself again suddenly.

"I thought there was some reason for them. But what's the Cinderella Club been doing?"

"Nothing at all—but some of these mothers like to get together and tell each other how terrible we are. They rather have it in for me," Pamela ended innocently, raising to his her gray eyes and still wet lashes.

"Perhaps you flirt with their sons," he suggested.

"Or with the men their daughters would like," she added, with an anxiously inquiring and maddeningly pretty little wrinkle on her forehead.

"Oh, you wouldn't do *that,* I'm sure."

"I don't *think* I would!"

"I'm sure you wouldn't take anything away from Maisie-girl!"

And with the programme shaking violently between them, they were laughing again, more helplessly involved than before.

"I didn't hear you, Mrs. Broome!" Pamela checked her mirth short; her tone was apologetic, she turned about in real concern.

"I only asked you if we mightn't share the joke, dear, whatever it is!"

"It was nothing at all," said Pamela, sobering. "It was just——" Her voice quivered treacherously. She stopped, perforce, and grew red, ready to burst.

"Pamela, don't forget you're going to bring an icebox cake to the sale, Tuesday!" Carol, desperate at the sight of this complete monopoly of the desirable young man, said from behind.

"I won't. But I'll see you a dozen times before that!"

"Can you cook, too?" murmured Chester.

"How do you mean, 'too'?"

"Well, I've heard you make engagements to play

tennis, to swim, to cook—you're going with somebody
to look at a hat on Monday, you've promised dances
you and Miss Catherwood are having a French lesson—what *don't* you do?"

She smiled at him, turned back to the track. The
"cold-blooded" pony race was on. The fog blundered
about, soft and warm, and the riders appeared suddenly, strange, tall flying shapes, from the left, plunging out of solid mist.

It did sound popular, it did feel sweet, to be so de-
sired, so much in demand. After all, there was nothing
like one's own crowd, one's lifelong, loyal friends. A
great wave of happiness and generosity went over
Pamela, and she turned about and included the others
resolutely in the conversation.

But it was no use. It was no use. In no time at all she
and Chester were cut off from them again, in a world
of their own, murmuring, glancing up briefly, half
smiling. The words were nothing, the glances could be
seen by everyone about, the smiles were ordinary
smiles. But the sum total made heaven itself.

"Are you enjoying this? Do you know I'm enjoying
it more than anything else I've ever done in my life?"

"I'm liking it, too."

"I don't know," he said, youthfully ineloquent, "I
don't know what makes it so. But I'm just—crazy over
this Rodeo and this place, and"—his voice fell—"and
you," he said.

Pamela could not answer. Her heart beat slow and
thick, with an exquisite, painful little twist to each
throb. The Rodeo swam in a brilliant blur of colours
and movement before her; she felt secure, pretty,
young—felt herself, as it were, her own body and soul
and personality, deliciously atune with the world.

Happy, confused, she looked down once more at the programme, where, between advertisements of restaurants and candy stores, the cowboys and horses were listed.

"I must find my darling little Goldie Dunton," she said, busily. "He's a beau of mine."

"You don't have to go that far to find a beau, do you?" Chester said.

Pam shot him a sidewise glance.

"Oh, say you so?"

"Get your box all right, Pam?" called a fine-looking silver-headed man from a neighbouring box.

"Oh, yes, thank you, Judge!" she called back. "And M'ma said please to thank you. She is surely going to be here to-morrow!"

Chester saw the Mayor come up and pay his respects to the Raleigh twins; the cowboys touched the brims of their heavy big hats as they cantered by; everybody in the place appeared anxious to greet the slim girl in the white coat and blue felt hat.

"That's Judge Beaver," she would tell Chester. "That's old Señor Pajos, from the Three Bar Dot. That's the Molino outfit, over there by the fence, with the red rosettes on the horses' ears. My darling little Goldie is with them—see, with the purple bands on his sleeve. And that's Gregory Chard on the claybank; he'll come up here pretty soon—he does every year— and we'll discuss the fog and the crowd. He looks like a ragbag, but he owns the Molino ranches, and there's nobody in the country that can ride like him. He always dresses like that—he seems to think the horse is all that matters!"

There were no intermissions in the shrieking and plunging sequence of Rodeo events; races began while furious bulls or blinded bronco horses were still in the ring, and in any interval a "high-school horse" would be walked solemnly out before the grand stand to curtsey and waltz, or bawling calves with boys astride them were loosed from the chutes to plunge madly across the field. An old covered wagon and a rickety stage coach, visibly disintegrating, came racketing about the track, with pioneer women in hoopskirts and scuttle bonnets laughing on the front seat, and the eight-horse teams raising clouds of dust to mingle with the fog.

Presently young Chard's beautiful horse was indeed pacing up the course; Gregory reined him in with some small trouble before the Raleigh box, and the girl leaned over its railing to pat the black-maned head.

"Hello, Miss Pamela," said the rancher, grinning nervously, showing big white teeth in a copper face. Immediately he seemed to feel the smile too wide, for he scowled and added the next words sternly, austerely, his lips nervous. "You ought to hear my boys kicking at the fog," he said gloomily.

"Hello, Gregory—you remember Chester Hilliard, Mr. Porter Hilliard's nephew?" Pam said, indicating the man beside her with a jerk of the little blue hat.

"How do," said Chard, with a strange contortion of countenance. "Pretty foggy, huh?" And suddenly, to his own horror, he burst into a loud laugh. Instantly he sobered, again frowning heavily. "I hear you were down to Coffee Bob's last night, Miss Pamela," he said when Chester turned to Maisie and a general conversation in the box gave him an opportunity to speak to her alone.

"Oh, did that adorable little Goldie tell you?" the girl asked shamelessly.

"Some of the boys were talking about it," Chard

said severely. "That seems a funny place for—ladies to go," he added awkwardly, trying to laugh naturally.

Pam laughed, quite without effort, plunging her hands deep in the pockets of the white coat. And, if anything, she was prettier when she laughed than when she was serious.

"My mother agrees with you, Gregory," she said.

"As for Goldie Dunton, he's nothing but a little runt —I may have to ship him down to the Tia Juana place —he isn't worth his salt," Gregory pursued unhappily. "He's all right riding round out there in a purple shirt, and he dances all right, the boys tell me, but you—why, you wouldn't have anything in common with Dunton, Miss Pamela. I'm not saying anything against him, but—why, he's just a sort of—of kid, really—he's not got any brains where cattle is concerned——"

She read aright his blundering phrases, and his flushed face, and the big gauntleted hand that nervously played with the claybank's mane, and her eyes danced.

"Oh, I liked him!" Pam said regretfully.

"Well, I think he's going South," Gregory said, inexorably, vaguely, looking beyond her. "I certainly would like to come into town and see you some night, Miss Pamela," he added, in a voice made loud by his uneasiness.

He had a general impression that every person in the box, and some in the neighbouring boxes, heard him speak, and that the girls were all laughing at him. Laughing and red-faced himself, he pulled up his horse with a suddenness that made the animal plunge wildly, and tore away. Pam saw him no more that afternoon, the long straggling entertainment was almost over anyway, and if Gregory Chard chose to ride darkly

about the outskirts of the Fair Grounds, and reach a
back road, and gallop the lonely ten miles between the
Rodeo and the rancho all by himself, nobody missed
him and nobody cared.

All the way home his cheeks burned as he reviewed
the few words he had exchanged with her. He had not
intended to make any allusion to her visit to Coffee
Bob's: it was none of his business. What a fool——!

She and her crowd were probably doing something
amusing to-night, going somewhere—someone had said
something about a restaurant. He, Gregory Chard,
had gone to school with the Beaver boys; there was no
reason why he shouldn't telephone Harry or Bill and
say carelessly, "By the way, I may have to come back
to town to-night. Where are you all going? I'd like to
drop in for a little while."

Why not? Why not? They couldn't—and, anyway,
they wouldn't—kick him out of a public restaurant. He
might not sit next to her, but he would see her, see the
lovely tumbled curls on her head, and hear her voice
—that throaty, deep, delicious voice with the laugh
just under it. He might even dance with her. If she
had danced with that poor little simp Dunton . . .

Better, why not telephone her direct and say off-
handedly, "I'm going to be in town to-night, Miss
Pamela, and I'll be pleased to take you wherever
you're going."

Once home, he lighted two lamps in his room, ripped
off his rough clothes, plunged into a hot shower. Afterward he dressed himself in fresh linen, took a pair of
brilliantly polished shoes from a damp, plaster-lined
closet, and laced them up carefully, tied a new blue tie
accurately, combed his thick heavy black hair wet and
flat, and put on a quite new suit, large, stiff, and ex-

pensive; a suit of chocolate-brown tweed, with a flare to the trousers, a suggestion of padding on the broad shoulders, a general effect of being just a shade too small and snug for this big man.

And having reached this point, and having read on the face of his bedroom clock the hour of seven, suddenly Gregory sat down, on the edge of his bed, and fell into deep thought.

A dog wriggled her way in from the living room, flattening her beautiful setter-red body in an ecstasy of devotion on the floor at his feet, and Gregory dropped big fingers to her silky head and fondled her, without seeing her, without knowing that she was there.

The fog had cleared now and a livid sunset was fading away beyond the warm, dreaming blue surface of the Pacific. The light shone red as blood on Gregory's walls, dimmed and faded. There was soft summer dusk in the open patio outside the shuttered windows.

"Suppose she just said that she was dated up already?" he said, and shuddered. "What of it?"

The dog stirred, and he patted her head.

"But what'd be the harm in my driving into town in the car and asking her?" he demanded aloud. "It wouldn't hurt me to have her say she couldn't go. Girls get asked lots of places they can't go.

"She looked awful pretty in that outfit. I'll bet she's changing her clothes now—she's upstairs in that room with the two bay windows, brushing her hair and changing her dress. She looked awful pretty to-day, all right."

He glanced at the telephone. He imagined himself laughing easily and naturally when he got her number, and saying, "I've just about made up my mind that it's time that you went to dinner with me, Miss Pamela!"

So simple. So normal. He would hear her rich, surprised little voice.

"Oh, hello, Gregory! Why, I'd *love* to go!"

"I couldn't take her to the Arms, because the fellers all dress for dinner there," he mused. "But there's lots of places I *could* take her," he thought.

For a long, long time he sat motionless again, staring at the telephone. Then quickly, heroically, he snatched the instrument and asked the operator for Pamela's number. But immediately he cancelled it.

"Let that number go, I don't want it," he said hoarsely, his upper lip wet, his hands shaking.

"I can keep on trying, Mr. Chard," said the operator's voice pleasantly.

"No, don't bother—don't bother!" he said hastily. He made up his mind that if the bell rang he would not answer it.

He was still sitting, deep in thought, when one of the Mexican women knocked on the door and addressed him in Spanish.

"Señor, will you be here for dinner, your honour?" she asked.

"Yes. Yes, I'll be here for dinner, Teresita. I'll be out in five minutes," he called back.

When he came out, in little more than that time, for his solitary meal, he was clad in his old corduroys and the shirt that he had worn to the Rodeo.

CHAPTER III

"ARE you happy, Pam?" . . . The girl did not answer, except by raising her gray eyes smilingly to the black eyes so near them, and tightening her soft, slim fingers on the hand that held her own.

"Are you happy, Pam?"

"Haven't these been wonderful days?" Chester Hilliard said tenderly.

There were ten places at the table, but all the other diners were dancing, and Pam could respond without any danger of being overheard.

"The most wonderful days of my life!"

"This is Saturday night. Can you believe we've known each other, really, only since Thursday?" Chester reminded her.

The girl shrugged, smiled, was silent. She looked into his face, glanced about the room, and taking out her little vanity case began to repair the ravages that the long evening had left even upon the freshness and beauty of nineteen.

It was almost eleven o'clock; they were all dancing at the Arms. The group had dined there at a late

eight o'clock, and for three hours had been breathing
the hot, food-scented air, dancing on the crowded floor
deafened by the steady droning of the saxophones and
drums; eating, drinking, and smoking.

Now the girls looked pale and jaded, and the men
had reached a stupid, flushed state, almost of torpor.
There was little conversation; they confined their remarks largely to monosyllables, and by mere nods and
shrugs carried on the business of filling glasses, passing and lighting cigarettes, and rising for dancing.

The air was thick with blue cigarette smoke that
wreathed itself silently about the room, dimming the
glaring colours of great artificial flowers that were
twisted on heavy cotton vines on a sort of lattice overhead, and softening the effect of the little lamps that
glowed in skirts of gold lace on every table. This room
was called *Italia Lontana;* its decorative effects were
indeed as distant from anything truly Italian as might
be imagined.

Here and there among the green-painted lattices
wistaria blossoms and Japanese lanterns were hung,
and on one corner a large coconut tree had been
erected, to support dusty limp cotton leaves and a
somewhat moth-eaten monkey.

The waiters were dressed in white duck with coloured sashes; the cigarette girl was in a complete
Turkish costume, and some of the smaller edibles, pep-
permints, tiny biscuits, ripe black figs, all described by
the management of the Carterbridge Arms on the
menus as *"spécialités de la maison,"* were distributed
without charge by two sloe-eyed, creamy-skinned,
thick-lipped little Chinese girls, in black alpaca trousers and gay coats.

There was a big crowd to-night; Sam Billings had

had some trouble in getting a table. But, as always, the insistent Cinderella Club had had its way and had been placed in a sort of bay, close to the dancing floor and in view of the entire scene.

Dancing, encores, the clapping of hands, the cabaret numbers—all were familiar to boredom to Pamela Raleigh, yet she watched them lazily, indifferently, hour after hour. It was always the same, Saturday night at *Italia Lontana*. There were always the "pony girls" in their eternal sailor suits, the Russian woman with her gold and red lacquered zither, and Yvette, haggard-faced, thin to emaciation, dressed principally in a ruffled Elizabethan collar and satin bathing trunks, slashing furiously at her violin—wholly, delectably, enchantingly French, thought Carterbridge, among whose women there prevailed a vague enthusiasm for everything French.

In a jumble of mashed and melting desserts on the table were crumpled napkins, ashes, beauty cases, and many glasses, some of the last half filled with a pale yellow drink. As the girls and men came back to seat themselves between dances they drew these glasses toward them, lighted cigarettes, put their elbows on the table, and regarded each other sleepily, kindly, and in silence.

The men's collars were wrinkled and wilted on this unusually warm night, and every last trace of freshness had departed from the girls and their clothing. Little satin dresses were crushed and limp and streaked with perspiration; the beautifully crisp heads of three hours ago had become stringy and untidy, and the paste and rouge stood up visibly upon the weary young faces. And still the white young hands scratched matches, reached for tall glasses, unscrewed the tops of lipsticks, and smeared the red paste upon silent mouths.

"Little more?"

"No, it's just right, Harry."

"Maisie go?"

"She had to, at eleven, poor kid. And that was a special favour!"

"These are all Luckies. Give me one of yours, Sam."

"Whew! It's hot."

"I'll say it's hot."

"What's become of that Miss Runyon and Allerton?" Chester asked in one of the times when he and Pam were alone at the table.

"They're probably outside, in Bill's car. That's—that's quite an affair," the girl said idly. "She just came to our table because she happened to be here," Pam added, raising her eyes after a moment of smoking and staring at the dancers through the smoke, to meet his ardent look. "It's rather an understood thing," she went on, "that the Cinderellas don't—*pet*."

Chester blew out a long feather of blue smoke, turned to look at her seriously, and nodded.

"They do, here and there," Pamela amended it, after thought. "Everybody does, of course. But I mean that they don't always do it, as Doris does. The Cinderella Club is almost twenty years old: some of the mothers belong—almost all the younger married crowd here belongs. We're really the junior Cinderellas—but in a way it's a débutante club . . ."

Her voice drifted into silence. Either because she was a little younger than the other girls, or a little healthier, the man noted that she still retained the exquisite creamy clearness of her skin, and the soft, lustreless cap of wavy, tawny hair was as lovely as ever. But she looked tired.

"Well, the Rodeo's over!" he said, looking at her over the match as he lighted a twentieth cigarette.

Her eyes moved to his; she did not speak.

"It'll always seem, to me, to be *our* Rodeo," Chester went on.

"Wonderful!" Pam said briefly, dreamily.

"Are you sorry it's over?"

"It's been——" She hesitated. The pageant of the long hours marched before her, from that enchanted tea hour when she and Chester Hilliard had met again after ten years; she nineteen, and queen of her little world ne back from the East, with the glamour of a great Eastern college behind him, and the glamour of being his uncle's nephew ahead.

Since then they had seen each other during all of their waking hours, they had shared meals downtown, at Maisie's house, at Sue Rose's house. They had packed themselves into dusty, hilarious motor cars, they had sat at the Rodeo, looking down, from the royal box that was always at the Raleighs' disposal, at the sunshine flashing on the horses' restless flanks, the heavily charging bulls, the churning bright lines of the cowboys and cowgirls, the meadows—dotted with farmhouses and eucalyptus trees—beyond, and the transparent, opalescent, gracious line of the coast range beyond again.

Always together, while the hot summer day waned, and the mountains turned blue and purple and gauzy gray, and the crowd drifted back to bunting-draped Carterbridge, and the first dew fell pungent and sweet on the dust.

They had shared paper bags of ripe black figs and heavy muscatel grapes, shared casual sandwiches and waffles; they had watched the pink lights begin to shine

out on Carterbridge's festal streets, and Chester had
parted from Pam at her doorway only long enough to
go to his uncle's house and change his clothes, even as
Pamela was slipping off the day's draggled little garments and making herself beautiful once more, for the
summer night.

He had come to know something of her, the tall fair
girl with the wide-open gray eyes; he had seen her
sweetness with the faded little pretentious mother,
with the graceless, lovable brother; "Cart seems so
much more than seventeen minutes younger than me,"
Pam told him seriously

And he was quite at home now in the faded Carter
mansion; he knew the smells of the old carpets and the
rep curtains, knew that the three charming, unpracti-
cal persons who lived there had once been the great
folk of the town, and that there was reason indeed for
the aristocratic fineness of Pamela Raleigh's skin and
the proud lines of her high cheek bones and throat

He knew her very wardrobe; he liked the blue hat
better than the "burned orchid" one; he asked her to
wear the gold evening gown that seemed to blend so
miraculously with her creamy skin and bright hair.

Of him, the girl knew almost nothing, except that he
was that particular Hilliard cousin who had been sent
East to school and college, and who had spent his vaca-
tions with a mother and stepfather. He was straightly
built, straight of glance, he had a pleasant touch of
something a little more cultivated than was Carterbridge's custom in manner and speech, and he had a
delightful, a most amusing and breath-taking inde-
pendence. The thought of being conspicuous, being
criticized, never seemed to occur to him. He would

stand in the street eating a sausage roll, grinned at by the crowd, and grinning back imperturbably; he would plunge into a Rodeo procession and endure the ensuing indignities with great enjoyment; he would consult fortune tellers, surrounded by draperies of red tablecloths and large charts of the human palm—it was all "fun" to this newcomer out of the East, and his enthusiasms doubled the others' fun.

Liking all this, she liked too the cut of his mouth, the clothes that were not noticeably new, but noticeably right, the crisp decisions made in his crisp, confident voice.

And both liked the thought of having found each other; liked the fact that the other members of the group quite philosophically consigned Pamela Raleigh to Chester Hilliard, now, and accepted the probability that her fair head and his dark one—there was only an inch between them—should be always together.

"It's been what?" Chester asked patiently, after a while.

She brought herself out of deep thought with a jump.

"I was thinking what fun it has been," she answered.

He had ground out his cigarette; as he leaned on the table his voice was close to her ear, and heavy with sentiment, and smoke, and food, and drink.

"And you know I like you terribly—*terribly,* don't you?"

The girl's elbows were on the table, her lips against her locked hands. She nodded, smiling mysteriously.

"I *hope* you do!"

"I think you're the most beautiful person I ever saw!" Chester breathed. "And the finest!"

Pale hands, pink-tipped, like lotus leaves that float,
Down the still waters where we used to dwell . . .

the music sobbed. The crowd was dancing slowly,
rhythmically, the lights had been lowered, and waves
of green and pink were sweeping the smoky, odorous,
close room with the precision of heavy ocean swells.

"You asked me if I was sorry the Rodeo Week is
over," Pam said, raising her eyes slowly, knowing her
power over him, revelling in it. "No, I don't think I'm
sorry. It's always a wild week—it's been especially
marvellous this year, but there's a sort of relief in
going back to normal life again. We're not—wild, like
this," her glance included the dancers, and the smoke,
and the long glasses. "We don't do this all the year
round," she said. "Maisie's mother won't even let her
do it on great occasions—my own mother isn't any too
keen about it. There's a lot of talk about the younger
generation, but it's mostly nonsense. We're not prudes,
that's all. We dance at the Arms here almost every
afternoon, of course, when it isn't too hot, but we don't
even do that very often in the summer—it's more fun
to go out to the club and swim.

"I was reasoning with my mother a few days ago. I
told her that we didn't have chaperons because we had
sense enough to take care of ourselves, and that, as for
drinking and smoking, men have always done it, and
it's only prejudice—old-fashioned Victorian prudery—
that stirs up all this hullabaloo about the girls doing
it, too."

Chester was not listening.

"You have the most beautiful mouth I ever saw in
my life, and you know I'm crazy about you!" he said
slowly, steadily, a little huskily, his eyes, shining with
emotion, only a few inches from hers.

Pam laughed, and was silent for a minute.

"Petting," she presently began again, "is entirely a matter of taste. From the time I was a—well, a mere infant, I've hated being kissed—I've loathed it."

"Perhaps the wrong person has tried it on you, perhaps that was the trouble," Chester said, in a tone that was heavily charged with significance

"Being mauled—being kissed—ugh!" Pam said, with spirit. "But I don't do it simply because I don't *want* to," she went on, quick to defend the attitude of her generation, "and not because I think it's immoral. Immoral! Why, there infinitely less immorality in facing things and using your own judgment than in all their mawkish, mysterious——"

Suddenly she was tired, bored, sleepy, broken.

"Take me home; it's after eleven, Chester," she said, turning to him beautiful black-lashed gray eyes heavy with sleep and weariness. "Let's get out of this; let's get some clean air into our lungs! Is everything paid for? Come on, then, now—while the others are dancing."

She caught up a wrap; they were out in the quiet side street, where Chester had parked his uncle's smart little roadster.

A hundred yards away the Camino still boiled and seethed with the end of Carterbridge's great week; the cowboys, the calliopes, the radios and movie theatres, the waffles and doughnut kettles were still going full blast. But here there were peace and shadow, and Pam and Chester, breathing deep, could look off to the east, where the black mountains were slumbering, enormous and motionless, in the warm moonlight, could look up at throbbing millions and millions of stars, and the flung scarf of the Milky Way.

The cool, clean air struck gratefully on their aching, hot temples; the car was open, and as they drove along Pam gasped with sheer relief and delight. On the wide seat she disposed herself snugly.

"Say, we can't lose this," Chester said. "Let's—I'll tell you, Pam, let's go up the grade—and take a look at the town!"

She did not speak; she did not have to speak. They turned at the corner; moved smoothly under the heavily scented foliage of the great trees, traversed the factory district, silent under the moon, and passed the old Mission, whose gracious arcades and mellowed tile r   ˉ had weathered the storms of a hundred winters.

Suddenly church bells poured forth an unfinished choral; the half-hour after eleven.

"That particular chime always makes me feel late," the girl said. "When I was a little girl, Sunday mornings, walking to church, hearing that always meant hurrying to be in time. It always sounds to me as if it said, 'You're just too late—you're just too late—you're just two late!' "

"I'd have liked to see you, you little prig, all clean and fresh and smug."

"I *was* a little prig, I guess. We were twins, you know, and my father and grandfather had been—well, anyway, everyone made a fuss about the Raleigh twins." Pamela looked up innocently to the stars, and her voice had a pure, childlike quality as she went on: "I rather think I'm something of a prig now, Chester, really. I'm awfully proud, you know; I like to pronounce things right, and have things fine—and have people fine, too. And I'm an awful snob about family —I can't help it. It's not all imagination that certain persons *are* finer and nicer than others, and that if you are a gentlewoman and read good books and know something about music—don't you think it makes a difference?" she broke off to ask, a little self-consciously.

"Sure I do!" he said youthfully, obligingly. "Now that fellow at the Rodeo, who was always grinning like a chess bishop, that big butter-and-egg man———"

"Oh, Gregory Chard! Oh, yes. But he"—Pam persisted, a little disconcerted—"he really is a gentleman, or he ought to be."

"Well, that's what I mean. Roughneck as he looked, you could sort of feel that there was something there —feel sorry for him!"

"I do," Pam said carelessly. And then again, in awe, "Chester, what a night!"

The road simplified and became a ribbon of creamy gray, rising in long spirals on the enormous flank of the mountains. There were meadows on each side, no buildings anywhere, but here and there great oaks, furred by the warm moonlight, threw blurred shadows on the brown grass, and all the way a stout, short fence of heavy poles, painted a ghostly white, outlined their path.

The air was sweet with Indian grass and tarweed; at one turn of the road a group of hill ponies, their heads flung across each other's shoulders in a long line, stared at the light in coltish terror, and when the reassuring darkness returned galloped in headlong confusion down the hill. Sometimes cattle, roused from sleep, looked stupidly across a fence rail. But they met no cars; Carterbridge's latest visitors had been gone hours ago. The Rodeo was a tiring festival; its hours were rustic hours.

At the top of the long grade Chester stopped the car, and turned it to face the town, and beyond the town the sea, and they sat there, with Pam's head resting against his shoulder, and his arm about her, for a long time.

Far below, the lights of Carterbridge lay in a general central blur, with the long lines of the Camino and the trolley system crossing it. An orange brightness hung over the city, all about it for a radius of two or three miles, scattered lights marked the residential districts, and beyond these again lay the occasional bright single light of an isolated ranch.

Over all the lavish moonlight poured itself in unearthly glory, the patterns of the oaks near by lay like lacework on the road, and to the west, a vague, pearly shimmer beyond black hill shoulders, was the sea.

"Heavens, what a night!"

"And think of being shut into that inferno at the Arms since dark, with all this going on!"

There was an interval, then the girl said composedly:

"I told you I didn't like people to kiss me."

"Not even the top of your darling bare head, when you've taken that scratchy, beady band off?"

"Not even then."

"But *why?*"

"I told you why."

"You're a little touch-me-not!" he said, rubbing his chin against her soft hair.

"Look, Chester," she said suddenly, indicating the long valley that descended between wooded hills at an angle from the road, "that's Hatter's cañon—that's where Hatter's Pavilion is!"

"Oh, don't tell me that old place is going again!"

"Going? It's never stopped. A lot of us went down there last New Year's Eve, hoping for the worst, but nothing happened at all."

"Do they still have that nigger band? I went there once when I was in high school—I thought I was a heavy blood, of course. I remember those fellows."

"In the red uniforms, yes. And old François wanders about telling you what to order. Sometimes it's thrilling, and sometimes it's dead flat. The last time I was there we all almost died of boredom."

Chester removed his arm from her shoulders, touched the ignition, and turned into the side road.

"Well, come on," he said, "let's go!"

"Oh, I'd love it!" Pam exclaimed, suddenly awake and alert. "I'll bet they're having a marvellous time there to-night!"

"I'll bet they're tearing the paper off the walls," Chester said with a laugh, and the girl beside him laughed excitedly, too.

"We don't have to stay, if it's dull——"

"Nope. We can just get a quiet table, somewhere in a corner, and look on until we see how it goes. Still have the same old white tablecloths and iron knives?"

"Oh, yes; no *Italia Lontana* at Hatter's."

"No monkeys in palm trees?"

She laughed again.

"No; and no confetti or souvenirs or cover charges. But people flock up here Saturday nights: movie stars and millionaires from Hollywood—everyone——"

"When you get there you'll have plenty of time to fix up your hair and all that, while I'm getting a table."

"Oh, that's all right." She gave a little wriggle of felicity on the seat beside him. "Chester, this is fun!"

"Do you realize, my dear little girl, that *anything* you and I do together is fun?"

They coasted down the long grade on gravity, and there was no sound except occasionally the long sigh of the expiring night. The little clock on the running board announced an even twelve, and the air grew perceptibly colder. Pamela sneezed, and Chester gave a sort of shudder.

"Chilly, huh?"

"Night in these mountains always is, even in July. M'ma told me to bring my heavy coat, but it was so *boiling* hot before dinner," the girl said. And presently, "Funny we don't see any lights, Chester—oh, my gracious, I believe it's shut!"

CHAPTER IV

FOR they were in the very dooryard of the inn now, and instead of the long lines of parked cars that usually filled it, the windows gushing hospitable lights, the sounds of voices and music and dancing feet, there was absolute darkness and silence, not a car in the yard, not a lantern hung under the brooding old trees, not a spark of light to break the tremendous bulk of the old wooden building, looming over them stark and black.

They got out of the car, crossed patches of moonlight that seemed strangely leprous and unnaturally white, far down in this cleft of the hills, and walked to and fro aimlessly, as if a chance look here or there might discover what obviously was not here to-night.

"Gay Scene Number Three Thousand Two Hundred and Eighty," the girl presently said, on a gale of giddy laughter.

"Well, isn't it? Look, Pam, is that a light over there by the barn?"

"It's creepy," she said decidedly, suddenly close against his shoulder.

"Ah, you darling! But let's see who this is. It may

be an old Chink caretaker or something," Chester's
unalarmed voice suggested hearteningly.

Still uneasy, and with wary steps, she accompanied
him to the low shed and they opened the door. Pamela
had her first hint of real apprehension when two
tramps looked up from a greasy pack of cards, in a
nest of hay, their unshaven grinning faces revealed in
yellow lantern light.

She clutched Chester's arm, but made no sound. The
oddly assorted quartette, a handsome boy in dinner
clothes, a beautiful bareheaded girl in a light opera
wrap, and the two disreputable, bloated dere' :s,
faced each other.

"Hello, mate!" one of the men said in a wheezing
voice.

"Hello, there! Nobody living here now?" Chester
asked confidently. And Pamela's heart beat more nor-
mally for the sound of his unalarmed voice.

"That's about the size of it, bo," the other man
said, leering.

"How much money would you and a pretty girl like
that one carry about with you, mister?" asked the first,
straightening up as if he meant to rise.

Chester shut the door abruptly and, guiding Pam
with a firm arm, almost ran to the car.

"We might as well get out of here; they might be
ugly," he said quietly. "Get in, Pam—that's all right,
I'll open it. Jump in. Why, there's nothing to be
scared about," Chester added, as the blessed roar of
the engine commenced and the faithful wheels glided
through the black mouth of the old gate. "I wouldn't
mind taking on both of the old bums at once. But it'd
be rotten for you."

The lights picked up the winding road, the trees went by them in a vanishing procession.

"Whew! What an experience," Pam said then, with chattering teeth.

"I suppose the place was raided and shut. But someone was talking about it to me only yesterday."

The strangeness and darkness and fright of it were a long mile behind them now. The girl laughed out suddenly.

"We'll tell the others to-morrow that we came down to Hatter's to-night and that it was wonderful!" she said.

"What'd that old guy say about money?"

"Something about how much did a gentleman like you carry round with him."

"No, but he brought you into it, too, the old crook!"

"Oh, yes, he said a young gentleman and a pretty girl—— What *is* it, Chester?"

He had stopped the car on the steep up grade, punctiliously drawing to the right-hand side of the road as he did so.

"I hope it isn't—Lord, I hope it isn't engine trouble!"

"Of course it isn't!" Pam said cheerfully.

The man got out and in the darkness investigated the opened hood. Pamela, at the wheel, followed his directions anxiously, and Chester more than once came back to spring on the running board, lean across her, and anxiously manipulate the switches and gears.

"Here, I know how to drive!" she reminded him.

"We'll be in a fine fix if I can't start her!" Chester muttered. "Now, listen, you touch the starter when I sing out."

No use. No use. Nothing succeeded. Pam saw a

beautiful madrone tree, brightly lighted by the car lamps, leaning over the road at the turn ahead, and said to herself that in a few seconds they would sweep by it and be on their way, and she would forget it. But just now it seemed to be imprinted on her vision. A bending and mighty madrone, with pale green rounded leaves and a gloomy rich red trunk.

"Gas!" Chester said, struck. He went to the back of the car, and Pam heard him striking a match. In another few seconds he was back again, his face pale and anxious, his black hair dishevelled, and a streak of oil across one cheek. "Not drop. We're out of luck," he said simply.

"Where's the nearest station?" Pam asked gallantly. Her heart had given a strange drop at the news; she was tired and very cold, and all the fun seemed to have dwindled out of the expedition. But she would not weaken; they would have to see this through somehow.

"Oh, Lord, back in Carterbridge, probably!"

The girl whistled with lips that were cold and trembling. She looked ahead and saw the madrone, brightly green and maroon in the gush of white light. The moon had disappeared long ago, and down in the cañon they could not see the stars for treetops.

"What to do?" she said seriously, sensibly.

"Well, thank God, you aren't going into hysterics anyway," Chester said. "Gee, this is a simple thing to happen," he added boyishly and fretfully. "The tank's leaking, evidently, for I had a lot of gas this afternoon. However, it doesn't matter how it happened, the thing is how to get home."

"How far are we?"

"About—well, it's thirteen miles to the top of the grade, from Carterbridge, and we came down about four or five—we're about seventeen miles from town."

"Seventeen miles." She repeated it quietly, but her soul was sick within her. "Maybe we could walk to the top of the hill, to the highway, and something would come along?" she suggested.

"I don't dare try it, Pam," he said. "You in those high-heeled slippers and that light coat. You might get your death."

"Well, it's not much warmer here in the car," she suggested, trying to keep her teeth from chattering.

"But what *would* come along over the Los Antonios grade?" the man asked, biting his lip, shaking his head. "The last bus goes out at about six, and between one and five there wouldn't even be a milk wagon!"

"Is it one o'clock, Chester?"

"Five minutes past."

Pamela, thinking hard, stared into space. And the immovable madrone tree, brightly lighted, smote upon her tired eyes and filled her with despair. She was evidently destined to see that tree for a long, long time.

"I'd put up the curtains and the top, and we could simply wait here," Chester said. "But it's too cold. And even then we'd have to climb up the grade in the morning—about four miles I should say—to get any help."

"Sit here all night! Oh, we can't do that," Pamela said decidedly. "M'ma would simply throw a fit. Whatever we do, let's not do *that*."

"What *can* we do?" Chester asked, in a level tone.

"Well——" She began briskly, her tone wavered. "But we can't—M'ma—everyone——" she stammered, thinking it out. And for the first time he heard fright in her tone. "Chester, there must be some way?" she asked pleadingly.

"We can't go back to Hatter's," Chester said. "I don't like those old fellows down in the cow shed. They've probably got a bottle of something there, and you don't know what they'd do. We can't sit here——"

"But even if we *did* go back to Hatter's," the girl said in alarm, "there's nobody there."

"Well, I suppose we could dig out some blankets— I'm worried for fear you'll be sick, Pam."

"I won't be sick. Chester, I've got to get home—before morning—somehow. You don't know Carterbridge—it'd kill M'ma. Let's start walking."

"In those shoes?"

"I can take them off! I can walk barefoot!"

He did not answer her. He had been standing in the road while they talked, leaning over the door and playing idly with the gas control on the wheel. Pam had turned herself about on the seat to face him. They had lighted the little roof light, but they could barely see each other's faces. The madrone remained before them, bright and changeless, pale green leaves and rich dark trunk.

"Gosh, this is a mess to have got ourselves into!" the man said bitterly. And for a while both were silent, staring into space darkly.

"That road that said 'Private,' Chester, that we nearly turned into on the way down? Where would that go?" the girl presently said, without much hope in her voice. "They might have gas—or a car we could hire."

"No; I know that old place—that's one of my uncle's places. I remembered it as soon as we passed it.

There's not been anyone there for years; he was telling me about it to-day," the boy said. And then suddenly, "Say, but there's a house there! It isn't so terribly far away. That's our best bet, I guess."

She got out into the road, feeling stiff and chilly. Chester, investigating the pockets and cushions of the roadster, found a small flashlight and appeared immensely heartened.

"If we can't make it, we'll come back here and sit it out. I don't even find the curtains—but we might get the top up. Here——"

"Oh, Chester, I will not! Your coat! I have mine."

"Yes, but yours is nothing—here, put it on, put your arm through there. Even with both of them you haven't got as much clothing on as I have. Come on, now, we'll be all right!"

They turned out the car lights, locked the transmission, walked past the madrone, and on into the inky blackness upon which the flashlight's little disc of pale yellow fluttered like an ineffectual butterfly.

"How you making it? Shoes awful?"

She spoke strongly, naturally.

"No; I'm fine. They're as comfortable as can be!"

More turns, more turns, more road always ahead.

"Isn't it the limit the way you can get yourself into things like this?"

"Well, isn't it? I was just thinking."

They walked on; Pamela in the two coats was shaking with cold.

"You always get out of things somehow!"

"I know."

"You're an awful good sport, Pam," he said, more than once.

"Well, I feel as if it was my fault."

"Yours! You hadn't anything to do with it. It was *all* up to me."

"Awful road."

"Rutty!"

The dreary little light found a gate; Chester recognized it with satisfaction.

"This is it—'Private Road—No Thoroughfare,'" he said. "It ought to be right here."

They went on, the road growing worse and worse. Pam felt as if she were in a hideous dream. A quarter of a mile, painfully followed, brought them to a bridge, the ashes of a burned barn, fences, a windmill, and a small, dreary building recently used as a farmhouse.

No need to ask if it was empty: most of the window-panes were broken. The black interior looked through them fearfully.

Chester climbed in; there was a heart-chilling wait. Then he unlatched a kitchen door, and Pamela went in over rough boards, into a black vacuum that smelled of rotting apples and mice and ashes and decayed wood.

"Buck up, now, old girl. There's a stove here, I just fell against it. We'll start a fire—we'll be all right!"

"Oh, I'm fine," said Pam's voice. He could not see her face.

She was so cold that she could not use her hands for a few minutes. Then she tore into shreds a little card-board box that had been on the table and dropped them, by the feeble light of the flash, now lying on its side on the rusty stove, into the mouth of the opened lid.

A smoke-blue flame rose, wavered, rose again.

"That's the stuff!" Chester said, splitting a wooden

fruit box with his bare hands. "Take the flash and scout around and see if there's a lamp."

She found a short candle—another few inches of candle. Shudders of cold shook her; her hands were shaking as she held the broken tips to the flame. The wavering, trembling light illumined the dark little kitchen.

A terrible little room, bare and smoke-darkened and empty. But there were a shaky table and two chairs and some battered odds and ends of china and pots.

The fire sputtered vigorously, crackled, dropped, and settled in its box; the red stove plates leaked aureoles of blue smoke. Chester was still wrenching and smashing at his kindling. Pam fussed with dampers. The smoke cleared away.

"That's the stuff—I'll fill that kettle there. Maybe there's some tea or coffee somewhere," Chester said.

"Chester——" She was stacking the shattered box sides beside the stove. "Don't go away. This place scares me!"

"You poor kid, you, and you're being such a sport! No, I won't go away. I just want to look into these rooms here—it's all one floor."

He carried one of the candles away. Pamela sat, huddled together, shivering. The fire crackled, a faint heat began to break the frozen closeness of the desolate room.

Chester returned with his arms full of sour and odorous blankets, which he spread about to air and dry.

"Now we're all set. We'll be comfortable in here in no time! Golly, she burns, doesn't she?"

"Chester," the girl said impulsively, in a voice that shook a little, "you're wonderful!"

He was exploring the horrible closet; she saw from the glance he flung her that he liked her praise. Presently he came toward her with a canister.

"Smell that. Is that tea?"

She sniffed it; broke into a forlorn laugh.

"It's tobacco, I think."

"Well, wait a minute——" He returned to the closet. "There must be something in here!" she heard him mutter.

He came back with a dark glass jar, tightly sealed, wrenching at the stuck zinc top as he came. It opened with an escaping jerk of thick contents.

"It's a sort of chow-chow or sweet pickles or something. It's pickled currants, I think. Chester," Pam said gratefully, humbly, again, "you are wonderful!"

The kettle was boiling now, and the warming blankets were more odorous than ever. Chester found two cracked cups, filled them with hot water, mixed a portion of the rich dark pickle in each.

"Try it!" he said encouragingly.

Pamela, sipping, looked at him over the cup.

"It's hot, anyway. What price that chicken Maryland and the small blacks we left behind us at the Arms, now?" she asked.

"Oh, don't! Say," Chester said frankly, "this is a funny break, isn't it?"

"One of those things that's very easy to get into and hard to get out of," Pam answered with a rueful little smile.

"Hard to get out of is right. We'll have to stay here until daylight, and then I'll get up to the top of the ridge as early as I can, and flag something—if it's only a hay wagon."

"To-morrow will be Sunday. There won't be any

hay wagons. But there'll be something," the girl mused aloud. "Heavens!" she said under her breath, looking down at the draggled satin dress, the ruined slippers, gray with summer dust, her own bare arms, and the light folds of the evening coat that had been torn by brush and soaked by dew. "I'll present a charming picture to any rescuing party," she observed philosophically.

"Gee," the boy muttered, with a philosophic laugh, "it makes me sick!"

"Bad luck," Pam said stoically.

"I know. But why the deuce did it have to happen to us? Just to run out of gas. It makes you feel like a fool!"

"I sha'n't mind anything," Pamela said with a long, weary sigh, "as soon as we're home again and have got it all straightened out. I don't think my mother will worry, because I often stay with Carol or Maisie. . . .

"Oh, she won't worry. Another fellow and I were lost in the Blue Mountains for two days once, but we were all right; we had our guns and some chow and a blanket," Chester recalled.

"But that was boys! Girls are different," Pam admitted.

"Shucks, girls are just the same. There were some girls who came hiking through our camp two years ago —young kids, too. There were three of them, hiking along with packs as calm as you please! Pretty, too. The fellows couldn't get over it."

"But that"—she protested again—"that was *girls*. It's this"—a gesture indicated him, herself, and the closed four walls of the room—"this is what'll make M'ma wild!" she said.

"She'll have to be wild, then," Chester said hardily. But he looked somewhat concerned, nevertheless.

"These blankets are all right now," he said. "Wait a minute!" He disappeared into the adjoining room again, and came back dragging a flat, dirty mattress. "Roll yourself up in the cleanest of these things and lie down here and maybe you'll get some sleep," he said sensibly. "Don't look so scared; we've got to stay here anyway, and you might as well be comfortable. If you think there's any chance of getting out again to-night, just put your nose into that front room there —it's an ice box."

While he talked he had flattened the terrible pallet on the black floor and disposed some of the blankets upon it. He stoked the fire and put the kettle back. Now, removing his evening coat, he wrapped himself Indian fashion in an old gray blanket, and lay down on the floor, with his head resting on the slight elevation of the mattress, at its foot.

"That candle won't last more than a few minutes longer, better make yourself comfortable while you can see. Big luck for us that they didn't take their stove away," Chester said, with a long weary yawn.

She took off both coats and spread them over him.

"Here, you take these, anyway. Have you a watch, Chester?"

"Yep. But it's home on my bureau."

"Mine, too."

The girl rolled up a small end of bed covering for a pillow, wrapped herself up in the cleanest of the blankets, and stepped out of her slippers. Her hands felt dirty and sore, her bare shoulders cold. The last candle end, melted into a cracked saucer and standing at a drunken angle, flickered wildly in its last fight for life.

"The warmer this room gets the more awful these blankets smell," she said, when she was lying down.

"They seem to have used them in the chicken house."

She was not too tired, too uneasy, too cool, to laugh feebly.

"I was thinking they probably used them for a dog's bed."

"Well—better than freezing."

"What should we have done, Chester, if there hadn't been any shelter or stove, here?"

"Hiked back to Hatter's and broken in and taken our chance on the old hoboes getting gay," the boy answered, after a pause.

The candle guttered out. The room was lighted only by the red eye of the stove, burning brightly. It was comfortably warm, Pamela could feel the stiffened muscles of her weary body relaxing, even among the horrors of the old dog blankets.

"We'll get back to-morrow, early," was Chester's final sleepy statement, "and we'll send someone after the car and keep our mouths shut—that's all!"

Almost immediately he was asleep, and the sound of his deep breathing, not quite a snore, mingled with the steady sucking sound of the fire.

But Pam lay fiercely, feverishly awake. Her exhausted body, tortured by her untired brain, rested without stirring among the thick, coarse coverings, her bright eyes roved about the dreary little room, its stained walls and smoked ceiling revealed by the fitful firelight.

Horrible, horrible place. And she was destined never to forget it, never to have one detail of this frightful night forgotten.

All sentiment—all romance had vanished long ago.
Toward the man who lay sleeping, with his head almost touching her feet, she felt a strange coolness;
their sharing of this escapade had seemed to put an
incalculable distance between them. They had been
something more than friends in the box at the Rodeo
this afternoon and at the Arms a few hours ago. They
were less than that now.

"Keep our mouths shut about it!" That was the
man's way out.

She was lying on a mattress on the floor of a dilapidated little deserted cabin, up in Hatter's Cañon, alone
in the night with a young man—a man she had been
dancing with, flirting with, all this mad week. She,
Pamela Fairfax Raleigh . . .

A vision of her own room at home crossed her seething mind. A big, quiet room into which nobody had the
right to enter but her own slim, fine, utterly secure
and independent self. Her books, her wide bed with its
fat pillows and much washed blankets, her quiet awak-
enings in mid-morning, with the pear-tree shadows
moving on the worn carpet . . .

They were at the Arms again, and it was very hot
and smoky and stupid. Bare-armed girls dancing—
dancing—in a blue film, their carefully curled short
hair jarred out of place, their lips heavy with paint,
like Japanese women . . .

She was telling Maisie all about it, gaily, adventur-
ously.

". . . tramps—fearful-looking creatures! so I assure you, my dear, we got out of *there!* And then—
perhaps a mile up that frightful hill, still four miles
from the summit—imagine our discovering that we
had no gas!

". . . behaved like a perfect gentleman, but then of course he *would*. There was simply nothing else for it, and so off we started. My dear, with one flashlight, in the pitch black of night! Imagine——

"What else would you have had me do, M'ma— start walking seventeen miles home in those old gold slippers?"

Red flashes on a black, stained ceiling. Outside the soft sigh of a summer night wind among trees. Inside the crackle of a sleepy fire and the steady, aspirated sound of a man snoring. A young man in evening dress and herself, in her own best formal attire, shut into one room alone . . .

To-morrow she would be back in safety, back in her own room, with the jointed gas jet above the bed and the worn old mellowed carpet on the floor and the tree noises outside, rustlings and drippings and sometimes, in a storm, mighty creakings. And M'ma would be in the next room.

Astonishing thing, home. Home, where one be- longed. Where one's presence was never the cause of criticism and question.

". . . and you're such a darling to see it like that, Sue Rose, because we had no choice! I mean it was the most innocent thing—the sort of thing we're doing all the time, you know. And if one other girl had been along, of course it'd have been merely *fun*. As for Chester, he couldn't have been finer."

She was warm, tired, she had almost reasoned her- self into reassurance. When this adventure was over, and she had had a bath and rested and explained it all to M'ma, and when the stalled motor car was back in the garage, then under what circumstances would she meet Chester again?

Perhaps he would come in for supper to-morrow—
or to-day, rather. M'ma would cream eggs in her own
inimitable fashion, and they would fix sweet potatoes
with marshmallows. She would wear her Chinese bro-
cade, a much-washed, soft pink.

The full horror of it rushed over her again—she
was spending the night alone with a man. And no girl,
in Pamela's simple argot, could "get away with *that*."

"My dear, you heard about Pamela Raleigh?"

"No, *what?*"

". . . alone there all night, with that boy! Some sort
of cabin or farmhouse, or whatever it was, but not
another soul there! They'd started for Hatter's as if
that wasn't bad enough, and the place was closed down.
In the first place, they'd been dancing at the Arms, in
that Italian room, you know, and I suppose neither one
knew what was going on—anyway. . . .

"Well, Pam Raleigh can't say she wasn't
warned. . . ."

This time next week it would be all forgotten. Perhaps nobody would ever hear of it, anyway. Perhaps
M'ma hadn't telephoned to Maisie, and she—Pam—
and Chester would get a lift into town upon the milk
wagon of some unsuspecting Portuguese or Chinaman
from the strawberry ranches. She would slip into the
house before sleeping Carterbridge was aware that another day had dawned at all, and be upstairs, undressed, and in bed—safe!

"Pam, how late were you last night?"

"Oh, the latest yet, M'ma dearest! I'm ashamed to
tell you."

"Well, I should think you would be. Yo' goin' to
get into trouble if you keep this up!"

"I know it, darling, and I'm *not* going to keep it up.

It's all a waste of time; I've come to that conclusion once and for all. Hereafter——"

Hereafter. Why, what more did girls need, or ever really want, than friends, and simple good times, and companionship, and swims and summer, and movies, and tennis—and into bed at ten o'clock, to go off safely to sleep? What was the *object* in——

"Oh, my God, get me out of this! Get me out of this without killing M'ma!"

She had wailed it, almost audibly. Chester turned, raised himself on his elbow, stared dazedly about the room. Pam could see only the silhouette of his head in the gloom.

"Pam! All right?"

"Fine!"

"Been asleep?"

"Just going off."

"That's right. You're a good sport!"

"I wish you'd take another blanket, Chester. I'm really warm."

"Oh, I'm all right." He settled himself uncomfortably, twisted, lay still. "This is a nice jam to have got ourselves into, isn't it?" He yawned largely, unashamed. "We'll just have to keep our mouths shut about it," he said. And immediately he was snoring again.

She was one of the girls who had to keep her mouth shut about something, now. Pamela Raleigh had sometimes wondered what that felt like. Something to hide . . .

CHAPTER V

PAMELA lay motionless, her hands locked behind her head on the heaped pillows, her eyes stern. She was at home again, she was in her own room, in her own bed, where she had so longed to be. But there was no peace in her face. Her jaw was firmly locked, her forehead faintly knitted, and her gray eyes fixed on space. She was remembering.

Remembering the dawn breaking cool and dewy as she and Chester climbed the four miles to the highway, remembering a cool rough morning wind that struck upon her fatigue and stiffness like repeated blows. Remembering the sudden dazzle of sunrise, when at last they reached the hilltops, and that her skin had felt hot and prickly, and her eyes sore with smoke and strain. Far down toward the roofs of little Los Antonios she and Chester had been able to discern two cars coming along in the warming and widening light; they had congratulated themselves. The adventure was all but over now. A lift from either car—and one or the other would surely grant it—and a quick smooth passage down into Carterbridge, and thanks and good-byes—and the thing was concluded.

Standing there, watching the tiny black beetles flash

74

through trees and into sunshine again, get captured by the hills' green wet shadow, and once more emerge, following the line of the stout little white fence posts, Pamela had lived, a dozen times, through the stages of home-coming.

She would creep in, through the fragrant, wet, sleeping garden, she would find the side door unlocked, slip through the odorous close halls and up the stairs, be undressed in half a minute's time, and plunge deep —deep—deep into bed. Let M'ma come in then, if she would, let her scold, let the party dress be a wreck and the slippers useless, let anything, everything be disgraceful to remember and impossible to explain—but let it be *over!*

The sun had smitten her eyes, but she had faced eastward bravely. It was from the east that the little crawling cars had been moving, coming steadily toward the waiting couple on the hill.

"I may have to call you my wife," Chester had said. "If it should be some gossipy-looking woman——"

"Hardly, at this hour, I should think."

"Well, who would it be, so early? It's only half-past five."

"One of the forest rangers, maybe. They go off duty early Sunday morning—he might be coming down to town for the day."

"Well, maybe we won't have to make any explanation at all."

"We can just say that the rest of the party is waiting in the car," Pamela had suggested.

"Some night, huh? Glad it's over?"

"It isn't over, yet." Her smile had softened the pessimistic words. The car had come near enough to be signalled, now. They had gone into the centre of the

narrow road, their shadows lying in long lines behind
them, and waved to it.

This was the moment, in the whole terrible experience, that Pamela most hated to remember. Her
thoughts brought her to it inexorably; she met it with
an inner writhing, a sort of mental nausea.

Oh, why—why, in the history of the whole luckless
evening, why hadn't some guarding angel warned her,
and warned Chester to wait for the second car! Why
hadn't she and Chester, climbing the hill so fast, so
impatiently, been delayed only another ten minutes—
or started another ten minutes later? Why hadn't they
hidden themselves in the shrubs and underbrush beside
the road, to see who might be coming up the hill so
early before they hailed him?

Too late now! They had hailed him, and he had
stopped, peering out of a small car curiously, blinking
through strong glasses, puzzled and surprised. Dr.
Broome.

Dr. Broome who had been called to the Los Antonios sanitarium at two o'clock in the morning, and
who had been spending the interval in a hot, white op-
erating room, fighting—fighting—fighting, and losing
the fight for an indispensable life. Dr. Broome, hurrying home for another two hours of sleep, thinking only
of his good warm bed, and amazed to see beside the
road two figures in the early morning light: a pale,
bedraggled, bareheaded girl, in a shabby evening coat,
torn stockings, and dusty slippers, and a rumple-headed
boy . . .

The Hilliard boy—old Porter's nephew—and Pamela Raleigh!

"Oh, Dr. Broome, how lucky——" Pamela had
stammered. "We—we—will you give us a lift home?

I didn't recognize your car—we ran out of gas—we've been having the most terrible time——"

The doctor had got out of his car, his fine, bearded face full of concern.

"Anyone hurt?" he had asked briefly.

"No, no, we didn't have a wreck. We just ran out of gas!"

"Who was with you?" the man had asked sharply, glancing down the Hatter's Cañon road, as they, explaining, had glanced.

"No one else," Chester had said quickly.

"Just you two?" Dr. Broome had asked, perplexed.

"Yes, we—we thought we would see what was going on at Hatter's, just for fun," the girl had begun bravely, desperately. "And they are closed. Did you know that, Doctor? When were they closed?"

He had been paying no attention to her words. Instead his piercing gaze had moved from one to the other, mercilessly noting the details of their tumbled heads, their tired eyes and white faces, and their incongruous costumes.

"I see," he had commented drily. Pamela's face had blazed in a sudden agony of shamed colour. There had been no misreading the significance of his glance and tone.

He had stood silent a minute, and although Pamela had strained for some easy words, and Chester more than once had cleared his throat, the silence had spread and deepened like a horrible spell.

"Well, get in, Pamela—get in, Hilliard," the doctor had said then briefly.

Chester had opened the car door for Pamela. And at this moment the second car they had seen had passed them, a low-hung roadster, with two cheerful, long-legged college boys stretched on the front seat.

If that might have been the first car! Or if they had waited for it! No use to think of that now.

She had got into the doctor's car, and Chester had taken his place beside her on the back seat, and in wretched silence, like two criminals going to jail, they had driven the long miles down the hill.

Pamela, lying in bed in the quiet summer morning, loathed the recollection of her own futile efforts to win the grim, bearded, weary man who was at the wheel to friendliness and understanding.

"After one such experience as this," she had said ruefully, smilingly, "I can assure you, Doctor, that one is quite willing to agree that 'Mother knows best'!"

And she had laughed gallantly, philosophically.

But the doctor had paid no attention whatsoever, except by a faint shrug of his implacable back. And Chester's eyes, when her own sought them, had been grim and troubled.

Chester had been delivered first at the old Hilliard house, which showed not a sign of life in the early morning. There was still dew on the beautiful groomed lawns and shrubs, but no leaf was stirring: it was going to be a hot day.

"Latchkey?" Dr. Broome had asked, harshly.

"Yes, sir. And thank you a thousand times," Chester had said stiffly. And he had come about the car and shaken hands with Pam. "Good-bye. I'm terribly sorry I was a dumb-bell about the gas," he had said simply and penitently. "You've been an awfully good sport."

"How do you get in, Pamela?" the doctor had asked her unencouragingly, when they were driving on.

"M'ma leaves the inner side door open. At our house we haven't—" she had tried to laugh—"we haven't much to steal, you know!"

But no answering smile or glance had reassured her. The man had taken her to the side gate and had accepted her thanks in silence, his eyes quietly fixed on her face as she stammered and blundered.

"Doctor—there really is an explanation of this—it isn't as bad as it looks."

"It looks—pretty bad," he had said, pursing his lips, rubbing his gloved thumb to and fro on the wheel.

Again the blood had flamed in her tired face.

"But anyone—anyone," she had said, rallying her spirit, "might run out of gas."

"Not any girl of nineteen, alone with a young man," he had said decisively, relentlessly.

"Well, I wouldn't have chosen a Saturday night, after a dance, to have it happen!" Pamela had admitted, with a brave attempt at a joke.

"No, I suppose not. Well, you are not my daughter, Pamela, and perhaps," the doctor had said, detached and cold, "this isn't the time or place for a discussion of what a girl may or may not do, nowadays."

She had thanked him again, escaped hot-cheeked and with a boiling heart into the house. And the remainder of the reality had been just what she had planned: her mother sound asleep, her bed awaiting her, pillows and oblivion and solitude at last.

But for the mischance that had brought Dr. Broome up that hill, the experience might well have been over, now; Pamela might once more have carried off the honours.

As it was, she found the memory of those two cars in that dazzling morning light the insufferable turn of

the screw. The encounter with tramps, the long wait in
the road, facing that eternal madrone tree, the stumbling search for shelter in the cold night, the hideous
hours, stiff and miserable and frightened in the shanty
kitchen, with that nightmare of a stove smoking and
crackling, and Chester Hilliard's black head at her
feet—all these she might have weathered, as girls
nowadays did weather the incredible.

But Dr. Broome, grimly, silently entering into the
last act of the drama—Dr. Broome, who had warned
her only a day or two ago that her way was not the
safe way! Oh, what would he do, whom would he tell,
what would happen now?

She put her hands over her face.

"I wish it were the middle of next week—I wish it
were the middle of next year!" she said, aloud.

Carter was breakfasting in the kitchen when she
went downstairs an hour later. Battered shades had
been drawn at the windows against the heat and light
that penetrated even into the Raleighs' overgrown garden, and the honking of distant motor horns and the
sleepy clucking of chickens fluffing in the warm shade
of the big trees came softened and subdued through
breathless, motionless summer air.

"Hello, Cart."

"Hello, Pam. Say, you look swell!"

She had indeed dressed with unusual thoroughness
and care, brushed the soft thick mop into its usual curly
order again, got herself into the freshest and trimmest
of little cotton frocks. She put down her tray and began to distribute dishes and equipment from it: the salt
cellar, the spoons, the sugar bowl.

"Maisie telephoned about half-past ten o'clock. M'ma tell you?"

"No." Pamela turned from the sink, interested. "What about?"

"They were all going down to the beach, or something."

"Oh, yes. They did say something about it. But I'm sunk. I couldn't have gone," the girl said wearily, washing cup and plate by holding them under the running hot water.

"What happened last night?" Carter flung aside the voluminous folds of the Sunday newspaper. "M'ma waked me up at about four, and came in and asked me if I thought you'd stayed with Maisie or Carol, but I didn't know."

"Oh, we got out on the road, near Hatter's there, and ran out of gas——"

But for Dr. Broome—but for Dr. Broome, this might indeed have been the accepted story, as little suspected by all her world as it was by her brother, who finished his coffee, brought his plate and cup to her at the sink, dispersed sundry crumbs with a beating gesture of his big, raw young hand on the table-cloth, and picked up a tea towel.

The bitter mischance of it—the evil moment that had brought her and that particular car together, across so many miles of space and so many uncounted minutes! Her eyes were dark and bitter with rebellion against fate.

Suddenly, subdued, friendly Chester Hilliard was in the kitchen. He was pale, as Pamela was, but he looked fresh and groomed again, and handsome in white flannel trousers and dark blue coat

Pamela's heart gave a throb of pleasure as she saw him. He was her companion in trouble, anyway, and the mere sight of him reassured and quieted her heart.

He came in and sat on the table edge, near Carter, and Pamela turned her back to the sink, rested lightly against it, while they talked.

"Well, how goes it?" he asked, with a keen glance.

"Fine," Pamela said non-committally.

"Hear you had a break-down last night—tough luck," Carter said.

"Ran out of gas. It was my fault—I'm just a fool," Chester answered.

"Where'd you have to leave your car?"

"Out on Hatter's Cañon road. But I sent Mike from O'Connor's right after it—it's safely back in its little home, now," said Chester, grinning.

The two men began to compare notes as to awkward situations arising from the commonest of motor oversights. A man and his wife had been stuck in the mountains and caught in a regular blizzard last winter, and had been found dead, with their arms about each other, a few days later. And if he'd had one gallon more gas . . . !

"Coffee, Chester?"

"Have you got any there?"

"No. But it'd only take a second!"

"Oh, no, don't—don't. I'll smoke, if I may. Say, what about this picnic to-day, down at the beach?"

"I heard something about it. But I don't think I'll go—M'ma wanted me to go out and call on the Weatherbys—their mother died," Pamela said. And with a significant look she added, "But you go.

"You go and play the game," said her eyes. "Dissociate your name with mine—be attentive to Maisie

and Sue Rose—blot out that unexplained interval last
night as completely as you can!"

"I think you're quite right, we don't want anything
to appear odd," his look answered, before he said
aloud, carelessly:

"I thought I would."

There was a little more idle conversation, then she
walked with him to the side door and they stood there,
for another few words.

"All right?"

"Yes, fine. Only I feel a little dazed and shaky."

"Same here. I got some sleep though."

"Oh, yes; so did I."

"Did you sleep at all in the night?" he asked, in a
quick undertone.

"No." The scene came back to her, and she shuddered. "Maybe a little, I don't know."

"Mother wild?"

"No; she was awfully decent. She always is." Pamela's tone was flat and toneless. "It isn't my mother,"
Pamela added apathetically; "it's Dr. Broome. He's
Maisie's father, you know. And Maisie is my best
friend. And they're terribly strict—they're the most
old-fashioned people in this town!"

"You mean the old fellow—what's his name—
Broome—who gave us the lift?" Chester asked.
"Why, *he* won't do anything!" the boy said reassur-
ingly. "What, after all, could he *do?*"

She considered this, beautiful serious gray eyes
raised to his.

"Well, *that's* true."

"Sure. That old bozo was probably thinking about
his patient. My cousin Jessy Stokes was in the house

this morning—she stopped in on her way home from church—and she told my uncle that she'd met Mrs. Broome and Mrs. Broome said that the doctor was all broken up; he'd been fighting all night, with blood transfusion and all that, for some woman who had small kids—a girl they all know—in Los Antonios——"

"Not Ursula Younger!" Pamela was conscious, through all her sense of sympathy and shock, of a real relief that she could feel anything but the insistent presence of her own trouble.

"That was the name."

"Oh, I'm so sorry." And she was sorry. But under the sorrow was a healthy sense of being, personally, saved. The world was still going on, there were other things to think about than Pamela Raleigh and her indiscretions. "M'ma'll be heartbroken," Pamela said. "And the Broomes were awfully fond of Lou. Here comes little Florence Broome now," the girl added, as a nicely dressed Sunday-prim child came through the gate. "Hello, Flops.—Her mother is probably writing to M'ma about Ursula," Pamela said, in an undertone. The child came up.

"Mumsie sent you a note, Pamela," the little girl said, smiling shyly at Chester. "And will you please tell me if you can?"

Pamela tore it open, absorbed the few words at a glance. It was written in a light, pretty flowing hand, on engraved paper, with "Hazelawn" at the top.

DEAR PAMELA:

Will you come and see me for a few minutes early this afternoon, on a matter of real importance?

Faithfully your friend,
FLORENCE PAULSON BROOME.

There was something about it—the very feel of it, the cool, direct question, the formal signature, that made a little chill come across the warm, balmy garden, and Pam's eyes were faintly clouded as she looked from the note to the waiting child.

"Tell Mumsie that I'll be there just as soon as I can change my dress!" she said.

Florence junior walked away, and Chester said:

"When do I see you again?"

"Chester, what do you suppose Mrs. Broome wants to see me about? Maisie usually sends me a message, or telephones. Do you suppose the doctor has told her about last night?"

"Well," Chester submitted sensibly, unalarmed, "what if he has? She'll probably make a kick and give you a call-down—she struck me as taking herself pretty seriously, yesterday. But what of it?"

"Yes, I know." And she was heartened again. "Well, I'll go and see, anyway," she said with a long sigh.

CHAPTER VI

S HE walked to Maisie's house—a short three blocks.
Bees were humming over the flower beds and
hedges, in the hottest hour of the hot midsummer afternoon. The town hall clock struck two.

There were very few motor cars astir in the green,
shady streets. Carterbridge dined, on Sunday, at one,
and afterward usually sat or lay panting in porch
chairs or hammocks until the processes of digestion and
the increasing coolness of the afternoon made possible
a run to the beach or a game of bridge.

It was a horrible house, Pamela had always thought,
the Broomes', and this afternoon her mood was not
calculated to make it appear any prettier. It had been
built on the site and in the garden where a lovely old
brick house had been torn down. It was of the innocuous type of lumber called "rustic," painted white and
trimmed in gray; it had plenty of bay windows and
large unimaginative plain windows, nice curtains, nice
porches, clean-looking columns and railings.

Inside were wide hallways and polished floors and
rugs, flowers and leather-covered limp gift books and
hand-painted lamps on mahogany tables, framed sepia
photographs of the Coliseum and the Parthenon, a

player piano, potted plants, and comfortable dining-
room, library, and reception sets of fine furniture.
Everything was good without being in the least dis-
tinctive, and pretty in the fashion of too few years ago.
Pamela, in whose home nothing had changed for fifty
years, was always sharing with Maisie the latter's
anxiety to "do something" to the Broome house. But
new wall papers, and sets of Stevenson, and orange-
net window curtains somehow never seemed to strike
roots there, never seemed really to change the wide,
square-cut, airy place; it was always just a house, with
wall papers and books and curtains in it.

Miss Maisie was away, and the family was at dinner, Nan, the waitress, said; would Miss Raleigh
please to wait? Miss Raleigh pleased to do anything
agreeable, yet she waited with a sick heart.

She, Pam Raleigh, asked to wait, like a casual patient or caller, or agent, in the Broome house! Why,
all her life long she had been running in and out here
like a member of the family. They always asked her
to join them for ice cream or puddings when she came
in at meal times, and the doctor always facetiously assured her that the dermatological institutes could do
a good deal for a face like hers, and Mrs. Broome always praised her for not dieting, in the silly way the
girls all were nowadays, and sometimes the baby came
and sat contentedly in her lap, and Pam gave her
sponge cake and spoonfuls of ice cream.

But evidently there was trouble to-day. Perhaps
they all felt badly about poor Ursula. Anyway, presently the baby could be heard making her weeping way
upstairs; things were going badly indeed in the usually
serene Broome household. Pamela began to hope that
the matter about which Florence Paulson Broome

wished to see her might be quite dissociated from any indiscretion of her own.

But Mrs. Broome, flushed and uncomfortable from the meal and the domestic unpleasantness, looked unfriendly and severe when she came in. She gave Pamela a stiff, brief smile, made more formal by her strong glasses, and turned from the girl's own smile to address the ubiquitous Florence, who was employing, in the doorway, all the comfortable leisure of an interruptive child with a real errand.

"Mumsie, Baby said to tell you that she was sorry and please to forgive her!"

"Well, you go tell Baby," the mother said, annoyed, "that Mumsie said that she was coming upstairs right away, and that is the only message she has!"

Florence, in horrid fascination for Baby's predicament and complete personal immunity from any of her own, departed with a dutiful nod, and Mrs. Broome said, coldly:

"Sit down, Pamela." She sighed heavily. "Pamela," she went on, making a resolute start, "Doctor returned from a night call in Los Antonios last night with—I think—the *saddest* news I have ever heard in the twenty-two years of our marriage!"

"You mean about poor Mrs. Younger?" Pamela said, hoping it was really that, hardly believing that anything so bad as its touching herself could be true.

"No, I don't mean poor Ursula," Mrs. Broome said, sighing again. And then suddenly, inexorably, "Pamela, did you spend last night at Hatter's Pavilion with Chester Hilliard?"

"Mrs. Broome—what actually happened——"

"I think I asked you a question, Pamela."

"Then"—the girl's voice came proudly and quickly.
—"then the answer is 'no,' " she said.

"No? But I thought——" Mrs. Broome looked
cheated. She bent a sharply suspicious gaze upon Pamela. In the silence the wails of the expectant Baby
could be heard in an upper region.

"Hatter's is closed," Pam explained shortly.

"Then," said Mrs. Broome, still sternly, "where *did*
you spend the night? Doctor, returning from Los Antonios, found you on the roadside, looking—well, I
wouldn't want your mother to know how!—at nearly
six o'clock this morning, alone with Chester Hilliard."

"It was foolish, and it was as unfortunate as anything could be," Pamela said, with some little dignity,
trying to hold back, trying to choose her words, "but it
wasn't anything more."

"Foolish? Nothing more than *foolish*—spending a
night away from home with a man you hardly knew?
Really, Pamela!" said Mrs. Broome indignantly, "I
am surprised at you. I cannot believe my ears."

"We were going down to the pavilion to watch the
dancing," the girl vouchsafed; "but the pavilion was
closed."

"And at what time was this?"

"This was—oh, about eleven. We were at the Arms
—I think Maisie had gone home."

"Indeed Maisie had gone home!" said Maisie's
mother roundly, with a sort of passionate pride.

Pamela remembered Maisie saying, "Darn it—my
mother thinks that the minute the clock strikes eleven
the immorality busts loose! I might as well be in a
convent."

Had that been only last night? It seemed months
ago.

"Maisie's daddy is very firm about *that*," Mrs. Broome was saying complacently. "Home at half-past ten—always chaperoned——"

Pamela looked at her, angry, scornful, the scarlet colour rising in her cheeks.

"Oh, Mrs. Broome, *when* have we been chaperoned—our crowd, I mean? I never in my life remember chaperons at the Cinderella Club dances!" she said impatiently, resolutely unimpressed.

"Don't you, Pamela?" said the other woman, flushing a little herself, but continuing to look steadily at the girl through her strong glasses, and maintaining her undisturbed expression. "Well, perhaps you other girls have not been aware of it, but my Maisie-girl has been protected for every hour of her happy, sunshiny little life!"

"Oh, *blah!*" was all that Pamela could think of in the way of a suitable answer, and as she dared not make it, she remained silent.

"It is from escapades like this most unfortunate one of last night," pursued Mrs. Broome smoothly, "that we are trying to save Maisie. Dr. Broome was simply —crushed, this morning. 'I would rather—' he said to me—'rather see our oldest daughter lying still in death, as poor little Ursula is lying, than find her as I found Pamela Raleigh!' Pamela—just a moment, you shall say all you want to, presently!" she interpolated, as the girl, nettled and angry, made a quick interrupting motion. "Pamela, are you going to tell your mother of this?"

"I *have* told M'ma, Mrs. Broome."

"Not the whole story?"

"The—yes, the whole story. There's no story *to* it!

It was just a—sort of combination—of most unfortunate—circumstances——"

"Most unfortunate indeed!" Mrs. Broome agreed fervently, as Pamela floundered. "What explanation did you give your mother—your poor mother," she asked, "of the interval?"

"Of *what* interval?"

"The interval between half-past eleven at night, when you discovered that Hatter's—disgraceful place! —was closed, and five o'clock this morning?"

"We had no gas," the girl explained patiently. But she was inwardly sick with terror and shame. "Coming up the hill the car—one of Mr. Porter Hilliard's cars —simply stopped short. What *could* we do? It was bitter cold—it gets frightfully cold between those mountains——"

"You sat in the car all night? That's—obviously— impossible!" ejaculated Mrs. Broome, nettled in her turn at not being able to land her fish more promptly. The girl was showing fight.

"No. There was a sort of—shanty, near there, that Chester knew of—it belongs to his uncle. We went there."

"How do you mean *shanty?*"

"Well—a little ranch house, down there a mile or two above Hatter's."

"Oh? I know that place. But that's a seven- or eight-room farmhouse; I should hardly call that a shanty!" said Mrs. Broome. "It's furnished, isn't it?"

"Well, yes—after a fashion."

"I think I've been down there with dear Jessy Stokes," said Mrs. Broome thoughtfully, pursing her lips. "They used to have a Portuguese man living there. There's no caretaker there now?"

How Pamela hated her! How she hated her!

"No, nobody at all. That was it!" she admitted, grudging every word, every concession. "If there had been a man there, anybody there—with an old horse and cart—anything! But there wasn't."

"So you made a fire and stayed there all night?"

The cruel shrewdness of the cross-examination seemed to shrivel Pamela's heart.

"Mrs. Broome, what else could we do?" she said desperately, youthfully. "When people—when people are wrecked on a desert island nobody questions them, nobody supposes that they intended anything wrong!"

"My dear Pamela, we are not talking of shipwrecks; they are acts of God. We are talking of a perfectly modern young girl, who, after a day at the Rodeo and evening of dancing, goes at midnight," Mrs. Broome recapitulated it with a relish, "to a questionable road-house with a man she hardly knows. If your father were living, Pamela," the other woman interrupted herself suddenly, "do you realize that he might send for Chester Hilliard to-day and demand that he marry you?"

"Oh, nonsense!" the girl said, bursting into uncomfortable laughter.

"If it were Maisie, I should feel it was the only possible thing," Maisie's mother persisted solemnly. "And Jessy Stokes," she added, playing a trump deliberately, "is of the same opinion."

Pamela's colour faded a little. It was all very well to have this spectacled matron, who retained, even after twenty-two years of married life, the academic ideals of the dean of a girls' school—which she had been— all very well to have her criticize and moralize in her own absurd way. But to bring young Mrs. Stokes into it was quite a different, and a much more serious, matter.

Jessy Hilliard Stokes had been the sister of that charming Jimmy whose death had indirectly brought Chester to Carterbridge a few weeks before. Her father, Porter Hilliard, was on every important directorate in town, and Jessy, married to one of the younger bankers of Carterbridge, was socially pre-eminent, president of the Cinderella Club, deep in theatricals and charities and concerts and golf and everything else that concerned the very nicest upper circle of Carterbridge society.

"Jessy came in here to speak to Doctor about poor little Ursula," Mrs. Broome said, seeing that she had made an impression, and pleased therewith, "and Jessy agrees with me in regarding it as—well, as most unfortunate, to say the least!"

"And I entirely agree with you and Jessy," Pamela said, trying to speak lightly and easily. "Mind you, Mrs. Broome," she asserted courageously, "a great deal more than what we did last night goes on at every dance—kissing and petting and all the rest of it! But technically—technically—it was wrong, and I'm heartily sorry. I'm willing to tell the girls that—to admit that I did a silly thing and that a miserable lot of accidents followed——"

"Willing, you mean, to tell Maisie and Sue Rose and Carol that you and a man you met Wednesday spent last night in the old Hilliard ranch house! Honestly, Pamela," said Mrs. Broome, "I don't know what society is *coming* to when a girl can say that she has no objection to confessing such an escapade to her friends!"

There was a short silence, in which Pamela attempted to look unconcerned and succeeded merely in looking rebellious. Then the girl said sulkily:

"I don't see what my having met Chester Hilliard last Wednesday has to do with it!"

"It has this to do with it. Doctor said two or three times that a grand passion—a really deep love—he could understand and forgive! But that to go off carelessly with a man you hardly knew—— No, Pam," the older woman said sharply, inflexibly, "it doesn't bear analyzing, my dear, and if you could have seen the tears in Doctor's eyes, and seen poor Jessy, standing in that very window, staring out and saying, 'I can't believe it of Pamela Raleigh!' you'd realize that it is very serious indeed."

"A grand passion—why, but that's nonsense!" the girl said, laughing nervously. "There's never been any talk of a grand passion between Chester and me—we're just friends."

"Well, I am afraid that you have done your friend a very poor service," Mrs. Broome said neatly, as she paused. "For Jessy feels now that it will be impossible to send him an invitation to the Cinderella Club—poor boy, he would, of course, have had one of them, if it hadn't been for this."

Now for the first time Pamela showed agitation.

"That would be a cruel and senseless thing to do," she said hotly, briefly.

"Jessy doesn't want to put it to the girls, she doesn't want to mark him or mark you," the older woman said, with an air of consideration. "She merely means to let the matter of his invitation drift, and she—I must tell you frankly, Pam—she feels that the only thing for you to do is hand in your resignation."

There was a moment of silence in the overfurnished,

bright room, with its books and lamps and vases and
etchings and clocks and trays and photograph frames.
Pamela, leaning forward in a rather high, uncomfortable chair, regarded her hostess steadily, with hostile,
shining eyes. Mrs. Broome returned the gaze equably,
her head a little on one side, her expression pitying, yet
firm.

"Resign from the Cinderellas?" the girl asked, in
a whisper, after a while.

"I really am afraid so, Pamela. That would be
better than being asked for your resignation, wouldn't
it?"

"But—but——" Pamela fell silent. "I couldn't imagine the Cinderellas—without me," she muttered,
blinking, biting her lips, clearing her throat.

"Jessy and I," Mrs. Broome said judicially, "feel
that that is the wisest thing for you to do."

"Why, but what would my mother think—what
would everyone think? Everyone knows it's my club—
everyone knows that I'm in everything the Cinderellas
do—the Mardi Gras and the theatricals and the Hospital Fund!" Pamela stammered. "I couldn't explain—
and besides, whatever the appearances were, I *didn't*
do anything wrong, Mrs. Broome."

Silence. Mrs. Broome continued to regard her
thoughtfully, dispassionately.

"Appearances matter, don't they, Pamela? It
doesn't concern you and me what people do, does it?—
but it does concern us what they *seem* to do. And *girls*
—girls must respect themselves, or how can any of the
rest of us respect them? Even on your own account,
Pamela, was that a fine thing—was that an admirable
thing to do last night?

"Now, my dear, you must make up your mind that

the simplest way out, and the quietest way out, is to resign from the Cinderellas," she went on, as Pamela, dazed, was still. "That means that there will be no discussion and no split. Jessy told me frankly this morning that some of the older crowd, the married set, have been pretty well disgusted with the way some of the Carterbridge girls and boys have been acting. She said to me that she *would not tolerate* certain things in the club. 'Even if he is my own cousin,' she said, 'Chester Hilliard cannot introduce immorality into Carterbridge.'"

"That," Pamela protested, scarlet-cheeked, "that is absolutely unfair! He's a stranger here—he didn't know anything about Hatter's—he only got here last Wednesday——"

"I'm afraid that you don't make a very good case for yourself there, Pamela. You *did* know about Hatter's, didn't you? But the whole case is this: We cannot —Doctor and I and Jessy and some of the others—if they knew—we *cannot* overlook this episode. We wouldn't be the right sort of fathers and mothers if we did. We *cannot* say that you didn't mean anything wrong and that it was a harmless escapade—no, it's too much. If things of this kind are to be tolerated, then there's nothing left of honour or decency at all.

"I don't want to be hard on you. Jessy herself said that there was no need for publicity, or discussion— nobody but ourselves need know. But you must resign from the Cinderellas."

It was a nightmare. She couldn't be awake, Pamela felt, here in the familiar Broome sitting room, listening to this.

She wet her dry lips, looked up from a study of the rug.

"What *reason* could I give, Mrs. Broome?"

"That your mother couldn't afford it, for one thing," the older woman said readily, unexpectedly.

The proud fair head went up again and Pamela's eyes shone black.

"My mother is glad to pay that twenty dollars a year—she wants us to have everything."

She felt her throat thicken and her eyes sting; she was going to add the last triumph to this merciless woman's conquest by crying like a baby before her.

"But your mother is a poor woman, my dear child. How much older are you going to be before you realize that?" asked Mrs. Broome compassionately. "Several of us, Mrs. Beaver and Mrs. Catherwood and myself, have been watching you for years, watching you spend your mother's little income for clothes like the other girls, pleasures and extravagances far, far beyond your means! Haven't you ever thought of helping her, Pamela, like a woman, instead of trying to hold your own with the few girls in this town whose fathers can afford to give them everything? There are fine things about you, my dear——"

To get out of this room. To get out of this room. To get home, to her own quiet room, and lie there until she died . . .

"Maisie and you were little-girl chums, and she loves you dearly," pursued the modulated, admonitory voice, "but even Maisie has said to me sometimes, 'Mumsie, if I were in Pam's place, I think I'd help you —I wouldn't want to see you worried——' "

"I don't believe it!" Pamela interrupted fiercely.

"Don't—how do you mean?" Mrs. Broome asked, bewildered and incredulous. "Don't believe *me?*"

"You must have misunderstood Maisie. She's loyal," Pam said desperately.

"She does love you, my dear, as we all did—no, I'll say as we all *do*," said the other, a little touched in spite of herself. "It's only that we want you to live up to the possibilities of your own fine nature, Pam. And now is your chance. Resign from the Cinderellas, get a good position downtown, stand by your dear little mother, who has had so much trouble! And Carter, too—Doctor always says that there is a great deal that is good in that boy——"

"I don't know anyone who thinks there *isn't!*" Pamela said, with a surprised and resentful laugh.

"I meant—about being expelled from the Cinderella Club," Mrs. Broome said delicately.

The girl flung up her head, looked at her with dilated eyes. There was a moment of silence.

"Carter! Why—why, what are you *talking* about?" Pamela said bluntly, too stunned to remember her manners.

"You knew that, Pamela?"

"Knew *what?*"

"That Carter—why, that was three weeks ago!" exclaimed Mrs. Broome, hearing, in the back of her own mind, her own sympathetic voice retailing these details to the doctor, later on.

Pamela, scarlet, was staring at her with a thinly veiled hatred in her eyes. The girl was breathing hard, her one conscious impulse was to say furiously, "It's a lie."

"Carter has been drinking disgracefully, Pamela," Mrs. Broome said gently, regretfully, "and in a special meeting of the directors this was decided on some time ago."

The girl took the shock bravely, swallowing once with a dry throat, raising her chin proudly, facing the other woman with a haggard, desperate young face.

"I'm sorry, I didn't know," she said briefly. She got to her feet, bowed jerkily, as a child might bow, and turned toward the door. "One thing more," she said, in a hard, resentful voice, "if I resign, there's no reason why my mother should hear any gossip—there won't be any talk?"

"Not unless you force it by making the club ask for your resignation, Pamela," Mrs. Broome said, cheerfully, rising also. "Some day, my dear," she added, "you may see this as a turning point in your life. You may see——"

"One more thing," Pamela interrupted, still in a hard, cold voice. "There *was* nothing wrong last night, and there was no thought of any such thing. If it's any satisfaction to you to know that you've ruined my life for *nothing,* you have it!"

"It was nothing to go to Hatter's at midnight, alone with a man, Pam? You've forgotten that part of it. The miracle is," said Mrs. Broome, "that doing the things that you do, you girls aren't continually in some such trouble." She laid her hand on the girl's arm. "We don't gain happiness by trying to force ourselves into positions that are not natural to us, my dear," she said. "The duty that lies nearest—that's the solution of all our lives. Far better hold a good position and lift the burden of responsibility from that little mother of yours than fight to hold your place in society—at too high a cost. Why, many of our finest women are not society women——"

"Good-bye, Mrs. Broome," Pamela said shortly, at the door.

"Good-bye, my dear." The older woman felt a little rebuffed, but the girl, of course, was hurt and shamed, and she could afford to be generous. She watched the slender figure go down the garden path, between the gillyflowers and marigolds and plumed phlox, and sighed. Maisie might feel badly about this. But it would serve to teach the unmanageable youngsters a lesson—scare them a little. And the penniless daughter of dreary little inefficient Mrs. Raleigh, be she ever so pretty and charming, was no great loss to the Cinderellas. Carterbridge's nicer society was growing fast, richer and more exclusive families were moving into town every year, and the Cinderellas had a most distinguished waiting list. The club was fortunate to be able to take so startling and so educational a stand with so entirely dispensable a member as little Pamela Raleigh. All for the child's good, too; she had been spoiled, she should have been helping her mother years ago.

CHAPTER VII

CHESTER HILLIARD came to dinner at the old
Carter house a few days later, and Pamela worked
herself almost into a nervous fever trying to make sure
that everything would appear at its best for his benefit.
She struggled with flowers, dessert and salad, dust and
dishes, all day long, and in the end looked tired and
excited, as indeed she was, and thought bitterly to herself that never had things gone so badly or the old
rooms looked so shabby.

They had to have the gas lighted in the frosted
globes high overhead; it seemed to accentuate the
dim, discoloured wall paper and the worn carpets, the
slitted red rep hangings that showed vistas of dark
overgrown garden through high, dirty windows.

"I don't know what we can do," Mrs. Raleigh had
said, in reference to this last detail. "We can't very
well wash 'em, an' if you haven't money for servants,
well, you haven't, that's all!"

When the meal had dragged itself to a subdued and
uncomfortable close, Pamela and Chester walked
downtown to a movie and had their first words together, alone.

"How goes it, Pamela?" the man asked sympatheti-

cally, as they went through the bright splotches of light
from the high street lamps and into the black shade of
the trees and out into the white light again.

"Oh, I guess I'm in Coventry, all right. And isn't it
ridiculous!" the girl said, with a philosophic laugh.

"It's a rotten shame!" Chester said warmly. "I
thought there was a Bolshevik movement?"

"Well, there was. At least, Maisie Broome simply
raised the roof when she realized what was going on,
but I believe Dr. Broome told her that if he heard anything more about it Maisie would simply have to leave
home—anyway, that's what Sam said. I don't know
how much Sam knows. Sam's mother, Mrs. Billings,
and Carol have gone to Tahoe for two weeks, you
know—I'm positive it's just to get away until the thing
blows over. Harry and Bill Beaver say they don't
know anything about it—Bill told me simply to forget
it and go on as if nothing had happened. But I can't,
of course," Pamela confessed, with a little laugh to
contradict her own words. "Perhaps it will blow over
and everything will be all right again, but just at the
moment it seems as if I were standing all alone—and
I don't like it!"

"It's so darned unfair!" Chester protested. "Whatever you did, I did, and nobody's ostracizing *me* that I
can see!"

"Well, with men it's different. And you're new here
and hardly know them, anyway. But I believe you're
not to be asked to join the Cinderellas."

"Yes, and a lot that matters, with *you* out of it!"

Pamela was silent for a moment. Then, in a voice
not quite steady, she said:

"That sounds mighty sweet to me, Chester!"

"It'll all clear up!" he said confidently.

"I suppose so." But she sighed wearily in the dark.

The film was good; she followed it interestedly and was happy again, sitting close to Chester, forgetting her troubles for a little while.

Afterward they walked home together, in the balmy summer night, and Pamela thanked him, at the Raleigh gate, for "standing by her."

"What else should I do, you poor idiot?" Chester said. But he was pleased nevertheless. "Aren't you going to ask me to come in?" he demanded, so blankly that she laughed her old laugh again.

The girl sat in a porch chair, and Chester on the top of the porch steps with his head against her knee. The moon rose and shone down into the old garden through the tall, motionless shafts of the eucalyptus and pear trees. The silver light poured and dripped through the trees and formed itself in silver pools in the garden; the world was transfigured and turned into a magic place of strangely black shadows and strangely white lights.

There was a scent of old-fashioned drowsy flowers in the garden, stock and wallflowers, roses drenched in dew, and citrus verbena. Chester sat sideways, so that by glancing up he could see the blur in the gloom of the porch that was Pamela's white gown, and the little pearly oval that was her face. She had taken off her hat, and a dim pink light through the old-fashioned strips of frosted glass that framed the doorway and the fanlight above shone dully on her tumbled, lustreless fair hair.

Coventry was forgotten now, and all the agonies and changes of the past week. She was nineteen, and the man was only a few years older, and it was midsummer night. The moonlight throbbed and throbbed like a living, beating thing, upon the garden and upon the scented, dewy, sleeping world.

After a while the man put his hand up, and she slipped her fingers, smooth and warm and young, into it, and they sat so, murmuring, murmuring, murmuring.

Presently, her hand still gripped in his, Pamela slipped down to the seat beside him, and he put his arm about her, and she rested her head on his shoulder. Chester bent his head and kissed her, slowly and deliberately, and although Pamela's breast rose quickly and she expelled her breath on a long sigh, she made no protest.

"We are companions in misfortune, Pam," Chester whispered.

"And misery," she whispered back, with a little laugh, "loves company!"

"And I love you," the man added, very low.

His lips were upon hers again; she could not answer. Her head back, her eyes closed, her beautiful body supple and soft and sweet in his arms, for a blissful half minute she gave herself up to love and youth and moonlight, and the sorrows of yesterday and to-morrow were forgotten in the perfect moment of to-night.

"You do love me?" he murmured.

"I do love you," she breathed.

"And nothing else matters, does it, Pam?"

"Nothing else in the world!"

From upstairs her mother's sleepy voice called her, and Pamela and Chester shook themselves free of the dripping silver-white moonlight and the black lace shadows, and, confusedly laughing, the girl lifted her flushed and fragrant face for a last kiss, and Chester, her hands gathered tightly in his and pressed against his heart, stooped over her for a moment, ran down the steps, and lifted his straw hat with a last good-night.

Then he was gone, and Pamela went upstairs, through the close hot house that retained all the warmth and odours of the long day, and into her black dark bedroom, whose only light was supplied by the streaks of silver moonshine that crossed the high windows.

She went to one of these windows and knelt at its open sill and rested her elbows there. The moon was overhead now, and straining down through the branches and heavy leaves of the trees. Its eerie light picked out from all the shadowed details of the side garden below a bench fallen against the latticed wall that had separated the flowers from the vegetables, when there had been flowers and vegetables and a gardener, many years ago. Wall and bench and flowers were all sunk in a general neglected jumble now; the collapsing lattices threw delicate patterns, like lace, across the path. The deeper shrubbery, where old palms were caught in the savage long streamers of roses gone crazy, and where twisted muscular-looking oaks were hung with a hundred luxuriant creepers, had the aspect of an actual jungle.

Pamela made no coherent prayer; she was hardly conscious of coherent thought. Once a whisper broke from her.

"Oh, my God, I would be so happy! I would be so *good!*"

"I've never seen Daddy so sad or so stern," Maisie told Sue Rose Catherwood some days later. "He never said an ugly word. He said I was to be as nice to Pamela as I could, if we met, but he said I wasn't to go to her house or have her at ours. I cried—well, simply floods! My father told Mumsie—but she didn't tell me that until after—that he would cut off my allowance like a shot and send me away, if there was any nonsense. You know," Maisie continued, in the full flood of mournful and romantic confidence, "my father's my guardian until I'm twenty-one. I get my grandmother's money then. He said he didn't wish any harm to Pam——"

"I know!" Sue Rose said, sighing. She had always been jealous of the intimacy between Maisie and Pamela, always eager to break into their charmed circle. And now she couldn't help enjoying the chance to have Maisie all to herself and this new and thrilling bond to hold them together. "Mother said," she went on, "that Pam had done the one thing that couldn't be forgiven. Isn't it terrible? It seems like a nightmare that it's *Pam!*"

"And everybody seems to know it," Maisie said. "My mother told me because the minute I heard that Pam had resigned from the Cinderellas I wanted to rush right over there—so she *had* to. And I guess Jessy Stokes told quite a few. We're going up to the lake next week, until this blows over, and the Billingses are, too. Sue Rose," she added suddenly, in a changed, somewhat self-conscious tone, "do you suppose they'll get married now?"

"Pam and Chester?" Sue Rose asked alertly. "Yes, I suppose they will," she answered unhesitatingly. "Because, look, what else can they do?"

"It doesn't seem quite fair," Maisie said lightly, dreamily.

"You mean that she should get him, after all? No, but she will!" Sue Rose said darkly.

"Do you think he's attractive, Sue?" Maisie asked hesitatingly.

Sue Rose answered slowly, deliberately, her eyes far away.

"I think that without exception he's the most fascinating man I ever saw in my life," she said.

"Yes, I do, too," Maisie said, in a low tone.

"Look, here's the way I feel about him, Maisie," the other girl said suddenly and honestly, "I feel that if I could have—you know, could *get* him," Sue Rose went on, floundering, "have him fall in love with me, and—and marry him, why, I'd never want anything else in the world. I'd never want to travel or marry a title, you know, or anything like that! I don't say everyone would feel that way, but that's the way I feel."

"Yes, I feel that way about him, too, Sue Rose," Maisie said very simply.

The confidence made them feel suddenly close, and they looked with a sort of shamefaced pride at each other and laughed, as if even to admit an unrequited devotion to Chester Hilliard was a distinction

"The old Carter house is going to be sold, you know that," Maisie said, after a while.

"I know it. And Elaine Mulligan said that Pamela asked her for a job," Sue Rose added.

The other girl looked genuinely shocked.

"What—in a hat store!"

"Oh, well, I guess she just thought she'd fluff around and sell hats to her friends."

"Well, Mrs. Beaver said that she telephoned her —Pam did, I mean—and asked about the kindergarten work, and Mrs. Beaver said that she was really glad to be able to say conscientiously that they took only trained teachers. I guess the Raleighs are pretty hard up!" said Maisie.

"Oh, well, if she marries Chester she'll be all right!" Sue Rose said jealously. And this piercing thought hardened Maisie's heart, too, and she told herself that, no matter how poor she was, Pamela Raleigh always had a fashion of coming out on top.

CHAPTER VIII

COMING into the darkened side door of the old Carter house on a drenching January afternoon six months later, Pamela Raleigh made a little sound of pleasure as she saw a familiar hat and overcoat hanging there.

She took off her damp outer garments hurriedly, fluffed her damp hair with all ten spread fingers, and looked expectantly into the kitchen.

"Hello, Chester!" she said, colour coming into her tired face. "Nice to find you here!"

"But he won't stay to dinner; he's dinin' with Jessy," Mrs. Raleigh, who had the unfortunate habit of always greeting the tired or weary members of the family with whatever depressing news there was, added promptly.

The older woman was at the stove, struggling in uncertain lamplight with a sizzling pan; Carter, at the table, had folded his long, lean young arms before him and rested his face upon them and upon the crumpled evening paper. Chester was seated by the window, against whose shining black panes trickled and dripped the little twisting worms of the rain.

Pamela saw that he was in evening dress and went suddenly weary and discouraged again. He came often to the old Carter house, he was unchangeably her friend, but he never wore evening dress when he came. To-night he was going on somewhere, unless they could persuade him to stay.

"Hello, Pam," he said, not rising. His affectionate and easy status here was that of an older brother now. "How's the world?"

"The world is wet," Pamela answered, kissing her mother, inspecting the pan critically. "Deary, you have too slow a fire under that," she murmured. Then, more audibly, "What's happened to the gas?"

"They're movin' the mains the first thing to-morrow," her mother explained, "an' they've turned us off!"

"No more gas in the old Carter house," Pamela commented patiently. Carter looked up sleepily, burst into laughter, and buried his head again.

"Moving the mains—that's a good one!" he said appreciatively.

"I had Cart find some of those ole lamps down cellar," Mrs. Raleigh explained, wiping her hands on a limp strip of apron and tapping her son on the shoulder with a small, veiny hand. "Come on upstairs, Cart, an' make yo'self presentable," she said, "an' we'll leave Pam to persuade Chester to stay for dinner."

"That was sufficiently obvious," Pamela commented drily, as her mother and brother went out. "The pains poor M'ma takes to leave you and me alone!"

"Lucky, though," Chester said, "for I really wanted to see you, for a minute."

"Not really?" The explanation stung her. She couldn't help the little bitter, ironic laugh that went with the words. The man's expression changed to one of grieved reproach.

Quite unemotionally he put his arm about her and kissed her on the mouth, and Pamela submitted rather than invited the caress, her own face not losing the patient, scornful, and weary look it had assumed as soon as her mother left the room.

"Now, don't take that tone, Pam!" Chester pleaded, half affectionate and half sorrowful, and yet all the while maddeningly uninvolved.

She blinked her eyes, braced her shoulders, and drew a long breath. It was becoming increasingly difficult to maintain a philosophical calm and self-control with Chester as her fortunes dwindled and sank and his own steadied and rose.

"You're tired, dearest," he said tenderly.

Kisses and tenderness and "dearests." And all so automatic in these days—so lifeless, somehow! Pamela, taking a stale half loaf from an old tin box fancifully lettered "Cake," was conscious of a heavy-hearted wish that she had never met him, never let him kiss her, that Jessy Stokes's stunning cousin was still to be encountered—and won.

"No, I'm not tired," she said briefly, sturdily. She wouldn't sue for his sympathy, and yet she wanted it so terribly to-night. "Well, I finally worked out the Raleigh family's indebtedness," she observed, with a sudden change of topic, an effort to make the conversation quite impersonal. "And it's"—she pared a crust carefully—"it's awful!" she finished with a laugh.

Instead of answering, Chester came to her, and tak

ing the knife gently from her hand, laid it on the table and put his arms about her.

"Look here," he said, refusing the change of topic, "don't you like me any more?"

The girl, conscious of a suddenly thickening throat, was silent for a minute, her fingers on the lapels of his coat, her breast against his own, her beautiful thick lashes raised above the serious gray eyes to his lovingly troubled look.

"Of course I like you," she answered resentfully, almost impatiently.

"But, then, why do you act like this with me, dear?" he pleaded.

He had asked it a hundred times in the last few months, and on every occasion she could only answer, as she did to-night, "I don't know."

"Is there anything I *could* do that I'm not doing?" Chester asked.

So perfect—so impeccable—so little to blame for it all! She hated herself for holding him; she could not let him go.

"No-o," she admitted reluctantly.

"Well, what is it, then, dear?"

"Oh, nothing—" Pamela answered, already soothed by the touch of his big arms—"Only—I never should have let you in for this," she went on fretfully. "You —you'd have a much better time if you didn't come here—didn't worry about us!"

"Pam," he said, his eyes reproachful, "have I deserved this?"

He was acting, of course, she told herself scornfully. But then, wasn't she acting, too? Hadn't she been acting, in the very beginning last Rodeo Week, when she had pretended to be so much in love, and

had let Chester kiss her, and had talked love talk—
hours and hours and hours of it—to him? Weren't all
girls just acting, during those wild "crushes" and
"cases" and "rushes" that formed the very prelimina-
ries to their friendships with men, nowadays?

After a decent girl had permitted a man to kiss her,
embrace her, sit for the long hours of summer moon-
lights with her cuddled up in his arms, there was little
left for her to concede. Pamela had given Chester all
these privileges, eagerly, unthinkingly, instantly, and
during the months that followed, those painful months
of social and financial reckoning that had made this
year different from all the other years of her happy
life, she did not quite know what to do.

In six days of love-making she had reached the wall
beyond which she must not go; six weeks of the same
kisses, the same endearments, the same embraces had
brought Chester and herself to the high tide of that
young passion that should have been taken at its flood.

Unfortunately for them this could not be. His very
meetings with her were more or less clandestine, the
relationship between himself and his uncle still unsettled and precarious, and the affairs of the Raleighs in
a lamentable condition. Carterbridge society was dili-
gently criticizing and snubbing Pamela Raleigh; nothing was established and nothing normal.

Woman fashion, Pamela had begun to long for the
visible evidences of his devotion, for the flutter of the
engagement, the presents, the stir of wedding plans.
And these had not followed.

But a time of pain and uncertainty had instead set
in, a time when she more and more doubted her power,
or her right, to hold him, and when everything in his
life conspired against her to draw Chester away from

her. Almost every day now brought her some new proof that Carterbridge had forgiven him his share of the long-ago escapade and was taking him once more to its heart.

Under the circumstances, Pamela couldn't be happy, gay, provocative, daring, any more. She had angry moods, scornful moods, bitter times when she told him—told Chester, himself so handsome and groomed and secure—to go away from her entirely.

She knew wretchedly that the day would come when he would take her at her word; she knew that her kisses, three months after the Rodeo, had meant less to him than the first delicious kisses had meant, and that to-day's kisses, six months after the happy summer, were less significant again. It was something of a pose with the handsome, much-courted young fellow now, this attitude of loyalty and devotion to poor little Pam Raleigh, who was down and out. He told Jessy and his uncle and whoever else betrayed curiosity or dropped hints that he liked Pam Raleigh better than anyone else in town. And afterward he told Pamela, and she praised him. But despite her praises Pamela did not want that sort of attention. She wanted him to be breathless, ecstatic, proud over the triumph of winning her, not patient, gentle, mildly reproving of her moods, even sometimes critical of her despairs.

"You mustn't take it so hard, Pam," he said kindly, to-night, when they were seated at the kitchen table, working over her accounts. "It's hard lines, of course, but everyone has a turn at it. I've had an awfully stiff time at the bank, getting started, and nobody ever hears *me* complain!"

A protest rose in her heart, but she stilled it and

made herself smile; made herself seem careless and merry again.

"Well, here's the horrible total!" she said cheerfully, making figures firmly with her pencil, resting the eraser against her lips, and looking up at him wide-eyed. Glorious eyes, in this lamplight, Chester thought.

"What is it?" he asked aloud.

"Seventeen eighty-five and taxes next month one seventeen," Pam repeated. "Nineteen hundred and two. It sounds like a year!"

"That's everything?"

"Everything." She nodded seriously, like an uninvolved child.

"What might your mother get if the house sells? It's partly hers, isn't it?"

"Not one penny. It belongs to the bank, and the arrangement was that she was simply to live along here and pay taxes, as a sort of rent—about twenty dollars a month."

"Which she didn't pay."

"Which she hasn't paid. But, of course, she's had absolutely no income at all. She sold that strip off the back of the property about six years ago, and she's been living on the capital ever since."

"And overdrawing."

"And overdrawing. And my grandfather practically owned Carterbridge," Pamela commented unemotionally.

"I know. It seems funny!"

She put her elbows on the table, rumpled her hair.

"I don't know what to do about it!" she said childishly. "They've turned our gas off here; we'll *have* to get out, now. I don't suppose there's a chair or a bed

in the house that would bring ten dollars at auction—
they were talking of an auction. But people don't
build rooms big enough for furniture like this in these
days. All my grandfather's books are fine, fine print
and water-stained and swollen out of their bindings;
they aren't even fuel! My grandmother's Canton
china set might bring a few hundreds, but everyone
can get Canton, nowadays—it isn't as if the Chinese
ever changed anything or stopped making it. I really
—honestly, Chester, I don't know exactly how we're
going to live, or where, much less pay off nearly two
thousand dollars in old bills."

"Well, now, let's see," he said, resolutely encourag-
ing, looking at the pencilled calculations again. "In the
first place, your credit is good. Everyone knows you
will pay—eventually. That helps."

"I don't know why everyone *should*," the girl said
frankly. "We certainly haven't given much reason for
that idea. I was looking at some of those little old-
fashioned cottages down near Broome Street to-day,"
she went on, "and I notice that rent in advance is one
of the rules. Thirty-five a month, but they're not bad.
Of course, they have rough floors and no closet space
and all that. But even that would be quite a responsibility as things are now."

Her thoughts wandered. She was near enough to
him to catch a pleasant aroma of shaving soap and
toilet water. She thought that Chester was looking his
best to-night—like all handsome men, at his handsomest in evening dress.

"Where is it this evening?" she asked.

"I'm squiring Jessy to-night—Jack's away. I think
it's bridge at the Forbes's."

She imagined him in the handsome quiet rooms of

the Forbes mansion: his sleek black head and fine
hands, the subdued lights at the card tables, the click
of the cards as they fell.

"Do you like bridge, Chester?"

"Kinder."

"And I'll bet," said Pamela wistfully, "that you play
well."

"Good enough to get by with this crowd," he answered indifferently.

"It seems to me they're—forgiving you, Chester."
She had to say it, although it hurt her to put her fear
into words.

"They needn't distress themselves!" he said coolly.

"Before Easter—" Pamela's elbows were on the
table, her chin in her palm, her eyes fixed on him—
"Before Easter they'll ask you to join the Cinderella
Club; you'll see if they don't!"

"I should like—" he lighted a cigarette—"I should
like a chance to decline the honour!" he said.

"No, no; you wouldn't do that, and you mustn't do
that," the girl said. She put out her fine hand and laid
it on his for a second, making no other acknowledg-
ment of the loyalty that was so exquisitely dear to her.

"The Cinderellas are extremely subdued," he told
her. "They're all in theatricals, you know, and doing
writing games—puzzles and quizzes and all that. They
have dances once a month, but they go out to the Country Club and come home at about midnight, as sober
as judges!"

"And I suppose Mrs. Beaver and Mrs. Broome
take great credit to themselves!" It sounded bitter, but
she couldn't help it—she *was* bitter.

"Oh, yes—and Jessy. They're the upholders of mo-
rality, all right. Jessy treats me as if I might break out

into larceny or violence at any minute. She'll take me
to these dead-and-alive parties, like to-night, and fill
me up with chocolate layer cake and fruit punch—and
we usually win an ash tray or a green glass mayonnaise
dish, and then coming home she'll sort of cuddle up
against me in the car and purr at me, 'It *was* fun,
wasn't it, Chester? And *aren't* they nice, kind, simple
people, and isn't it a sweet home?' "

"I can hear her!" Pam said. "But, then, why don't
you stay here with us, Chester, and have some dinner
here?" she added impulsively.

"Oh, I couldn't. Jessy'd never forgive me."

"She has a rather low opinion of your character,
anyway," Pamela said persuasively.

"I know. But I couldn't do that!" His tone was decided; he was not even considering it. And suddenly
Pamela felt like the girl of the other world—the girl
who importunes and coaxes, the girl to whom a broken
engagement means nothing, and her cheeks burned
red in the dim black and red lamplight of the shabby
old food-scented kitchen, and she was still.

"I wish I had the last half year to live over again,"
she managed to say presently, as Chester, made
wretchedly uncomfortable by her emotion—sympathetic enough, but in deadly fear that she would break
down into real sobbing—began to make little marks
and quirls on the paper before him with his fountain
pen.

"That—experience of ours hasn't anything to do
with all this money trouble, Pam," he said somewhat
brusquely.

"The ostracism, you mean, the being dropped overnight?"

"Well, if you want to call it that!"

She did not dispute it. But she knew better. She knew now, when it was too late, how easy—how exhilarating it would have been for the Pamela Raleigh of a year ago to encounter this reverse of a mere material fortune, to state frankly her money problems to kind Mrs. Beaver and intelligently helpful Mrs. Broome and friendly, admiring Jessy Stokes, who had always called the seven-year-younger Pam "one of her kids." They would have advised her, stood behind her; their loyalty would have supported her through the picturesqueness of hospital training or a partnership in some pretty tea shop, all orange and black china, and gold gauze curtains.

Chester felt troubled, almost angry, at his own helplessness. He knew Carterbridge better, now, than he had known it six months ago, and he appreciated far more clearly than Pamela did the desperate nature of her situation. He knew that her mother was involved to the last stretching of creditors' patience and bank and personal credit. And he thought it was too bad!

Meanwhile he had also become acquainted with the affairs of Maisie Broome and Sue Rose Catherwood. Sue Rose would have a large fortune; Maisie be independent. It made a girl safer, somehow, a nice little bank account, responsible persons back of her, her pretty little signature on checks.

"Well, perhaps I ought to move on," he said, putting away his pen.

Pamela had assumed a large limp apron, and in the dim lamplight she was assembling the inevitable bread and butter and sugar bowl on the kitchen table. The kettle had been singing shrilly for some time.

"I went down to the *Express* to-day and talked to

old Foster. He said the usual thing," the girl said, breaking eggs into a bowl.

"Which is——?"

"Oh, that they'd take my name and address and keep me in mind."

"Can't you stay, Chester?" Mrs. Raleigh said, returning.

"I really can't, thanks, Mrs. Raleigh."

"Pamela, what you thinkin' of that you don't keep him?"

Pamela did not answer in words. She nodded an understanding good-bye to Chester, who slipped away, and presently asked her mother, who had fallen into a discontented sort of silence, whether Miss Rogers had telephoned about the position of matron at the school.

"Perhaps they've changed their minds about that," the girl said, filling the teapot and drawing up a chair as her mother shook her head.

"Well, I'm just as well pleased," Mrs. Raleigh said. "It's an awful dull place for a girl yo' age; runnin' the holidays an' managin' the laundry for those little girls!"

"It's a *job,* M'ma dear."

"Yes, I know it is, but, my gracious! isn't there anything but money in the world nowadays? I never did hear girls talk as mercenary as you do now, Pam. No matter what you made, it wouldn't be enough. Why aren't you content just to have a good time, like you use' to be? You an' Maisie and the other girls use' to be real companionable, an' I guess you had as much as they had, even if yo' home was a little shabby. But now it's money, money, money," said Mrs. Raleigh resentfully, "always tellin' me how much I owe and sittin'

round here so ole-fashioned and quiet! I want to tell
you you'll never get married, Pam, if you keep this up.
Boys don't like girls that are always talkin' ways an'
means—you mark my words. What you need is to forget all this business worry, and get yo'self a new dress
and begin to enjoy yo'self again. I'm going down to the
bank to-morrow an' have a talk with ole man Stokes
—you see if I don't—an' I'm going to tell him what
I tole Judge Beaver. 'When my father Tom Carter
was alive,' I tole him, 'we didn't hear all this talk
about interest an' taxes! My own house,' I tole him,
'that my father built—an' here they go puttin' a big
sign right out in the garden, where anyone but a child
could see it, sayin' that this desirable corner property
is for sale, suitable for apartment house or office
buildin'!' "

"M'ma, it'll be very comfortable in a smaller place,"
Pamela said soothingly. "This room is the only room
in the place to live in, in winter—the halls are simply
ice boxes. I saw one of those Broome Street cottages
to-day, and it was nice and sunny——"

"What I can't understand, Pam, is you an' Carter
takin' sides with the bank against me!" her mother
complained. "They'd never dared come here and begin
to tear down the stable fence like they are if you
children had felt like I feel about it. I always hoped
you'd be married in this house, Pam, like I was—it's
a beautiful house for a weddin', and it lights up so
pretty at night. All you've got to do is raise yo' finger
and you could have Chester Hilliard; everyone knows
that!—an' yet here you are talkin' about gettin' a job
an' movin' down to that place near Chinatown, where
there's nothin' but stores an' boardin' houses. He *is*

in love with you, isn't he, Pam?" she asked, a trifle uncertainly, as the girl, drying the few dishes, wiping
the sink, neither turned nor spoke.

Pamela answered slowly, honestly, "M'ma, I don t
know whether he's in love with me or not!"

CHAPTER IX

S HE argued the question incessantly with herself,
her mother was not the only one to ask it. It
gnawed at her heart day and night; it was with her
waking and sleeping.

"Everything has been so upset—so unsettled," she
would reflect. "He couldn't say anything very definite,
poor fellow. But he must—he must still care, it *must*
be that we are working along toward a marriage—
there can't be any other explanation!"

He *had* been in love with her until that fatal Saturday night. He had had what the girls called a case on
Pamela, on those sun-flooded, radiant days of the
Rodeo, last year. He had walked beside Pamela, sat
beside Pamela, talked to no one else, he had bought
her peanuts and sodas and pennants; they had had a
photograph taken together, with a background of
charging bulls and wild horses. Pamela hated to look
at that picture now, at the smiling man in the white
flannels and the happy girl in the loose white coat.

They had laughed incessantly in those days; there
was little laughter now. Chester came to see her loy-
ally, and they talked in the old kitchen, or Pamela
spread a tablecloth, so big that it had to be doubled

four ways, in the dining room and he stayed to dinner. But somehow the confidence and bloom and laughter were gone.

The first casual investigation of M'ma's finances had been enough to still Pamela's laughter, for one thing. It appeared that M'ma, having exhausted every available shred of capital on all sides, had proceeded to exhaust every available shred of credit as well. M'ma had borrowed right and left, ten dollars here, a hundred dollars there. The house was gone entirely: it had not been theirs in any sense for actual years. Worse than all was M'ma's attitude toward her liabilities.

"Just tear that ole bill up. I don't believe they're ever goin' to ask me for that ole eighty dollars."

"But, M'ma, you owe it!"

"Well, in a way I do, an' in a way I don't. The very sto' that man has stands on property that belonged to my father."

And M'ma would purse her lips and raise her lean little face proudly, as one who could launch very thunderbolts of retaliation at her creditors, if nobility of birth had not forbidden.

Small wonder that Pamela could find little cause for laughter in these days.

"Just keep a stiff upper lip," Chester would urge her. "This will all pass—when they get tired of it. Something else'll come along to keep these old women buzzing, one of these days. Don't lose your nerve, Pam—you'll work out of it. Before you know it you'll have a job, and Cart'll be working, and you'll have moved out of this big, cold place and be in comfortable quarters, and I'll be vice president of the bank—and we'll show 'em!"

It was heartening beyond words; indeed, she felt as if she could not have weathered the hard, dragging months without Chester's encouragement; felt that she must have gone into melancholia, into fever, without him. But it wasn't love-making, any more.

And meanwhile, to the debts were added, of necessity, more debts. The three Raleighs must eat, and there were microscopic expenses of gas bill, M'ma's newspaper, money for Cart's trip to San Jose, when he made an unavailing journey there in search of a job.

One day Pamela walked into Mockby's big department store, and asked for the employment office, and talked to a pleasant, tooth-sucking, shrewd little gray man who apparently liked the duty of telling pretty girls that salesmanship was a fine art and that Mockby's wasn't taking on any extra hands now, anyway. The holidays were the busy time—nothing now until the Easter rush.

"We have a sort of club system here; might not work everywhere, but it does with us," said Mr. Woolcock. "The girls practically manage it themselves. I believe I've had a title invented—'consulting manager.' That means that any girl in this shop can walk in here at any hour—put her problem to me, whatever it is, make a clean breast of it . . ."

There was more of this. Pamela, listening with the new mannerliness that she was painfully and slowly acquiring, was reminded fantastically of Alice and the Mock Turtle. Presently, like Alice, she rose respectfully and thanked Mr. Woolcock for his interesting history. But her cheeks were blazing and her heart cold as she walked out of the store.

Nettie, of "Nettie's," more kindly and sympatheti-
cally, told her the same thing.

"It's this way, dear. There are weeks when Mrs.
Harrison and I don't make our rent, and that's the
truth! I had that girl we called Julie in here, paid her
fifteen a week, and I had to let her go. We said then
we'd never pay more than ten and commission. . . ."

Ten dollars a week. That wouldn't even be rent.
How did people live in this world, Pamela wondered.
Everyone—everyone one passed in the street was
alive, and had had breakfast or lunch a few hours ago.
Women buying early asparagus, and men parking cars
beside the curb—how did they do it?

She hated to go back at night to the gloomy house
with the dark trees about it, and the little complaining
woman in the kitchen. Mrs. Raleigh's attitude had become one of melancholy triumph.

"You an' Cart think you're such wonderful man-
agers, but I don't see anything wonderful about it, if
you ask me! Things went on a good deal better the
way I had 'em!" she would say.

Pamela began to read the advertisements in the
morning paper. "I never thought anyone did that except immigrants right off the steamers," she said to
Chester one day, "but desperate maladies demand
desperate remedies!"

"Do the best you can and then forget it!" was Chester's advice. "If things go wrong at the bank, I just
wipe 'em out of my mind and go out and play golf or
something! That's the only way."

"I'm boring him with my troubles," she thought,
chilled and proud. And she made herself talk of other
things. But presently, looking up from her soup, she
saw him quickly, furtively looking at his wrist watch.

It was a Saturday afternoon, and they were lunching at the "Kopper Kettle," as they almost always did before a movie on Saturdays. But spring was coming in a rush now, and movies were flagging. Chester's thoughts had gone to the Country Club, where Jessy had asked him to play golf to-day, as a special mark of favour. He had said that he would make it if he could.

"You've got an engagement?" Pamela asked, almost reading his thoughts and flushing sensitively.

"No, honestly not." It wasn't a real engagement; he had just said he would come if he could. And the possibility, as the time passed, continually fretted at his thoughts.

Not that he cared, especially, to accept the favours of the Country Club. But these were wonderful near-spring days, and he loved the game. And more than that, Jessy, in her benighted little smug way, had been showing a really pathetic desire, of late, to reinstate him, to restore him to social favour. He had played golf with her a few Sundays ago, and as they went from green to green they had passed other golfers, playing, and had exchanged greetings. "Hello, Jessy —oh, how do you do, Chester, how do you do? Isn't it? What would Easterners give for a New Year's Day like this?"

Sue Rose Catherwood, in a bright scarlet coat and the smartest of white wool skirts, and lazy little Maisie, with a muffled fur collar about her friendly little face—well, they hadn't said anything or done anything significant, after all; it had all been casual enough. But it was his own language that they had spoken—pleasant talk of tea and bridge and golf scores—these girls who were what girls should be, young and gay, untroubled by financial and moral problems.

And his own girl, tall and lean and tawny and brimming with her own peculiar sweet vitality, ought to have been among them, he had thought. It was a shame that Pamela Raleigh hadn't a comfortable income and a dad behind her and all the other things that girls needed to be happy and safe.

To-day, with the sensitiveness of her response to all his moods, she suspected something of this and quickly, without a change of expression, set him free.

"I'm sorry I can't go to our usual movie this afternoon," she said. "M'ma's in bed with a heavy cold, and I'm going straight home. Chester," she drew his attention suddenly to a newspaper clipping taken from her purse, "do you suppose there's anything in this? It was in last week, and you see it's in again to-day."

Chester was glad of the change of topic. They read the advertisement together.

WANTED: on country ranch, middle-aged companion and helper for elderly woman. Must understand plain cooking and have no objection to care of invalid. Ideal position for right party. Highest references required. Salary $100. Telephone Beachwater 88.

Chester had been slowly shaking his head. But at the last words he suddenly became interested.

"That salary rather raises the tone of the whole thing," he observed. "But what do they want, a nurse or a cook or a companion, or what?"

"Well, that's just it. You know how women are worked on those country farms"—Oh, ask me to marry you, tell me you love me! her heart pleaded. Then it'll all be so easy—then nothing else will matter! Tell

the town straggled into detached small cottages,
almond trees and scarlet Japanese quinces were already in bloom. Maples and locusts were still as bare
as whips, but the willows down by the Broome Street
bridge were a faint and delicate green, and there were
tulips, clean and cool and tall, in doorways and windows.

Pamela walked for an hour after Chester left her
—left her duly to board the two o'clock trolley. She
saw nothing definite, only a blur of homely streets and
shabby houses and vague walking shapes that passed
her. Her thoughts moved as fast as her steps, and
they were wretched thoughts. She felt like a creature
baffled, caged, chained, who could not get free.

How could she possibly marry Chester or expect
him to marry her? What of M'ma and Carter, then,
and that hideous eighteen-hundred-dollar debt?

Carter must get a job, of course. But why didn't he?
Why didn't he see the situation and spare his sister
something of its anxieties? He was twenty years old.
A man of twenty ought to be responsible. . . .

Chester's uncle was paying him a nominal salary of
fifty dollars a week. If he were retained in the bank as
a junior in the family his income would be much, much
more.

But until his prospects were definite, it would be
madness for him to marry. Unless he married
secretly . . .

The word caught her fancy, and she followed the
line of thought it suggested. If he were married
secretly and she and Cart and M'ma went to Mrs.
Pettys's at twenty-seven dollars a week, and Cart immediately got a job for a hundred—four times twenty-
seven . . .

It couldn't be done, even then! And meanwhile she had no job, and Carter had none, and none of them had any money, and the debts were growing hour by hour.

Pamela stopped at a grocery; she had one dollar and sixty-five cents in her purse. To-morrow was Sunday. And in the dark big kitchen of the Carter house there were three eggs and some butter—not much butter— and the cold string beans and half a loaf of French bread and some raisin bread. Coffee, tea, sugar—they had those. But matches—there hadn't been a match in the house this morning—and milk and cornstarch; no vanilla, no chocolate, no cream for the chocolate pudding even if one made one . . .

"A dozen of the rolls and the can of tomatoes and the matches and a quart of milk. And will you send them, Mr. Sykes?"

Fifteen and fifteen and fourteen and ten. What a horible thing money was, anyway! Just a little of it, flat and soiled, must be in the purses of all these women. The little dead exchange one must have in order to live. Dollars and cents—why, these were food and breath in another form, and without them food stopped and breath stopped!

She was frightened on the last block of the walk, frightened as she went down the sunken, sodden brick steps into the jungle of the garden, frightened about money and life. And suddenly a salary of one hundred dollars a month seemed enormous; it seemed the difference between life and death. To earn one hundred dollars a month one ought to be glad enough to wash steps or take one's seat in a galley.

"Must understand plain cooking and no objection to waiting on invalid." Pamela experienced a pang of terror. Suppose somebody else already had the position!

Once at home, she went straight to the telephone. It was to be taken out any day now, but the telephone company had not yet sent for it, and the operator answered her call as promptly as if the Raleigh bill had been paid, instead of ignored, for seven months and a half.

"Hello. It's in answer to that advertisement in the *Star*," Pamela said.

She had some little trouble in getting an answer. There appeared to be confusion at the other end of the line; then she was told briefly that the man who had placed the advertisement was not there.

Would they please tell him that Miss Pamela Raleigh knew of a very good woman? They said they would. Pamela hung up the telephone and went into the kitchen.

A kitchen without food in it, without cooking or warmth, was a chilly, dismal place upon a spring afternoon. Pamela gathered the lamps and filled them carefully, wiping their bases with a rag and placing the chimneys and globes delicately on the frames again. Afterward she washed her hands at the sink, rubbing them with lemon rind and spreading all ten fingers over her face to get the good clean citrus smell. She filled her mother's hot-water bag, carried it upstairs, was confident and gay with the invalid, came and went on a dozen household errands.

"Pam, you're gettin' to be the greatest *comfort*," said little Mrs. Raleigh.

"That's all I want you to say, Florrie!"

Down in the kitchen again, she opened a door into a large, damp, odorous storeroom; there were pota-

toes and apples here, rotting in boxes. Apples and potatoes from Joe O'Keefe, who had been Grandfather
Carter's young coachman forty-five years ago and was
a wealthy farmer now. Joe's two sons did almost all
the building of Carterbridge; James and F. P.
O'Keefe, Inc., would probably erect the building that
was presently to cover the site of the old Carter house.
Old Joe had sent the widowed daughter of Colonel
Tom boxes of apples and oranges every month of
every year that had passed since Joe, a dapper stripling
of twenty, had driven the colonel's handsome span of
blacks.

Pamela was standing here, studying the vegetables
stupidly, trying to estimate their preparation in terms
of butter and sugar, when there was a loud, firm rap-
ping at the kitchen door. She turned to look, took a
step toward it.

She saw, in the dapple of spring sunshine and tree
shadows, a tall young man in the opening; a broad-
shouldered person dressed like a rancher, in laced
boots, corduroy trousers, a well-worn leather coat, big
gloves, and a shabby slouch hat. His brown face was
lighted by a very white smile.

"Did you want——?" Pamela came forward, a
slender girl with tawny hair in exquisite curly disorder,
a worn old faded apron buttoned about her brief dress.
"Oh, hello!" she interrupted herself, with her own particular gray-eyed smile. "How do you do, Gregory?
Did you ring? I didn't hear you ring!"

Gregory Chard stooped to shake her slim hand,
white in his brown palm. He grinned nervously and
cleared his throat.

"I rang the bell two-three times," he said huskily.

Pamela glanced upward at the bells of the Carter

house, big bells aligned high up on the wall, once set quivering convulsedly by the jerking of wires, but silent now for many years.

"That door's never locked," the girl explained. "These bells haven't rung for years. How are you, Gregory? They're tearing us down next week, and we've sort of let things go. Do you mind coming into the kitchen? M'ma's sick in bed and I was getting supper."

Gregory Chard was not listening; his dark eyes were doing double duty, and his only possible answer was a confused laugh. She was so lovely, so slim and straight, with her tumble of beautiful tawny hair and her disconcerting eyes, that the only sound he heard was the drumming and ringing of blood in his own ears.

"What brings you into Carterbridge?" Pamela said kindly, conversationally, hoping to put him at his ease.

"There was a directors' meeting at the bank," he answered, "and the boys from the ranch 'phoned me your message, so I came right over."

She looked at him a little bewildered. He's a perfectly stunning-looking big creature, she thought, losing touch with the conversation in her turn. Heavens, what a clean brown skin, and what bad black eyes! And he has exactly an Englishman's voice —well, he has English blood. You seem to me a very dangerous combination, Señor Chard—— "I wasn't listening!" she broke off, smiling, apologetic, her beautiful head tipped to one side.

"You left a message about the servant," he repeated patiently.

"A message—about a servant——" She was utterly in the dark for a minute, then the truth came to her like a flash. He had put that advertisement in the paper, and he must never know that she had meant to answer it herself!

Pamela thought rapidly as she sliced bread and put away the groceries.

"Was that you, Greg, at the rancho? It sounds as if you were getting married," she said, with her gay laugh.

He laughed uncomfortably himself in return, turning very red.

"I guess you aren't asking me that seriously," he said. "I guess you're kidding me about that—getting married."

"Why shouldn't you get married?" she demanded.

"Well, I guess there's plenty of reasons—I guess nobody would have me, for one thing," he answered, with his awkward air of hilarity. And immediately he became preternaturally solemn again, and scowled at the floor, clearing his throat importantly.

"Was it for yourself that you wanted—this servant?" the girl questioned.

"No, it's like this." He fumbled in his pocket, and drew forth a folded sheet of letter paper covered with writing in a fine, close hand and very black ink. "This is a letter I got from my grandmother a few months ago," he said.

"Your grandmother!"

"Yep. Didn't you know I had a grandmother?" He grinned again.

"I didn't know it, no. I knew—I thought—your father and mother are dead, aren't they?"

"Oh, long ago." He was talking more easily now, when he had something to say. "My mother was Maria Aindini—that place I've got now down South was one of the Aindini places. But this is my father's mother.

She's English—she's Mrs. John Fox-Brooks Chard; she's about eighty."

"And coming to America?"

"Coming to California. She used to live here, here in Carterbridge, when my father was born—she thinks it's still a village, with dirt roads and the post office in the grocery store. She came to America about ten years ago, when I was a kid about fifteen, and I went on to the East and spent the summer with her."

"I didn't know that!" She was a little impressed. The English grandmother and the trip East seemed to give him a little importance.

"She's old—she'll probably sit in a chair a lot, but she's really a——" He hesitated, looked at Pamela with wide-open eyes, and shook his head from side to side. "She's tremendous!" he said seriously.

"She sounds so!" the girl said, laughing at his manner.

"And with her—she's on her way here now—are her grandson, Bob Charteris, my cousin, and his little girl," said Gregory.

"Her grandson and a baby! No wonder you need help!" Pamela said, laughing again.

"She's not a baby, Audrey Charteris; she's about fourteen," said Gregory.

"Good gracious! And how old is the grandson?"

"Oh, he's—he's about thirty-five or -six, I guess. My grandmother was married when she was sixteen, the first time. He was wounded in the war. He's an invalid. His wife is dead."

Pamela's attention was riveted at last.

"Do you tell me that an old, old lady and an invalid man and a young girl you never saw are all coming to visit you?"

"Well, it isn't exactly a visit. They're—they sort of intend to stay," Gregory said somewhat uncertainly.

"To stay! At the ranch!"

"Well, that's what my grandmother says here." He looked at the letter helplessly. "She says that she and Bob—she calls Colonel Charteris Bob—want to try California, and that an English girl they know is teaching in a Santa Barbara school and the little girl could board there, and they're sick of coldness and fogs and streets and taxes and war debts and everything—and they—well, anyway, they're on a Dutch ship, coming through the Canal, and they get here in about ten days."

"And will you have them go to the Arms?"

"Oh, no—my grandmother hates hotels. They're coming right down to Molino. I've had some rooms cleaned up. . . ."

She had a vision of the rancho. Old plaster-walled rooms, cowboys, slipshod Mexican servants, cattle, mud, barns, and mildewed haystacks. And plunged into it an aged woman, a crippled man, a strange little English girl, and—Gregory Chard, in his faded shirt and worn cords.

"Now, how about this servant?" Gregory asked.

The servant? She had almost forgotten the advertisement and the purpose of his call. She roused herself.

"You see," he said, "I've got nothing but those half-breed women down there, and, while they cook all right and take pretty good care of the boys, they can't do what an old lady would like. And besides, there's the kid. And then Colonel Charteris may be fussy. I wouldn't want her to *cook*—there's twenty of them there, now, to do that—but sort of tell them what to cook, do you see?"

"I see." She was thinking, eyelids half lowered, a faint frown on her forehead.

"Is she middle-aged?" he asked suddenly.

"Is she——?" Pamela had been thinking only of herself.

"The woman you know of?" he prompted.

"Is she——? Oh, no; she's young."

"I don't want a lady," he said flatly.

Her chin went up. Her face reddened.

"You don't," she repeated mildly.

"No, I don't want anyone," he explained, "who will pull a lot of class—be too good to do things. I want someone who'll help—I'm going to be in a lot of trouble if I don't get some help. I don't even know— oh, a lot of things. I don't know whether my grand- mother will want the little girl to sleep in her room, or how much covers they want——"

"Why, but, my dear Gregory," Pamela said smil- ing, "you surely can wait until they get here and ask them things like *that!*"

"Oh, well, a lot of things," he went on vaguely. "She may want her breakfast on a tray—my grand- mother, I mean—and Colonel Charteris, my cousin, may not come to meals at all, and then I can't sit down and eat with a kid of fourteen—she wouldn't like it, anyway."

"You'd have this woman—this servant—have her meals with the child?"

"Well, if she wanted to. I wouldn't care—I want her to settle all that. I've had the boys unpack a lot of my mother's china—it's French; I suppose it was brought to her mother in a sailing ship around the Horn. They broke a lot of it——"

"Oh——!" wailed Pamela, putting her hands over her face. "Oh," she laughed at him through her fingers as she took them down; "it was probably *Sèvres!* What are you *doing* down there!"

"Well, they only broke a soup tureen and some platters. And nobody uses soup tureens any more," Gregory said unexpectedly.

"How do you know that?" the girl asked, surprised.

He looked at her honestly, reddening slightly, as if he thought she might laugh at him again.

"I have a book about—well, it's called *Manners To-day,*" he said.

Pamela did not laugh. She was even ashamed of the impulse to do so. The poor blundering idiot, she thought pityingly.

"Have you sheets and towels and all that sort of thing?" she asked practically.

His face brightened; it was pathetic to see the eagerness in his eyes and hear it in his voice.

"I ordered lots of them, from catalogues——"

"Oh, Gregory, you're terrible!" the girl laughed again, as he paused, looking at her hopefully.

"Why, was that wrong?" he asked quickly.

"Well, it wasn't *wrong*. But—but it's such fun to shop!" Pamela explained youthfully.

"I hate it," he said, scowling.

There was a silence; Pamela's thoughts were busy.

"Gregory, could I help?" she asked suddenly.

He looked at her gratefully.

"I'd be awfully obliged if you would," he said. "And if you could get me this woman—or let me go see her——"

"You're talking to her now," Pamela interrupted impulsively, as he paused. It somehow sounded rather flat, and his blank, almost annoyed expression made her feel even further embarrassed.

"I mean—the housekeeper," he explained carefully.

"Yes, and so do I."

"Oh——?" said Gregory Chard, and the girl flushed to hear the slow-thinking man's resentment and suspicion creep into his voice.

"I ave to do *something*," Pamela went on, resolutely nd pluckily. "I didn't know it was you, of course But I answered the advertisement for myself."

The man's face was red.

"No," he said heavily and perplexedly, "that wouldn't do. I couldn't—I wouldn't allow—those servants of mine don't know anything—you're certainly kind——"

Both were now embarrassed, Pamela's face as flushed as his own.

"I would be delighted to try it, anyway, Gregory."

"Why, you——" His gesture indicated the Carter mansion, in whose gloomy and decayed shadow they sat. "You couldn't take a job like that!" he stammered.

No, of course not. Of course not. It was just a silly idea. Of course. They both laughed awkwardly.

"I guess you don't need money that bad," he said jocosely.

She hated him. She despised herself for betraying the family's need and poverty to this brown-faced, white-toothed man. In her anger she was more than ordinarily friendly and bright. She asked a hundred questions about his expected visitors, and promised to do her best to find him the right sort of helper, a middle-aged woman, practical and clean—Swedish, maybe, or a good German girl.

Gregory, speaking convulsedly between silences, evidently as uncomfortable as it was possible for a human being to be, nevertheless lingered so long that Pamela began to think that she would have to take him by the hand, give him his hat, and lead him to the door. Eventually she observed in desperation that she had to go downtown to market before the grocery closed.

Even this was only partially successful, for Gregory waited for her to put on her hat and drove her to the grocery in his big car. He waited for her while she bought butter, one pound, thirty-eight cents. They always needed butter at home. Pamela—in the still watches of the night—wondered if he heard the little controversy that took place; the woman clerk hesitating about charging the sale, the officious young man who came out from the glass-boxed office and reasoned with her—with Pamela Fairfax Raleigh—about the new regulations, suggesting that a payment be made on the Raleigh account before any more charges were made.

If he did hear this, Gregory made no sign. He and Pamela went afterward to Mockby's, where in the space of about twenty minutes be bought eleven rugs and ordered the curtains for seven rooms. Pamela stayed his hand from lace and velours; he became enthusiastic over soft rich English chintzes and plain net.

"In a hacienda, Gregory, everything ought to be farmhousey and simple," the girl reminded him.

"That's right."

"Now those—are these chairs frightfully expensive?" Pamela asked the salesman briskly.

"Yes, those are expensive, madam." The man bent, consulted the tag. "One hundred and ten," he said respectfully.

"Per hundred or per thousand?" Pamela laughed.

"Individually, madam. That's the only chair of the kind we have."

"You see how Spanishy it looks, Gregory. The black wood and the red cushion and the tassels. And——" she sat down in it, slender arms extended along its own black carved arms, beautiful young head thrown back —"it's deliciously comfortable," she said. "That's the sort of chair you ought to have, say, in the dining room, Gregory," she advised him. "It's Spanish—it would fit in."

"You could get more?" Gregory asked.

"Oh, certainly. But it may take us ten days," the salesman said effusively.

"I'd want eight."

They bought table runners and a steamer chair and an ice-cream freezer.

"It is such fun to spend money!" Pamela said, pretending not to suspect that the crate of chocolates in the gilded box tied with orchid ribbons was for her. Gregory, trying to buy it inconspicuously, laughed and became grave.

"I don't get much kick out of it," he said gloomily.

She saw him pay for the candy, four big silver dollars, and she grudged each one as the saleswoman expertly gathered them up. Afterward he drove her home and lingered at her gate, Pamela facing him, looking up at his bigness, the candy box under her arm. She was suddenly pale, constrained.

"I'm awfully sorry that you have to—to feel that

you have to—do something, Miss Pamela," the man said.

"Well, my mother happens to be in financial difficulties at the moment," Pamela answered brightly. "But they may clear up any time."

"If I could ever help out in any way," Gregory stammered in a thickened voice.

Her hands were cold, her head aching, her thoughts in wild confusion. Hardly conscious of what she was saying, Pamela thanked him indifferently. He was very kind, but things would be all right.

"Was that the little Broome girl, in the garden there, as we passed?" he asked suddenly.

Grimy twilight in the shabby street, hideous excavations a few feet away from the discoloured and imperfect poles that once, elegantly scalloped, had been the Carters' fence, gloomy jungle of neglected paths and collapsing garden behind her.

"Yes, that was Maisie Broome."

"She's a pretty little thing, isn't she?"

"She looked awfully pretty in that golf outfit, I thought."

"It looked kinder nice to see the doctor come in the gate and put his arm around her. Kinder fatherly," Gregory said, vaguely wistful. "I thought that little girl looked awfully cute going up through the garden with those two men. Was that her brother?"

"The other man? No, there aren't any boys in the Broome family," Pamela said. If he would go—if he would go—*if he would go!*

"Nice-looking chap," Gregory commented innocently. "I've seen that feller somewhere before, too."

"That was young Mr. Hilliard, old Bob's nephew—he's here from the East."

"Oh, that's right! That's who it is."

He went out to the big car, flashed up strong lights in the dusk; there was the deep roar of an engine, and he was gone.

Pamela stepped out of the path where the big street lamps, dangling high up among bare branches, would not shine in her face, and crooked her arm upon the top of a mouldering and vine-embraced old pedestal that had once held an urn, and put her head down upon her arm childishly and began to cry.

CHAPTER X

A RUBBISH fire was twisting a thick gray winding sheet about the Carter house when Chester Hilliard arrived there on Sunday afternoon. He found Pamela far upstairs in one of the big wings of the enormous attic, busy with trunks and boxes, wardrobes and old bookcases, all stored with the accumulated discard of forty long years.

On the roof a spring rain was pattering softly; the high branches of the pear trees outside the narrow dormer windows occasionally shook and shuddered in a breeze. The air in the attic was musty and cool, and the light dim.

"Carter!" the girl said, as Chester's head came above the level of the open stairway. And then in a pleased voice that almost disguised an undertone of constraint, "Oh, Chester—hello! You didn't go to the picnic?"

"Why should I?" In his cool tone there was also constraint, an attempt to appear faintly reproachful, faintly hurt.

"They called it off," she said, in her soul. "Be careful where you sit down!" she warned him, aloud; "it's simply filthy here."

"How long have you been working on this?"

"Oh, several days, off and on. Carter's supposed to be burning some of it in the back yard."

"Carter's doing yeoman service. He'll set fire to the whole place if he isn't darned careful."

"It might be a good thing if he did. Look at them—trunks and trunks of old letters!"

"Not worth keeping, I suppose. And when do you move?"

"Tuesday, I think. I'll be done here to-morrow. That heap there is for the auction, on Thursday, and all those old bookcases and desks are for the auction, and the books. Most of the books are so mildewed you can't read them, but the auctioneer told Cart that they gave a great tone to an auction—says people like the look of them."

Conversation. Conversation, just as if she and the handsome troubled-looking man sitting opposite her had just been introduced.

"What ought it all to bring?"

"He says about four hundred dollars."

A silence. Chester gave as much time, motion, and attention as possible to the lighting of a cigarette.

"Say, what do you think I did last night?" he said suddenly, with an air of recollection.

"Last night?" She did not quite dare add, with all the hurt and jealousy and longing that brimmed her heart, "I wondered all evening long—all evening long—where you were."

"I had supper at the Broomes'."

"Maisie?"

"Yep. You're not any more surprised than I am."

"All is forgiven," Pamela said, trying to smile and speak naturally.

"All is forgiven, apparently," he said, with a little laugh.

"How did that happen?"

"Well, I brought Maisie home from the Country Club about six, and we were standing at her gate, talking—talking about you, as a matter of fact," said Chester.

"Saying nice things, I hope." She tried to say it as she would have said it a year ago, confidently, indifferently.

"Saying wonderful things. There's a very loyal friend of yours," Chester said seriously.

"That's good." Her tone trembled a little, but he could not know that it was with anger and fear.

"She told me last night—however, I'll come to that later," Chester said, evidently enjoying the rôle of prodigal son. "We were at the gate when the doctor came home. And I was really surprised at the old boy's cordiality. 'Saturday night supper, very informal,' he said. I didn't know what to do!" Chester confessed ingenuously. "I thought maybe Mrs. Broome would kick me out. However, Maisie said afterward that her father was boss."

"He is when he does exactly what Mrs. Broome wants him to do," Pamela said drily. Chester flushed a little and looked a trifle dashed; after a moment he went on with his story.

"Well, anyway, she was cordiality itself—awfully nice—couldn't have been nicer. It's a lovely family to visit—four girls and their mother and father," Chester added innocently. "That Angela is a regular circus."

"Flops is the pretty one." Pamela made herself say it quietly.

"She's going to be a beauty. They were teasing Maisie last night—apparently they all love to guy each other. I never saw parents and kids so easy together," Chester diverged to comment. "They were saying that Maisie'd have to get married before Flops came along!"

"She will, I guess. Maisie's—awfully attractive." Pamela had begun the sentence intending to end it, "Maisie's going to come into a lot of money," but she altered it. No use in being catty.

"And listen, after supper I had quite a talk with Mrs. Broome, and she was really terribly nice," Chester went on. "She asked me about you—now, listen," he interrupted himself with a little laugh, as Pamela's head went up proudly—"I know when people are being nasty, and I know when they're being nice, and honestly she was being nice. She and Maisie and I happened to begin talking about you, and they were as affectionate as they could be. Tears came into Mrs. Broome's eyes when I told her what a rotten time you've been having, and she said—well, she said everything! In the first place, she said that she had no idea your mother had been sick, and that she was coming to see her—not this week, because the baby is having her tonsils out, but week after next. And then she said she was going to talk to me quite frankly, and she sent Maisie up to play one game of cribbage with her father —she says that since Maisie was two years old she's always gone in to have a little visit with him in the evening——"

Pamela put her head into a trunk, extracted a fat bunch of letters, flung them upon a pile.

"If she's at home," she suggested dispassionately.

"Well, of course! Those girls have got beautiful

manners, with their parents, anyway," Chester said, fortunately unsuspicious of the emotions that were raging in the heart so near his own. "Mrs. Broome was telling me about the family, last night—they're fine people, aren't they? I mean the Broome family didn't come to California as immigrants, you know—well, anyway, after Maisie went upstairs, Mrs. Broome spoke about you. She said, 'Why, Pamela Raleigh mustn't be allowed to take any position she happens to get through the papers!' She seemed terribly shocked."

"You told her that?"

"Well, just incidentally. I was telling her how up against it you were, and how hot it made me. She said —she really did say, right out—'I've been doing that girl a terrible injustice! I thought she didn't want to take a position,' she said. 'Why,' she said, 'we'll get her the right sort of job—I'll make it my business just as soon as Baby is home,' she said. 'Poor child! she must have been having a miserable time.' And then she spoke of your mother as an angel, 'but,' she said, 'she's not the person to control that spirited girl and boy. I asked Pamela Raleigh to resign from the Cinderella Club,' she said, 'and it was the hardest thing I ever did in my life. But I did exactly what I would want some other woman to do for my Maisie. She was going too fast, she was needed at home, and she was without a father to protect her. I did it,' she said, 'to help her to find her own soul, and from what you tell me,' she said, 'she has found it, and I thank God!' "

Well, he was a stranger to Carterbridge, and a man into the bargain. How could he know that he was turning a knife in Pamela's very vitals, that her whole being was writhing and wincing under the shame of it?

The girl looked at him tolerantly, patiently, betrayed by not the faintest quiver of an eyelash.

"She says you're to come to lunch, any day after Thursday, and have a nice talk about it, and that she's sure that she can help you find work very much better suited to you than taking a chance on some farm position where you would be horribly lonesome!" Chester finished upon an innocent note of triumph.

Like all sisterless men, the girl reflected, as she smiled encouragement upon him, he was simple and credulous with women. He had believed everything that Mrs. Broome had said, naturally, feeling himself important because she admitted him to her confidence and talked to him as a friend. Why, she could have told him that Maisie was three years old and a golden blonde and he would have believed it!

But it only made him seem dearer and more desirable, and achingly less accessible somehow, this infantile rustingness, and the fact that Maisie wanted him so openly did not lessen his value. He was just as kind, as companionable, as charming as ever, his brotherly manner just as heart-stirring.

"Get through up here, Pam, and come on down and make yourself respectable and come somewhere with me! Go on, now, you've done enough of this! I'll sit with your mother while you change your dress."

And sit with Mrs. Raleigh he did. Pamela, during her hasty ablutions, could hear from the adjoining room his pleasant voice.

"Well, it isn't as if it was for life, Mrs. Raleigh. Boarding houses are pretty much the same everywhere; even the most expensive isn't so much better than a place like Mrs. Pettys's."

"I know, but it seems so cheap an' common!" This

was her mother's sad little note. "I don't ever remember any member of our fam'ly boa'ding anywhere before, I really don't!"

"Yes, but it won't be any time now before Carter has a good job, and everything will take a turn for the better. . . ."

It was still raining, warmly and steadily, when Pamela and Chester started for a movie. There was really nothing else to do. They could hardly sit about the dank and dismal Carter mansion in the last hours of its imposing existence; it was cold and inhospitable, with most of its old furniture taped off into corners now, for the auctioneer.

The picture house was well filled in mid-afternoon, but Chester got loge seats, and Pamela, laughing and breathless after a three-blocks' run under an umbrella through the rain, was pleased to find Carol and Sam Billings beside her and the Beaver boys just behind. It seemed like old times, somehow. They all talked together between the films.

"What on earth have you been doing with yourself, Pamela? No one ever sees you any more!"

"Well, I'm trying to get a job, Sam, for one thing."

"Oh, what doing?"

"Anything, really."

"Are you taking a regular course in anything?" This last was Carol, precise and cool.

"Well, I may study kindergartening."

"That sounds interesting."

She had encountered her old crowd in this civil, accidental fashion several times during the past months; she had had a handkerchief at Christmas from Carol, and a leather desk calendar from Maisie, and a really handsome bead bag from Sue Rose. They did the same

for Doris Runyon, Pamela knew, who had been one
of them in high-school days, but who had early chosen
an independent and unedifying path, and had never
been asked to join the Cinderellas, or attend any small
party at anybody's house.

Doris, as always with Billy Allerton, happened to
be in the theatre this afternoon, and afterward was at
the Arms, where they all went for tea. Pamela was
sorry that on this particular occasion Doris should
join them; it made inclusion in the group absolutely
unimportant. Carol seemed nervous and said that she
had to go home early, nobody danced, and Chester,
who had been showing plainly his satisfaction in being
with these particular friends, delegated to Sam Billings the duty of seeing Pamela home and suggested to
Carol that he take her instead.

It was understood that Chester was always engaged
on Sunday evenings for the dull early dinner in the
Hilliard house. Pamela wondered wretchedly if that
really were his destination to-night. She thought that
she heard Billy Beaver say, "See you later"—it was
hardly likely that Billy had been included in the Hilliards' family group.

When Chester and Carol had gone the others sat
on, refilling their cups. The tea room was almost deserted on this wet Sunday afternoon; everyone who
had a home was glad to be in it a day like this. Pamela
suddenly felt homesick even for her own forlorn house,
and little M'ma, wheezing and asthmatic in the big
bed, with the purple and black cape about her shoulders, and Carter peering hopefully into an almost bar-
ren pantry for food.

Doris Runyon was with them, a harmless, vain,
vapid girl, always defending herself. Sam, glancing at

his wrist, presently asked Pamela if she would let
Billy Allerton take her home—he had to run. Pamela
said she did not mind it at all. Billy had a small car,
and she and Doris squeezed into it, laughing, rain-
spattered, and Doris pulled Pamela's face down and
kissed the other girl good-bye when they reached the
Raleigh gate.

Chester delegating his duties as escort to Sam, and
Sam passing them on to Billy and Doris—well, they
would not have done that a year ago! Pamela's face
burned as she went into the dark, cold house; she felt
almost sick with despair. She felt Doris's kiss—poor
Doris! Pamela rubbed her cheek. Twenty years old,
and she said to herself that nothing in life would ever
be right, or straight, or happy again.

"I guess I'm beaten!" she said grimly, tearlessly,
beginning the familiar, uninteresting preparation of
her mother's tray. "I guess I'm beaten. I don't know
what's the matter with me, or us, or the world—but
it's all wrong!"

CHAPTER XI

THE days went by, and their appointed events slipped into the past. When the actual moment of leaving the old house came, Pamela was too tired and sore and stiff to feel it much; it was all like a dream. The elms and pear trees were still throwing their heavy shade into the blackness of the garden; the old rep curtains hung in the same dusty folds, with worn slits and faded stripes up and down their stately lengths; the stairway carpet still bulged loose where the rods were missing; the old smells—of apples and dust and damp plaster and mice and upholstery—still lingered in the cold passages, and when the Raleighs went away the cuckoo clock was ticking bravely and gave forth in parting four wheezing chirrups.

"Never mind, M'ma," Pamela said, in a sort of apathetic sympathy, "it's too big for ten families. Much better make some simpler arrangement."

But Florence Fairfax Carter Raleigh made no answer; her veil hung down before her convulsed face.

"It seems impossible that we aren't coming back," Carter said, impressed in spite of himself. After all, he had been born in this house, like his mother before him.

The Raleighs took a taxicab to Mrs. Pettys's boarding house; it was an extravagance, but they could hardly take a street car and walk four blocks loaded with handbags as they were.

It was a cool, windy spring afternoon, everything looked harsh and clear in the wind. Dust and papers were blowing about Broome Street, when they reached it, and all the peeled and sun-faded ugliness of Mrs. Pettys's bay-windowed wooden house stood revealed. It was a double house, with wooden steps rising from the street to the parlour floor, and a basement beneath, in which the large dining room was situated.

Pamela and her mother had a large, long, dark room, originally a "back parlour," connected with the front parlour by folding doors, closed now. Their one window looked out upon the flat side wall of a factory next door, with a strip of back yards and a blossoming plum tree beyond. Carter had a small bedroom upstairs, just over the front door.

The windows of the basement dining room were dirty; the hands of the girl who waited on table were dirty; to Pamela the napkin she held felt dirty. She looked at her mother with more anxiety than she felt for herself. Mrs. Raleigh looked ill; she was hardly touching her food.

The waitress's thumb was in the soup as she set down a lurching plate. There were soda crackers on the table, and catsup, and saucers of some pallid, gelatinous substance that eventually was identified by Pamela as the dessert. Plenty of bread, and plenty of

rather strong butter with dots of white salt on it, and
stewed tomatoes, and boiled potatoes, and saucers of
chopped cabbage, and a strange stringy meat in a
smear of brown gravy.

"We'll get out of here right away," Pamela assured
her mother when they had gone upstairs again. Mrs.
Raleigh lay upon the bed, none too sweet a bed; Carter half sat, half lay at her feet. Pamela, lame and
tired and cold, moved about the room, unpacking suit-
cases. A glaring electric light, hanging from the ceiling, sent a gush of merciless brilliance into all of the
four ugly, bare, shabby corners of the apartment.

"What'd Mrs. Pettys talk to you about in the hall,
Cart?"

"Oh, she said that another time I'd have to tell her
if I wanted a bath right before dinner, because it used
up all the hot water and made the girls wild."

"H'm!" Pamela commented briefly. Mrs. Raleigh
closed her eyes. "We won't stay here, M'ma," the girl
said confidently. "We simply *can't*. I'll bring up your
breakfast in the morning and go out about ten and
see what I can find."

"Pamela," her mother said faintly, "I blame myself
for this, dear."

"Oh, nonsense! Now, don't start *that*."

"Yes, I do, dear. For we ought to have ole friends
—the kind you can stay with, weeks an' weeks. . . ."

"That was the old way, M'ma. But nobody takes
whole families in nowadays. Think of the thousands of
boarding houses . . ."

They were silent, and a hundred depressing sounds
flowed into the dingy back parlour from all sides. The
sound of a radio in the front room, the sound of a
Victrola upstairs, and—still farther upstairs—the

wails of a small child being put to bed and slapped. From the kitchen came a loud clatter of dishes and pots and voices rising above them, the hiss of steam and the running of water. Pamela could hear a sewing machine buzzing somewhere—stopping, buzzing again. Motor horns honked in the street, voices sounded from all over the house; a woman's voice calling, "Harry! Harry!" and a child's shrill imploring: "Ethel, will your mother let you? Will your mother let you, Ethel?"

Persons lived here in this house, and in other houses like it, up and down the street. Pamela's soul seemed to faint within her at the thought.

"Well, they did not," a man's voice said loudly, on the other side of the folding-doors. "Well, you didn't know anything of the kind, because they did not."

A woman's voice murmured incredulously. The Raleighs could smell the man's cigar as if they had been in the same room with him.

"You expectin' Chester to-night, Pam?"

The girl gave a horrified laugh.

"I hope not! I wouldn't mind if he never saw this particular place. Just try not to worry about it, M'ma —we'll laugh at this some day."

The top of the large cherrywood bureau she was to share with her mother had been stained and nicked by decades of hard wear; wet glasses had left white rings upon its surface, and bottles of acids and corrosive drugs had been spilled there.

Upon it was spread a limp small towel, with three red lines at each end. The bureau drawers stuck, coming out with difficulty; they were lined with newspaper, upon which a faint drift of pink face powder and several crimped, fine hairpins still rested.

Mrs. Pettys came in, a florid-faced woman with a high-bridged nose and a keen eye. She and Pamela discussed rates, and Pamela explained that she expected some money from the auctioneer day after to-morrow. That was all right, then. Mrs. Pettys didn't know whether Miss Raleigh understood that rates were strictly in advance; it had to be that way, on account of Mrs. Pettys's waiting list. There was a delightful gentleman in the house who had been with her seven years, and he was extremely anxious, it appeared, that his brother and the brother's motherless son should occupy that very parlour in which the Raleighs were quartered. This widower was eager to pay fifty dollars a week for the privilege.

"I wish we'd stayed at home and taken boarders," Pamela commented mildly when the landlady had gone. Her mother, still lying with closed eyes, laughed forlornly, but Pamela, glancing at her a moment later, saw the glisten of tears on her cheek. The girl drew a cheap chair to the side of the cheap, wide, flat bed, and sat there, with her warm hand over her mother's.

Mrs. Raleigh sniffed and began to cry quietly; Pamela blinked the tears from her own lashes. There was a long stillness in the room, punctuated only by the unceasing and variegated noises from without.

Every time the door bell downstairs rang, Pamela's heart stood still. Her imagination baulked at the thought of Chester here. She had joked with him about a great many of the tragic events of the past year, but this was beyond a joke. Somehow, she could not make this seem funny, picturesque, dramatic—anything but sordid and painful and shameful. Decent folk ought not to be reduced to such straits, and if they were, at least they might spare their friends any participation in them.

Her fears were idle; he did not come that night or for many nights. Pamela searched for a new boarding house, and searched for employment, equally in vain. She walked the streets of Carterbridge, around this corner, up this block, through the Plaza, back again, to and fro, and it seemed to her like a strange town and a strange world.

Half unconsciously she avoided the street where the Raleigh auction was going on, where the mouldering books and the dusty Canton china, and the marquetry cabinets and the kitchen broom were all being sold under the hammer. She saw the advertisement in the papers; Mr. Massey, the auctioneer, must have put a great many more things in, she reflected. Seventeen complete china sets, four dining tables—the Raleighs never had that many!

Cars were parked, during the hours of the auction, up and down the block, but Massey told Carter that what brought the people was merely curiosity. The Raleigh furniture was too old-fashioned, too heavy, for them. "You can't get anything out of them," complained Massey.

"M'ma, dearest," the girl said sensibly and seriously, when they had been almost two weeks at Mrs. Pettys's, "we'll have to go away. I can at least wait on tables or wash hospital floors—but I can't do it here. Nothing but a miracle could save us, here—I mean that I can't think of the combination of circumstances that could pull us out. I think and think until I'm almost crazy thinking, and it comes out the same—I'm not trained for anything, and I can't afford to waste the time training. Either we'll have to borrow more

money, or we'll have to go away. And wouldn't you
rather go away?"

"I'd rather have stayed in my own home, that my
father built, an' have things go on as they were goin',"
Mrs. Raleigh persisted stubbornly.

Pamela did not go to see Mrs. Broome, but Maisie's
mother kept her word and, dainty and bewildered, duly
found her way to the unsavoury neighbourhood of
Broome Street. She took some pleasure in identifying at the corner of Mrs. Pettys's actual block the old
Broome mansion, now cramped in between shops, and
filled with quacks and dressmakers a~ palmists and
dubious agencies of all sorts.

They sat in Mrs. Raleigh's room; there was no central parlour in the Pettys home. Pamela put forward
the best chair for the visitor, seating herself on the
foot of the bed on which her mother lay. The girl
made no excuses; she was quite as conscious as was
Mrs. Broome of the odours of cabbage and warm
soapsuds and carbolic acid that permeated the halls
and trickled in under the cheap wooden doors; she
ignored them.

"And you're looking for something to do, Pamela?"

"I don't want her to work," Mrs. Raleigh interposed lovingly and fretfully. "I want her to stay right
at home with me!"

Pamela stroked the hand she held gently; she did
not raise her eyes. She would not give Mrs. Broome
the satisfaction of an exchanged significant look that
found M'ma absurd.

"Unfortunately, we can't all be choosers, can we,
Pamela?" the caller said pleasantly.

The beautiful gray eyes—Mrs. Broome said to herself that she had really forgotten how beautiful the

girl was!—were raised now, and Pamela looked the older woman fairly in the eye.

"We all know the proverb about—not being choosers," she said mildly. And then briskly, "Yes, I've been looking for something to do. Our affairs had been in a bad way for a long time; when they once smashed, everything smashed. M'ma and I may go to San Francisco, and I'll see what can be done there."

"Oh, I don't believe that's necessary, Pamela," Mrs. Broome said gently and thoughtfully. "Can't we find something for you to do right here?"

"I've tried—" Pamela would not be pathetic or pitiable if she could help it—"I've tried a good many places," she said dispassionately, "and there doesn't seem to be anything."

"The girl in Doctor's office is a graduate nurse—Miss Ramsay only uses the graduated kindergartners," Mrs. Broome mused aloud. "No, that wouldn't do—no, that wouldn't do. You play the piano, don't you, Pamela?"

"Pretty well."

"And speak French?"

"A little. Maisie and Sue Rose and I were all together, with Madame Ruyelles, you know."

"Maisie and I have worked on verbs together all winter," said Maisie's mother. "She's doing very nicely, *now*. I don't think she learned anything from Madame. They're all going to have such a trip together this spring!" Mrs. Broome diverged to say, with fond enthusiasm, to Mrs. Raleigh.

"Up to the lake," Pamela supplied rather than asked.

"Up to the lake. Eleven of them. The Billingses, and Sue Rose, and Maisie, and Jessy, and Jack. All

on horseback. They'll stay for a few days at the Catherwood cabin—such a lark. The girls are getting themselves up like regular cowboys, I tell them. Yes," said
Mrs. Broome, "it's going to be a great trip. I tell Doctor that I only hope they'll get home alive! But now
let's return to your problem, Pam," she added practically, bringing herself back from a vision of spring
woods, creeks, horses moving along corduroy road-
beds, and the laughter of youngsters set free in the big
mountains. "You say you may go away. I'm not sure
but what that might be a good idea. I had in mind a
position with dear Mrs. Parker, she's not strong, you
know, and she has those three sweet babies——"

"You mean as nurse?" Pamela said steadily, levelly.
Two spots of hot colour came into her cheeks.

"No, my dear, I don't," Mrs. Broome explained, a
little nettled. "Ada says she doesn't want a nurse, she
simply wants a general helper. She keeps no cook, you
know, and she said—she was very funny about it!—
she said that with a regular nurse she found herself
cooking to please the nurse. She wants just a friendly
helper, to do a little of everything—a companion,
really. The children are little ducks—such independent
creatures, all boys. They were having their spinach and
beef juice and whatever it was yesterday—Ada was
fixing prunes for them, and you *never* saw such little
monkeys! Ada says she wonders that they don't ache
all over when they go to bed at night."

"And what does she pay, Mrs. Broome?"

"Well, not very much, dear, I'm afraid. You see,
Roger Parker has just gone into that motor-supply
business for himself, and they're living very simply. I
think—I'm not sure, but I think Ada said twenty-five
dollars."

Pamela looked surprised.

"That's not much," she said dubiously. She was not in the least interested in the position; she remembered too clearly Ada Brookes of long-ago little-girl school-days, Ada superior and affected and playing the harp. No, she was merely being polite to Mrs. Broome. But even politeness had its limits.

"But, my dear," Mrs. Broome said defensively, "it isn't a question of what dear little Ada would *like* to do, it's really a question of what she *can* do! She's the most generous-hearted creature. And of course, you— or whoever took the position—would be absolutely a member of the family. I mean lunch with her, at the table, and all that. I believe she did say that Roger likes to have his dinner alone with his wife, but that's just because there were always a lot of things to talk over that wouldn't interest any outsider.

"It was only an idea," said the visitor, annoyed, as Pamela made no comment. "I wanted to help you to make a start—that's all it would be, a start—and help Ada, too, for truly, if something isn't done about that girl, she'll go into a decline."

The conversation veered, became general. Pamela was asked to go with Mrs. Broome to the door.

They were hardly outside her mother's door when the older woman said:

"Pamela, I must ask you this, dear; there's a reason for it that I can't explain. But was there ever an understanding—or an engagement—between you and Chester Hilliard?"

Pamela looked at her squarely, her chin high.

"Mrs. Broome, there's a rude old saying, 'Ask me no questions, and I'll tell you no lies,'" she said, steadily. "I suppose the rest of it is, 'Ask me questions you have no right to ask me and I *will* tell you lies'—if I must!"

The one balm contained in the memory of the wretched hour was the thought of Mrs. Broome's outraged face as she left the odorous Pettys hallways without another word.

Pamela told Chester about it afterward and was chilled by the realization that he had had Mrs. Broome's version first. She had tried to make it funny, but his gentleness and sympathy almost unnerved her.

"Yes, I know, my dear, but it mustn't make you bitter," he said.

She was silent, looking down at the hand whose fingers she moved nervously back and forth, back and forth, across a space of tablecloth. Presently she raised smiling eyes that were perilously close to tears, dewy gray eyes filled with the love and longing he was too blind to see.

"It's hard not to have things make you bitter," she said in a low voice.

"Of course it's hard. Don't think for a minute that I don't see *that*. But she wanted to be nice to you, Pam, and I gather that you simply wouldn't have it."

"She told you about it?"

"She just gave me an idea—she seemed so troubled that you were having such a hard pull, and she said— she was a teacher before she was married, herself, you know—she said that girls who wanted jobs didn't seem to appreciate that you *have* to begin at the beginning, especially when you've had no training. No, she didn't say an unkind word," Chester added, as Pamela remained silent, watching him with those tear-bright eyes, her lips firmly shut, "but she evidently felt that you misunderstood her, and it made her feel—hurt."

"Well," Pamela said moderately, "I'm sorry if I hurt her. What made me furious, of course," she went on, "was that she asked me if I were engaged to you. Did she ask you that?"

"No!" Chester said explosively, laughing a little forcedly. "You don't mean to say she asked that?"

"She did indeed."

The waitress interrupted. She had laid her large tray on a near-by table, now she wanted to know who had ordered the crab salad and who the pot roast, who the tea and who the coffee. The quick biscuit and stuffed potato went with both.

Pamela and Chester were dining at the Kopper Kettle, at Pamela's suggestion. She had written him, a day or two ago, and the prompt response and affectionate coöperation of his answer had had their own sinister significance to her. He was being "nice"; he was being "decent."

"I felt that I had to see you, Chester," she had said, meeting him.

"And if you hadn't written, I certainly would have," he had responded smilingly.

She was looking her loveliest, she had seen to that. The hat was two years old, but its broad brim and band of blue were exquisitely becoming to her black-lashed gray eyes. The soft curly ends of her tawny hair sprayed up against the dark blue straw, her skin was flawless, her mouth the one note of brilliant colour in her face, for she wore no rouge, and the new pallor lent her a beauty strangely mysterious and fine.

Chester did not return to the interrupted topic when the waitress went away. Pamela waited to have him do so; she presently brought up the subject herself.

"Yes, it evidently worried Mrs. Broome to hear that there was anything between you and me!"

"Ah, don't let it make you bitter, dear!" Chester said again, laying his hand over hers.

"Was that bitter?"

"A little. After all, they only want to help you, Pam. You've no idea how kindly—really affectionately —they speak about you. Maisie was almost in tears about it the other night. She said that you did nothing —nothing more than the rest of them—and that it wasn't fair; she says that she'll be twenty-one this May, and she says that the very first thing she's going to do is rush over to your house—wherever it may be. She's her father's ward until then, you know. But even the doctor is fond of you, Pam——"

"I can imagine it!"

Chester ground out his cigarette, laughing a little ruefully.

"Well, anyway, he spoke of you most kindly, Maisie said, and told her that if there was anything in the world he could do for your mother and you he'd be delighted to do it. And you're to be asked to Maisie's coming-of-age garden party, some time in the fall, I believe. I know you won't go, but you're to be asked."

Fall! This was April. . . .

"I wouldn't mind any of it," Pamela said, after a silence, "if——"

"If money was a little easier? I can see that."

"No, I wasn't going to say that. I was going to say——"

"You know it's much more a question of money than —than the other thing, Pam. There's no question that Dr. Broome and Mrs. Beaver and some of the others had been getting mad, last spring, because they thought the younger crowd had gone too far—they were spoiling for a chance to pick on somebody, anyway," Chester interrupted eagerly again, lighting another cigarette and waving out the match slowly. "But the main thing was the money. Your mother is a bad manager, and she'd been letting things run along pretty carelessly for years. But all that would have happened anyway, having to sell the house and board somewhere. You mustn't——" He was so fine, so secure, so sure of himself, smooth head, handsome, concerned face, big hand steadying his cigarette holder, new suit, new tie, pocketbook full of bills! "You *mustn't* let this thing get you," he said; "why, we all go through times like this—everybody has to take a turn at it."

"I don't think I would have minded," Pamela said steadily, her elbows on the table, her chin resting on her linked fingers, and her eyes, in the shadow of the blue straw hat, fixed on his face, "if—you remember what Mrs. Broome asked me?—I wouldn't have minded if I could have answered 'yes.'"

She had been saying it to him all night, tossing beside M'ma in the wide flat bed of Mrs. Pettys's back parlour, thinking—thinking—until she felt that her head would split. All night long she had been seeing herself seated opposite to Chester, had been hearing herself say courageously, "Chester, I wouldn't have minded, if it had been true. If I could have said that we *were* engaged."

And all night long he had answered her quickly, passionately:

"Why, then, you goose, *didn't* you?"

Now she had actually said it; the dream had so far

come true, but why was this silence spreading—deepening between them, like flood water? Pamela felt her throat thicken and her heart begin to beat slowly with shame and confusion and consternation.

There was a moment's silence. Then Chester, grinding out his cigarette, looked up at her and smiled and said quietly—no, not just the words she had planned for him, but they were almost the same:

"You mean to say you *didn't?*"

Hope, smothered in the ashes, sent up a spirit of renewed flame again, and the colour rushed back into Pamela's cheeks, and she was her most beautiful self as she said, half timidly, all eagerly:

"Oh, but don't you—do you—think it would have been—unwise?"

"Yes, I do," he said temperately, unemotionally. And Pamela's inner spirit shrank and withered again.

"I wouldn't like to say anything—definite until our plans are definite." Chester expressed it carefully, feeling for words, not meeting her eyes.

"Oh, *no!*" she agreed, with the proud quickness of a loving, helpless woman. Everything was to be on his terms that only she might hold him!

He was smiling at her, his own handsome, confident smile, with just a suggestion of reproach in it to-night.

"You haven't much faith in me, have you, Pam?" he suggested.

Her hand moved quickly, fell warmly on his own; the fingers tightened there.

"Chester!" she stammered, her cheeks hot.

"Well," he resumed, as the quick, denying echoes of the word died away, "why are you so impatient then, Pam? You're the most impatient thing!"

"I know. I know!" she said penitently, in the silence.

Chester, removing his hand from hers to pat it, monitor fashion, said mildly:

"Well, then, why *are* you?"

"Oh"—she tried to smile, her eyes watering—"it's when I don't see you—and the days go by——" she faltered.

For a full minute, looking at her thoughtfully, he was silent. Then, with a sudden air of resolution and reason, he began:

"Pam, dear, we *can't* get married now, can we?"

"Oh, no!" she agreed, over a quite different decision in the depths of her heart.

"You see that?"

"Oh, yes, Chester!"

"And your mother's plans are all undecided, aren't they? And I'm breaking my neck to get started in the bank."

"I know," she agreed, ashamed.

"So we have to be patient, whether we want to or not, don't we?" he persisted.

"Yes—I know. Of course!"

"And a lot of my work," Chester continued, "is— in a way—social. I don't like Jessy's dinner parties, nor to sit around making love to Mrs. Catherwood or Mrs. Beaver! What are they to *me?* But I've got to make a hit with my uncle—you see that?"

"Yes, I *do* see that, Chester!"

"And don't you see that we just have to wait?"

"Yes, I know we do. I'm sorry!"

And her heart was at rest again. The radio was playing something by Schumann, the little candles on the table wore red gauze ballet skirts, her orange ice was melting, twisting, slipping in its thick glass cup.

She was young and pretty, and Chester Hilliard was in love with her, and everything was all right.

"You see, I don't like secrecy," Chester said frankly, "and my idea would be to wait until we *can* be engaged, then *get* engaged, announce it right off the bat, and get married!"

Her mood chilled, and the old pain and fear and resentment stirred in her heart. She said, challenging his protest:

"Then I should have told Mrs. Broome that there was nothing between you and me?"

He was ready for her.

"Well, why not? What harm would it have done? It's none of her business! It would have shut her up, and it wouldn't have affected you and me—we would have felt just the same toward each other."

"Yes—of course—I see." But she felt sick with shame and doubt.

"You mustn't take this thing too seriously, Pam. It'll all work out," the man said, pocketing his change comfortably. Sixteen dollars in change. "It'll be forgotten by everyone, one of these days—everything passes, you know. We've just got to sit tight and let things happen for a while—that's our only way out. Eventually——"

He walked home with her; now and then she said, "I see," or "Of course. Of course not." At the battered Pettys steps he said:

"I'll see you again in a day or two. I've been terribly busy, but I'll not be so busy now."

"You're definitely in the bank now, Chester?"

"Well—it amounts to that. But that was a newspaper story. However, it looks good. Well—I'll see you soon."

"Don't you go on that camping trip up the lake?"

"Oh, yes—that's right—next Friday. That's true. Well, then, I may not see you until we come back. But long before that something will have turned up."

He was truly sorry for her, concerned, anxious that something should indeed turn up. He had given her all that any girl could ask of a boy twenty-six, a stranger in town. He had stood beside her, indeed, when her oldest friends had turned away.

Yet she felt suddenly blank and lonely as she went upstairs to her rear parlour bedroom. The night was warm, and Mrs. Raleigh had the window open; the plum tree's blossoms were gone now, or lost in new foliage, street lights and house lights and yard lights conflicted in a hundred angles and triangles across the black night.

"Have a nice time with Chester?" Mrs. Raleigh said, looking up from the somewhat complicated game of patience she was playing on the oblong table, a table that dated from the "Mission oak" era in furniture, twenty-five years earlier.

"Very nice."

"Where did you have dinner, deary? Arms?"

"No—the Kopper Kettle."

Pamela sat down, taking off the blue hat and throwing it carelessly on the bureau; her tawny hair was pressed in soft damp rings against her head.

"Hot, isn't it, M'ma?"

"It is—real close." Mrs. Raleigh began to detail some of the personal affairs of other guests at Mrs. Pettys's. She was interested in her own judgments of them as contrasted to Mrs. Pettys's opinions.

The dangling light harshly revealed the whole room: the red-striped towel on the bureau: the photo graph of Papa; the hairbrush with a yellowed ivory back, M'ma's initials delicately scrolled in black on the yellow; limp, flat bedspread on the limp, flat bed, nicked gilded balls decorating its white iron posts; limp, worn rug on the walnut-painted floor of cheap boards. . . .

"You're taking the whole thing too hard," Chester had said. "We all go through times like this."

"That red seven plays, M'ma."

"Well, so it does! Pam, Carter was real excited at dinner because he's got a position at last."

"Carter has!" There was wild hope in her voice. "Where?"

"With Otter."

"Otter? I don't know any Otter except the garage man."

"Well, that's it. Otter's Garage, down on Atterbury Street."

"But, M'ma, Cart can't keep books!"

"No, an' he isn't keepin' books. Either of these fives'll play, Pam, it always puzzles me so when there's two, because you might change yo' whole game. No, Cart says he's helpin' run the cars an' clean 'em!"

Pamela stared at the older woman in stupefaction. This serenity—this something like complacency, in the face of the fact that a Carter—a Raleigh—was working for black-handed, grinning Otter, in a garage!

"What are they paying him, M'ma?"

"Well, it's only ten dollars a week—to begin with. He's supposed to be there from about five until nine, when the other men are gettin' their dinners—and he was as pleased as Punch——" Mrs. Raleigh picked up a trey, studied her problem frowningly. "He was as pleased as Punch about it," she repeated dreamily.

Long after her mother was asleep Pamela lay awake, thinking of many things. Her grandfather, Colonel Tom Carter, and her father, the gallant Frederick Raleigh who had captured all hearts here in Carterbridge twenty-five years ago, passed before her vision—makers of the state. And their only male descendant was cleaning cars in a garage, jumping out of the driver's seat to let the owner step in, taking tips, murmuring, "Thank you, sir."

Sue Rose and Maisie discussing walking boots for the camping trip: ". . . and I've got to have another pair of those woollen stockings, Sue Rose—you can get 'em at Frink's."

Horses, the beautiful restless horses would be led about to side doors; Sam and Carol and Sue Rose would turn in the saddles, laughing, fresh, in the fresh laughing morning. "Where's Chester? He and Jessy——"

She saw the gauze-skirted lamps at the Kopper Kettle again, heard her own voice asking Chester to marry her. For that was the truth of it.

What did it matter, after all? In a hundred years . . . .

The street lights shone on her ceiling across back yards. Dingy lace curtains at the high windows twisted them into strange patterns on the discoloured plaster walls.

"If my father were alive . . . But what do people *do?* You have to have *some* money. M'ma is like a child, after all. Cart was pleased with his job, and so she was pleased.

"I can't study anything now—months without earning anything.

"Lots of girls must have faced this. I'm just pan-
icky, that's all.

"It doesn't mean he doesn't love me, just because he
isn't willing to ruin both our lives by jumping into a
perfectly crazy marriage. Why, if he'd been the one
anxious to try it I'd have said just what he said—that
it wouldn't really help anything.

"They'll stop at little hotels—they'll stop to swim
and have lunch at places. . . .

"Chester said that everybody took a turn at this
sort of thing. But that's not true. Maisie'll never have
anything like this to get through, nor Sue Rose—Sue
Rose with a million dollars!

"Well, I don't want a million. But I wonder what
it'd feel like to be happy, proud of yourself, and with
new hats and places to go?

"I'd get one of those linen outfits at Frink's, and a
little crush hat—sort of tan.

" 'See that my horse is gentle, will you, Chester?
I'm scared to death of horses.'

"Oh, my dear father, I wish you were here! I wish
somebody was here. . . ."

"There's a gentleman downstairs to see you, and he
give me his name, and there—! for all the good it
done me," said Mrs. Pettys. "But he says it won't
take a minute, and it's real important."

The girl who was brushing and straightening the
forlorn back parlour turned a suddenly paled face.

"Was it Mr. Hilliard?"

"No, it wasn't anything like that. A real short name.
He's in the dining room," said Mrs. Pettys.

"But you didn't have to come upstairs to tell me

that," Pamela said, remembering her manners after a blank instant. "Why didn't you just call up?"

"Well, I wanted to come in and have a little visit with M'ma, anyway. How are we this mornin'?" the landlady said affectionately.

Mrs. Pettys seated herself. Pamela took off her little apron, ran a comb through the curly mop of her hair, jerked her silk frock about expertly, flattening the collar, retying the stringy silk belt, and ran downstairs.

A young man in faded khaki, high boots, and a blue shirt turned from a contemplation of the dirty area outside of the dirty bay window. She saw the brown face wrinkle into a big smile that showed his white teeth. Gregory Chard.

He looked weary, anxious, supplicatory. His big sunburned face was wet with perspiration.

"It's awful," he said, almost without preamble. "My grandmother can't stand it—she hates California, she's going back to Essex as soon as Charteris— I think he's dying, poor fellow!—is able to move. The little girl cried last night—we didn't get dinner until half-past eight o'clock. I don't know what's gotten into the girls in the kitchen; they're acting like"—he paused—"anything," he said mildly. "I tried to get somebody in town here—couldn't get a soul! I telephoned San Francisco last week, and she said she'd send me a couple, a man and wife, Swedes, but they didn't come. So I telephoned again last night, and she said she'd positively have someone on the eleven o'clock train this morning. But I've just been over there—there was no one on board—just a thousand men coming to this darn' convention."

"But, Gregory, wouldn't your grandmother be happier at the Arms?"

"No, she won't go there, because they're full up with these Shriners, or whatever they are—they say there are two thousand men in town! That's a quarter of a man for every citizen," Gregory said ruefully. "I tell you it's awful. If you could—you said you'd be willing to—you don't *know* how grateful I'd be—you don't *know* how you'd help me———"

It was exquisite, to be wanted and needed. It was breath to her soul to think of escape—escape into this proffered atmosphere that held nothing of her old self and her old troubles. This big, simple, countrified fellow in his dusty boots and worn khaki breeches had his problem, too, a problem as different from hers as night from day. She smiled at him, and an old, long-ago picture of a girl at a Mardi Gras ball, a happy, popular, radiant girl, faded before this new vision of a rather pale, tall, fair-headed creature in a shabby, plain little silk gown, against a background of dilapidated boarding-house basement dining room.

"Could you come, do you think?" he asked, clearing his throat.

"If I could help."

"Oh, my *Lord*———" he said simply, almost a prayer.

"Well, then—wait for me. I'll get my hat!" said Pamela.

CHAPTER XII

L IFE is very simple, Pamela," said Bob Charteris
lazily. "It merely consists in learning how to accept the impossible, how to do without the indispensable, how to endure the insufferable. What could be
easier?"

Pamela looked at him quickly, thoughtfully, pursed
her lips to speak, and was silent. The man, lying back
in a steamer chair with pillows behind his head and a
light rug thrown over him, had closed his eyes. He was
silent so long that Pamela fancied that he might have
fallen into a doze.

The May sun had receded toward the western sky,
and there was exquisite blue shade in the old patio. But
light hung in great glowing clusters in the tops and on
the pink tassels of the pepper trees, and light lay lovingly on the soft old pink tiles of the low roof, and
struck in golden shafts through the mighty, shadowy
towers of the eucalyptus.

The walls of the patio were whitewashed, cream
colour under the clear purple-blue shadows; the little
balcony that ran around three sides of the open space
was supported by frail whitewashed poles. Gulls were
walking to and fro busily in the warm light; the windmill, out of sight, creaked and was still. And into all

the pauses came the steady, even fall of the waves down on the rocks.

He looked ill, the girl thought, taking this opportunity to study unobserved the only other occupant of the wide, silent space. He was less than forty—he looked nearer sixty. His temples were sunken and his cheek bones raised; the long thin line of his jaw looked sick, as did the thin, nervous long hands that were locked idly on the rug.

And yet he was not sick, he was not dying—he was just wrecked and left living. He could read books, and watch gulls, and sleep, and smile, and on some days, if there was no fog to choke him and no wind to shake his feeble legs, he could take his stick and get down to shore. That was about all; he thought it much. He listened to the Victrola, to the radio, to Gregory's stories of the ranch, to Pamela, even to the Mexican maids—he was well amused.

He had been a civil engineer and then a soldier. Now he was—this, and would never be any more than this. Sometimes he suffered, his breath coming in great whoops, his lean shoulders bent, his long fingers clutching his throat, and they all suffered with him. But most of the time he was serene and pleased with any plans they made for him, interested in their lives, like a child.

"I wanted 'Lisa," he said presently, opening his eyes to smile across a stretch of sunken old tiles at Pamela, sitting on the ground with an Airedale puppy in her lap. "That was all I wanted. Well, I had her—for five years."

The girl pulled the puppy's ears, looked up at the man intently. He had never spoken to her in this way before; she was afraid of stopping the current of his confidences by an interruption.

"She was a little creature—let me tell you about her," he said, the tips of his long fingers together, his interrogative, kind eyes on Pamela's face.

"I wish you would, Colonel Charteris."

"She was small, slim, you know—not one of these partridge women. But—I don't know, young. She wasn't so young, actually; twenty-four when we married, and just thirty when she died. Audrey was three when she lost her mother. 'Lisa came with her mother to visit at a country house where I was staying. You— you're what, twenty? You've never had the experience of having a perfectly commonplace house party suddenly take on a—a light. That girl—somehow she was like a little girl, rosy and sweet and full of fun— coming down to breakfast, riding beside me—— I'll never ride again. I don't know if I'm expressing to you what I mean," he went on, "that everything—the sunlight, the doorways, the garden, dancing, talk at the table, lunch in the woods——"

"Yes, I do know what you mean," the girl said, rapt, nodding her head, remembering a certain Rodeo Week.

"It was so strange. And strange to find that she felt that way, too."

He was silent a moment.

"I had to go back to the city on the Monday," he resumed, "and she came in to lunch with me on Thursday. A perfectly commonplace luncheon, don't you know? I think we went to the Ritz, yes, we did, that first time. But to see her coming toward me—I was in that big lounge there—you don't know London. But to see this woman—among all the others, coming right toward me—the look in her eyes, you know, and the feeling that nobody was going to interrupt us—we were going to talk as long as we liked! And her choosing what she wanted—it was really—" he blinked away smiling tears—"it was really most extraordinary!" he said, gulping.

"Well, we had a good deal of that, and then we were married, and I took her to Paris, and Venice—everywhere. And then we came back to a little house in the country; little brick place, with laurels, and a fireplace in every room. We unpacked books—the first Sunday."

He lay silent, his eyes closed again.

"We used to take walks," he said suddenly, "find violets and clematis, you know, have tea in earwiggy little inns. I was so happy that I'd notice other places in the city or at home, big places—rich places—and call her attention to them. It was as if I was saying to God all the time, 'There are thousands of others happier than I am—only let us alone! Lots of richer persons—there's nothing notable about *us!*' "

"It almost frightens me," Pamela said softly, in a stillness.

"It frightened us. And then Audrey came—her mother always called her 'the woman.' 'The woman's coming in to sit with us. The woman noted your absence last night.' Ah, my dear Pamela," said the man, with a break half of laughter and half of pain in his voice, "those were great days!

"We went into the war, and I was off, training. But we still had our little lunches—I'd see my girl coming toward me, so much more beautiful and wonderful than ever! And then, one June day, she wasn't there.

"I think I knew, then. I'd come home from Flan-

ders, this time; it seems they'd been trying to get me.
She'd had flu—was very weak, her mother told me
over the telephone. But she was better—she was
asleep—I was told to come straight home.

"She went on sleeping—that was all. I was sitting
beside her, holding her hand—it grew cool."

"You have Audrey," Pamela said huskily, after a
long pause.

"Yes," the man said briskly, rousing himself. "And
it's a nice thing to have—a daughter. But that's nothing like the other. Audrey's a good child, and she's an
attractive child—that's that. She'll marry, and I'll be
very fond of my grandchildren. But to expect to have
her take anything—any iota—of her mother's place is
nonsense."

And he shut his eyes again.

"But doesn't it—that wonderful thing—ever last?"
the girl asked.

"Doesn't seem to. Five years—ten—and then it's
over forever."

"Well——" Pamela hesitated, puzzled. "Life,
too?" she offered timidly.

"You're quite right," the man said approvingly.
"Change and loss are the laws of life, aren't they?"

"I suppose so," she reflected. "But—to be happy,
and not know quite why"—she stumbled on—"and
then to be—unhappy, worried—and not know quite
why about that, either——" She stopped, smiling at
him with anxious eyes.

"This doesn't make you unhappy, does it?" Charteris asked, indicating, with a shrug of his lean shoulders, the patio and the hacienda and the ranch whose
hundreds of acres spread about them.

"Oh, no!" The tears stood suddenly in her eyes.

"But—but it doesn't seem to be one's own life," she said. "This is like an interval, resting, thinking, preparing to get—started," she faltered.

"Things don't seem that way unless one is wanting to do something else," Charteris suggested.

Pamela considered. "Nothing definite," she answered, of her own case, "but perhaps just wishing that things would happen differently, that—people would do things," she said.

"You were very unhappy when you came here, weren't you?" the man asked suddenly.

Her eyes filled again, she looked at him through tears, smiling, and nodded her head.

"That's," he said, "why you could plunge into our problems here with so much courage. You didn't care."

"No," Pamela answered, "I didn't care. I thought you and Mrs. Chard would be going away in a few days, anyway, and as things went more and more wrong, I truly couldn't see why you stayed. It didn't seem to me to matter one way or the other, but I couldn't see why you didn't just—get out. But now I do care a little," she admitted honestly. "I'm glad it all worked out. It's the first thing I ever tried to do. And now that everything's working nicely——"

Her voice thickened, stopped; she left her chair and began to move the basket chairs into an ordered circle on the old stone flags, picking up a book here, a magazine there; Charteris, watching her, as tall and fair-headed and swift of movement she went to and fro, saw that she was fighting an impulse toward tears.

"Surely at twenty it wasn't all money—the trouble, I mean?" he asked, after a while.

"Why not?" Pamela asked, smiling, quite herself again.

"Well—it usually isn't at your age."

She took a hassock beside him, her body bent a little forward, her hands locked in her lap, a somewhat conscious smile in her eyes and red spots in her cheeks.

"No, it wasn't," she confessed. "I'll tell you," she went on, impulsively. "I—I made a mess of things—it was mostly my own fault. . . ."

He watched her while she talked, interested kind eyes—like a father's eyes—on her face. Sometimes he narrowed the lids thoughtfully, sometimes he smiled, once he pursed his lips to whistle and looked away. But he did not speak until she had finished.

"It's all ridiculous," he said finally, with a brief laugh. "It's just the kind of thing that small-town women of the calibre you describe enjoy enormously. But that doesn't make it any pleasanter for you."

"No," Pamela said ruefully, "that doesn't make it any pleasanter for me."

Her face was very serious, and she was frowning faintly, anxiously. But already she felt a tremendous relief, a great lifting at her heart.

"This position as my grandmother's companion came to you in the nature of a chance to escape, then?" the man asked.

"Oh, yes, I was desperate." Pamela was silent for a moment. "But I can't"—she added, presently—"I can't feel that I belong here. I'm always thinking of the others—Maisie and Carol and Sam and—all of them. I'm always thinking about what fun they're having, and about the time going by—days, and weeks, and—and I not there!"

"And it makes all this—here—seem unimportant?" Charteris asked.

"Well, yes. Nice," said Pamela, "you've all been

wonderful to me, and all that. But not—not *my* life."

"But you have got your bearings again, at least?"

"I don't know," she said. "I'm—out of everything. They're going on, doing the same old things—without me. And it doesn't—it doesn't seem fair!"

"But this man you like—this Chester Hilliard, that you think likes you, too—the man who was in that escapade with you—it seems to me he shows up pretty well—it doesn't seem to me that he could have done more than he did," Charteris presently said, watching her shrewdly.

"Oh, no, he was wonderful!" the girl asserted quickly. But there was a faint undercurrent of dissatisfaction in her tone, nevertheless.

"He doesn't come down here?" the man hinted.

"No, I've not asked him! I wrote when I'd been here about ten days. But I didn't ask him. He writes me every week. He's in a new job—and then they were all going off on a camping trip. . . ."

The statements contradicted one another; she stopped in a little confusion, with flushed cheeks.

Charteris, finger tips together, eyes fixed thoughtfully on her face, regarded her unsmilingly.

"It seems to me that I wouldn't feel left out of it all until I had at least asked him to come down here some afternoon," he said.

"I will," Pamela promised.

But in her heart she wondered. Would Chester like to come down here, to the ranch, a caller upon old Mrs. Chard's paid companion? Pamela, well as she felt she knew him, could not answer the question in her own heart.

She and Charteris had not spoken again when from inside the house the old lady called her. Pamela disappeared under the arcade of creamy, weather-worn pillars that ran along the south side of the patio; Mrs. Chard had finished her nap and wanted to come out for her tea.

She was a magnificent old figure, with richly curling short gray hair, spreading robes of silk, and fat, ringed, active hands. Her eyes were large, brown, liquid, and prominently set; her handsome old face looked brown beside the silver ripples of her hair.

"I suppose there's a good reason why Gregory keeps that parrot," she said firmly, as Pamela established her in her own basket chair and settled pillows about her. "It seems odd that the creature must screech every afternoon just as I get off. I'm no sooner in a doze than that bird perches himself—— What time is it, Bob?"

"Quarter to five, Granny," said Charteris. There was a moment's pause.

"Look in the dining room there, Pamela," said the old lady, then, startled. "His watch must be crazy!"

"No, that's right," Pamela assured her cheerfully, placing a footstool, moving a little table for the tea to stand beside Mrs. Chard's chair.

"Then I *did* sleep!" the old lady stated, in surprise.

"Oh, yes, you slept. And I slept, too," said Charteris. "I had a wonderful nap—out here under the peppers."

The old woman's eyes softened as she looked at him.

"I'm glad of it," she said in an almost tender tone.

"And that means that the poker-patience contest will go on until midnight, I suppose," Pamela suggested, capturing the wandering puppy and placing him with one swoop in the old woman's fine big hands, that began automatically to fondle him, even although

Mrs. Chard's bright eyes continued to study her grandson concernedly.

"Poker-patience passes the time, Pamela," said Charteris. "It's a great thing to pass the time. When you're a professional loafer," he added a little sadly.

"Or when you're a superfluous old woman," said Mrs. Chard, smiling at him.

Pamela put a book and a pair of eyeglasses on the tea table, close to the older woman's elbow.

"Everybody plays games," she reminded them, innocently. "Even the strongest and youngest people spend evenings and evenings and evenings at cards, and days of golf and movies and concerts. We have to amuse ourselves a lot—everybody, I mean. Children spend most of their time playing. . . ."

She paused, conscious of their appreciative eyes, and laughed, with the colour mounting into her face.

"True, Pamela," Charteris said. And she knew he was pleased.

Mrs. Chard spoke decisively, quite as if the younger woman were out of hearing.

"I declare I like that girl, Bob. She stands up to me!"

Pamela laughed and coloured again.

"But here's what I was thinking, Mrs. Chard," she said a little shyly. "I was wondering why you don't write your memoirs? That'd use any amount of spare time. About California, I mean, and Carterbridge—when it was just a village. It would be so interesting."

"I can't abide memoirs," said the old lady. "Never read 'em! The libraries are packed with 'em! Nobody reads 'em."

"But not that sort," the girl persisted eagerly. "You

—you remember everything so clearly—why, my own mother hasn't given me half such a clear impression of my grandfather as you have. And your telling us last night about the flood days——"

"Well, I may not be here very much longer," said the old woman evasively, as Pamela paused. Her grandson laughed disrespectfully.

"Now that you've got Gregory to spend a barrel of money on this place," he said, "now that you've had— how many men were here that day last month, Pamela?"

"We had seventeen men here one day, if you mean the day the piano tuner and the rug men and the plumbers and the radio man and the plasterers and the two gardeners——"

"The boy has plenty of money!" Gregory's grandmother interpolated, unashamed.

"Now that most of the remodelling and changing is done——" Charteris was beginning, again to be interrupted, this time by Pamela.

"Oh, but Colonel Charteris, we've hardly begun! Gregory wants to fix those four south rooms for Mrs. Chard."

"Well, all the more reason for our staying on here forever," the man said triumphantly, "and if you ask me my candid opinion, that's what we'll do. Sunshine, and the Pacific, and pepper trees, and gulls, and figs —I'm depending absolutely on your statement regarding those figs!—and poker-patience, and Audrey home for holidays——"

He shut his eyes. There was utter peace in the pain-racked face; there was deep content in his voice.

"You see!" said Pamela, with a little spreading gesture of the hands, to Mrs. Chard.

"Rats in the bedrooms running over Audrey's bare feet," briskly added the old lady.

"It wasn't a rat, Mrs. Chard, it was only a baby mouse!" Pamela protested quickly. "And Audrey said the next day that she never would have cried and made such a scene—she would have liked it and would have thought it was cunning!—if everything hadn't been in such a mess. She was tired out, and it was cold, and of course Aña and Anita were acting terribly. . . ."

Mrs. Chard, watching her, her brows knitted formidably but her fine mouth slightly twitching, made no direct answer. But to Charteris she said simply:

"I declare I like her!"

"Lovely place, Granny," Charteris said lazily, opening his eyes.

The old woman looked at him, moved her eyes reluctantly about the sheltered square of the patio, filled with mellowed warmth and light in the glow of the summer afternoon. The wide doorway in the western wall was opened; its arch showed a strip of old garden, a lane bordered with massive eucalyptus trees, and the level glittering blue line beyond, low down on the horizon, that was the sea.

The hacienda's three angles closed the square; narrow balconies upstairs were hung with passion-flowers, and starry clematis, and creamy banksia roses massed with bloom. The pepper trees were heavy with pink beads, the arches of the lower floor threw clean purple shadows, the whitewashed, heavy blinds above were opened; a Mexican girl, idling on a wide plaster windowsill, looked aimlessly out to sea; two men in faded overalls, with bright red handkerchiefs about their necks, were crawling about the discoloured flags on the patio, murmuring in Spanish occasionally, pulling the weeds that had sprung up between the tiles.

"I used to come down here long before I married Tony Chard," said Mrs. Chard. She mused. "I don't know whether anyone'd be interested in anything I could remember or not," she said irresolutely.

"Imagine—" Pamela said, with all the interest of the native born—"imagine Carterbridge before there was a post-office, and—what did you say the other day?—all willows and marsh below Broome Street, and no trolley——"

"My dear child, the stages used to go through twice a week when I got ... ."

"When was that, Granny?" Robert Charteris said, raising himself on his elbow.

"That was—well, I came here with your grandfather in 1876," said the old woman.

" 'Seventy-six!"

"Yes. Your grandfather was an Englishman, but I was born in Rochester, New York, myself. We came out here for his health—all the way round the Horn in a sailing vessel; we got into San Francisco in 1873. Your father was a boy of three. Robert's lungs got worse in San Francisco, and they told us to come down here—where it was hot and dry. We lived in a little wooden house in Washington Street——"

"Washington Street!" Pamela said, laughing. "That's where the packing plant is now, and Chinatown!"

"Well, that's where we were, and that's where Robert died, in '78, and the nicest part of town, too!" said the old woman sharply. "And afterward I married Gregory's grandfather and came down here. My gracious, it does seem a long time ago!"

"It seems like another world," Pamela said, wide-eyed.

"Yes; I married Antonio Chard—his father had been an Englishman, too," the old woman mused on; "but the mother was Spanish. And after he died, I took both my boys—Bob's father, here, and Greg's father —and went back to England. But Greg's father, when he was a young man, came back and married here. The Charteris family kept me in England—I was sick a lot in those years—but Tony, that was Greg's father, never wanted anything but this ranch.

"It was a great place, Molino, when I first came here. They had bullfights down here, and great feasts —everyone used to come down here and walk up and down on the cliffs. I remember a man—it was your grandfather, Pamela, come to think of it—going right into the sea after little Tony Chard. Tony wasn't five, because his father died when he was five."

"Tony. That was Gregory's father?"

"That was Gregory's father. Yes, he got fooling along the shore there, and in he went! There was a man named Catherwood——" she paused.

"Oh, yes; they're still in town—they're about the most prominent people in Carterbridge," Pamela said eagerly.

"Prominent, are they?" the old lady asked, pursing her lips, elevating her eyebrows.

"Oh, very!" Pamela answered innocently. "They and the Beavers and the Billingses and the Broomes. Oh, Mrs. Chard, do write about it—the prices of things, and the streets that the houses and shops were on, and about the beginning of everything. It would be so interesting!"

"It might be interesting to *me*," said old Mrs.

Chard, pleased with the girl's enthusiasm in spite of herself, "but it's fifty years ago—it wouldn't interest anyone else!" And abruptly, with an air of firing a gun, she added: "I'll think about it. Where's Gregory?"

"He had to go into Carterbridge on business." Pamela put her smooth cheek close to the black rubber beak of the big red and green and egg-yellow parrot; he sidled on her fingers, chuckled, gently closed his bill about the free finger she held close to it.

"Give him to me," Charteris pleaded, and Pamela carried him to the steamer chair and bent down and transferred the clinging feet to the invalid's long fingers.

"He's still rather worried about the puppy," she warned him.

"I'll remember!"

"I'll start Anita on the tea tray—Greg'll be home in time."

She went away, and Charteris said:

"That was a picture, Gran. That girl—with the bird——"

"Nice girl," the old lady agreed. "Fine stock. I wish Greg would see it."

"He sees it perfectly," Charteris said ruefully.

"Well, I wish the boy'd act, then!" his grandmother said sharply. The puppy whimpered; she soothed it without looking down. "I wish he'd begin—courting," she went on decidedly. "There's all the difference in the world between the way he acts toward the girl and the way he ought to act. The minute she looks at him or speaks to him the poor boy loses his wits completely. Why don't she see it? Why don't she put him out of his misery? I can't understand 'em—I can't see how two good-looking youngsters can go on, day after day . . .

"What he says doesn't interest her, he doesn't seem to be able to rouse her!" she added discontentedly, after a silence in which Charteris only frowned slightly and smoothed the parrot's slippery green feathers with his hand.

"I feel—" the man said deliberately, after a pause in which they could hear the soft, steady rush and recession of the sea, "I feel that I am about to betray a confidence."

Mrs. Chard shot him a swift, suspicious, hopeful look.

"She's discovered that she's in love with Gregory, eh?" she said in a cautious undertone, with a glance toward the grape-draped archway through which Pamela had disappeared in the direction of the kitchen.

"No, it's not that, I'm sorry to say."

"She suspects that the boy is in love with her?"

"No. Unfortunately, her affections are already engaged."

Mrs. Chard stared at the speaker, hostility in her eye.

"What you talking about, Bob?"

"It appears that all our little plans for them are to miscarry. There is a youth in Carterbridge."

"Did she tell you so?"

He nodded. The old woman bit her lip.

"No money, eh?"

"It doesn't seem to be quite that. I gather that she got into some youthful jam after a dance—whatever it was—the dovecotes were fluttered, and the youth, and Pamela too, frowned down, and ostracized——"

"I hadn't heard it!" Mrs. Chard commented, magnificently displeased.

"It appears to have broken her poor little heart. There's a rather ne'er-do-well brother, and there were financial difficulties, and the old home—the home of that actual Carter for whom the town was named——"

"My dear Bob, please remember that I lived in Carterbridge fifty years ago. I knew her grandfather before he was married—Tom Carter—and a handsome scamp, too. You can't tell me anything about *that* place!"

"I forgot. Well, anyway, the poor child's troubles appear to have arrived all in a heap, and she's suffering horribly from shame—mortification has set in. She tells me that she was at her wits' end when Gregory chanced along and asked her to come down here and run things."

"She must have been, to have been willing to have had anything to do with the conditions such as they were down here then!" said Mrs. Chard decisively. She was silent a moment. "They were snubbing her, were they?"

"They made a thorough job of it. She was asked to resign from the dancing club—she was pretty well dropped, I gather."

The old lady looked at him sharply.

"What had she done, do you suppose?"

"The usual thing. Out late, party dress, flat tire, and spending the night in some deserted old house beside the road. By bad luck, the man who picked them up in the morning was the father of one of the straitlaced girls of the town—Broome, I think she said. You know the name?" Charteris interrupted himself to ask, as his companion looked up.

"I know all their names!"

"Well, Mrs. Broome—who appears to be a lady of high virtue—led the opposition."

"Ostracized her, eh?"

"It amounted to that."

"The young people, too? They appear to be an obedient lot," Mrs. Chard commented scornfully. "She's been down here all these weeks, and not one of them has come down to see her. I hear her telephoning her mother, and she tells me that her brother had a position somewhere—in Bakersfield? Bakersfield. But I've wondered what sort of friends she had."

"Possibly they don't know exactly what she's doing here—she probably didn't say much about it, poor child."

"Of course, the mothers of any town have got a strong case against any girl who looks like that," the old lady said significantly. Charteris laughed. "But what about this beau of hers?" Mrs. Chard demanded suddenly, suspiciously. "Why don't he come down here? They didn't have a fight?"

"She represents him as everything that is loyal and concerned and fine," Charteris answered drily.

His grandmother studied his expression shrewdly.

"What's his name, Bob?"

"Hilliard."

The old woman's face lightened intelligently.

"I know *that* lot," she said, nodding. "There were two brothers, Robert and Jim. I know a great deal about them." Her significant voice sank, she sat silent, staring into space. "Are they engaged, Bob?" she asked suddenly.

"An understanding, probably. There was some question of his job, he's a comparative newcomer here, was educated in the East."

"And what's to prevent their getting married?"

"Money, I imagine. She has nothing, and he's working for an uncle. Money difficulties, and the fact that the important social group of the town heartily disapproves of her."

"The important social group! You don't mean these people she speaks of now and then, Broomes and Beavers, Stokeses and Billingses, do you?" demanded the old woman.

"The very ones."

"Tom Carter's granddaughter isn't good enough for 'em?"

"That was the impression she gave me," said Charteris, smiling suddenly.

"What's funny, Bob?" his grandmother asked.

"You, Granny. You look as if you were putting on your war paint."

Mrs. Chard bridled, sniffed, tossed her head.

"I'd like to manage her affairs for her for about five minutes," she said roundly. "Broomes and Beavers and Stokeses! I wonder how they'd like to hear about some of the things *their* families did in this town, fifty years ago. Carrie Broome would have been——" She paused. "Well, I don't suppose it was her fault; she was hardly responsible for what she did, poor thing!" she interrupted herself to say musingly. "As for that Hilliard lawsuit—I never heard of it until I went back to England, but I certainly——" She paused again. "I wonder how much these Beavers, in this generation, hear about old Harrison Beaver?" she asked presently, looking up.

"What did Harrison Beaver do?" Charteris asked, in high enjoyment.

"Never you mind what he did! Then there were the Catherwoods. She told me—you heard her a few minutes ago—that the Catherwoods were very important persons nowadays. Well, I can remember the day when the Catherwoods——" She stopped.

"You make my blood run cold!" Charteris said. "You're a terrible woman when you get roused, Granny. I can imagine nothing more awful—nothing more blood-curdling—for a group of these smug little social lights than to have a voice from the past speak suddenly among them, blasting their pretensions at the very root!"

He lay back, his eyes shut, his face one wrinkle of laughter. The green parrot sidled up and down his lax arm.

"I'll get Greg to put a little notice in the paper— I'll have 'em all down here!" the old woman muttered, thinking aloud. Charteris opened his tear-wet eyes, glanced at her again, and went off into another noiseless laugh.

Then there was a long silence, in the blue, sweet spring afternoon. There was an occasional sound of voices, or a dog's bark, from the direction of the cabins, and once there was a hysterical burst of chatter and the hissing of some overturned liquid on the stove in the kitchen; under and over everything moved the steady soft rush and murmur of the sea. There was a wind rising; they could hear it. The windmill creaked and splashed uneasily; the high, massed, dark sickles of the eucalyptus stirred.

But inside the patio all was peace; the old white-washed hacienda had dreamed in the California sunshine for a hundred years; it would dream on for a hundred more, its walls growing more mellow, its long lines of low tiled roof softer and lovelier. Great roses climbed it, and flung long streamers into the air; a passion vine, over the kitchen arcade, dangled its starry flowers of purple-blue across the tops of the heavy, wide-opened, iron-hasped shutters.

"That Broome family!" Mrs. Chard muttered finally as Pamela and Maria, carrying trays, came into view; "they were a fine lot! Those girls make another picture for you, Bob," she added.

"I am humbly appreciative of it," said Charteris, tossing the parrot toward his perch.

Pamela and Maria were walking slowly, burdened with trays; Maria's wide and light, Pamela's small and heavy—the silver pot, the kettle, the lamp.

Maria was a Mexican girl, short, dark, rosy, firm-breasted, sleek hair of sloe black, slim arms of brown. She had a scarlet handkerchief tied about her head, and her faded blue gown was open to show her brown throat; her white apron, a recent innovation, was longer than her short skirt.

Pamela, fair, tall, very earnest, was in white. Her beautiful gray eyes were lowered to watch the slightest movement of her tray, the thick long lashes sent umber shadows across her cheeks. Her mouth, the lovely chiselled mouth—"big enough for laughter, and for those superb big white teeth," Charteris thought— was shut and twitching, like that of a concentrating child. Her slim lean wrists, her nervous, fine, tense fingers, her whole body was intent now upon steering the lighted silver vessels she carried safely to the table, and she gave a child's long breath of relief when they were deposited there and, looking up at Charteris, smiled happily.

"You are a rare and lovely and beautiful person, all fragrance and curves and softness and firmness and glory," Charteris said, in his soul.

"What are you thinking about?" Pamela asked, arrested by his look.

"Something extremely agreeable."

"Tea?"

"Well, for one thing."

She poured his grandmother's cup first, and carried it across the patio. Maria was dismissed; Pamela took the toast, on its heavy green and pink plate, for a preliminary inspection.

"Is it still too thick?"

"No, it looks about right, now. Thank you, dear!" said Mrs. Chard.

The little garden meal was hardly commenced when Gregory Chard joined them; they heard his car humming across the flat meadows behind the hacienda, and Pamela put down her own cup and filled one for him. He came in through the patio doorway, wearing a weary, contented smile that showed his white, white teeth; he took his sombrero from his dark hair as he came in.

Pamela looked very slim and white and childish and fair as she stood before him, the smoking cup in her hands.

"Don't bother about the mail. Don't bother about the books—I'll open them. Where are you going to sit?" she said.

"But—what? I didn't hear you!" He was instantly transformed from the big, easy, half-Spanish ranchero to a stammering and flushing schoolboy. He laughed nervously. "Oh, I'll sit anywhere—here or anywhere!" he muttered.

She stood looking at him reproachfully, smilingly, over the cup.

"But that's *my* seat, and I have to pour tea!"

"Oh, that's right, that's right, too!" Gregory apologized, shifting to another chair. "Thank you," he said thickly, taking his cup.

"He'll not get very far with her *that* way!" old Mrs. Chard reflected scornfully.

"Poor kid!" Charteris thought. "If he *has* got anything, he takes good care that she shall always see him at his worst!"

Gregory was preternaturally solemn now, scowling as aimlessly as he had smiled before. Pamela, slim and white, in her garden chair, challenged him animatedly.

"How was it in town, and whom did you meet, and what's the news?"

"I met everyone," Gregory said hoarsely, sternly.

"Oh, why wasn't I with you! Oh, dear! Who—for instance?"

"Oh, the Billings girl—what's her name——"

"Carol!" Charteris heard the lift in her voice; her eyes were shining.

"Carol Billings. And she was talking about some plan to organize a Junior Auxiliary to the Country Club——"

"I didn't know that!" Pamela's voice dropped a trifle. Life was going on—fun was going on—without her!

"Yep. And there was some message for you. I wrote it down here——" Gregory was fumbling in his pockets, he did not see the light in her eyes. But Charteris saw it.

"Message for me?" The world was all rosy again.

"Yep, they wanted—you have a list, an invitation list or something for the Cinderella Club, and Miss Billings wanted you to mail it to her without fail."

"Was that all?" Pamela's voice was steady and quiet. But Charteris and his grandmother exchanged glances that appraised its significance to a hair.

"And then I ran into Maisie Broome and that feller she's engaged to," said Gregory.

"Maisie engaged!" There was electricity in the air; the colour fled Pamela's face as if it had been wiped out with a painter's rag.

"Yep—isn't she? To that red-headed Billings boy —Sam? I thought that was kind of understood," Gregory, having finally returned several papers to his pockets, said surprisedly.

"Maisie and Sam!" Her voice was fairly singing. "Oh, I am so pleased!" Pamela exulted. "What fun! Maisie and Sam Billings—imagine old Maisie engaged——"

"What was she afraid of?" Charteris wondered, watching the change in her. But the old lady knew.

"She was afraid that girl had gotten her beau," decided old Mrs. Chard. "Poor child, her heart's wrapped up in him. I must have a look at him."

Aloud she said:

"Gregory, I've been thinking it's about time that we let Carterbridge know that I'm here. The place is getting lovely now, and the roads are all right again. I think I'd like to give some sort of party down here in about two weeks. I'll write the notes myself. And I'll put a little postscript on each one: 'I want to speak to you about your Aunt Carrie—I knew your uncle at the time of the lawsuit.' They'll all come!"

"Sure—that would be great!" Gregory said, surprised.

"I may want—under the circumstances—to write my memoirs one of these days," said the old woman. "Just as well to brush up my memories."

Gregory was handing Pamela a letter—one of Chester's letters—and the girl had no eyes for anything else. But Charteris, grinning, sent his grandmother a long, eloquent look.

"Under the circumstances, perhaps you're wise, Granny," he said.

CHAPTER XIII

S HE puttered about Gregory like a child; from the
beginning of the day until the family good-nights
at half-past ten o'clock, Pamela was always beside him.

When Gregory came downstairs, by way of the open
patio, at eight o'clock, the slender figure in the striped
blue cotton gown was usually in sight; Pamela would
be playing with the puppy, the early sunlight glinting
down through the pepper tassels on her bright head,
or she would be arguing with the untrained gardeners,
her face flushed with eagerness, a weed in one hand, a
spear of grass in another, her anxious eyes on their
stupid Latin faces.

"They will not understand that we want the grass
and *don't* want the weeds!" she would tell Gregory,
walking in through the sunny and shadowy arcades
with him to breakfast. His grandmother always had
hers on a tray, but she liked to have Pamela bring it
in, and to have Gregory come in too with the paper,
just brought out from Carterbridge, and whatever
news was already afoot.

Charteris would limp out to breakfast in a low
chair, with a tray before him; Gregory and Pamela
shared their coffee and toast at the table. Then Gregory worked at his mail, his bookkeeping, while the girl
went about the house on a hundred errands. There

was never a time when the fair head and blue striped gown were in his neighbourhood that Gregory did not feel the world the sweeter, and never a time when she was gone for a few minutes that he was not conscious of missing her.

When he walked about the barns and corrals and paddocks at eleven, Pamela went too, her hands plunged in her sweater pockets, if the morning was chilly, and her little felt hat pulled snugly down, or, if the day was hot, with the sun gleaming on her tawny hair.

She was always companionable, always interested, sometimes contradictory and positive almost to the quarrelling point. She told Gregory that he spoiled all his men, and he grinned and admitted that it might be true. He watched her, down on one knee, mysteriously excited over puppies and the babies of the cabin settlement, and sometimes, if he had a few free minutes, they walked down to the sea—eternally seething and swelling slowly over the big rocks—and the bold gulls circled close about her beautiful head and extended hands, and she laughed out exultantly, in breezes and sunshine and fresh salty airs.

Every day she went into the kitchen, an l was dictatorial in the matter of sauces and trays. She threatened Maria and Anita and Aña with a Chinese invasion.

"If you girls can't learn to keep this place reasonably clean, he'll do it, I tell you! He'll get in two good Chinese boys, who'll be worth more than the whole pack of you!"

But she liked them, and they worshipped her. One word from Pamela to an old, old woman dreaming in the chimney corner, or spoken tenderly above a sick child, was enough to win all their hearts. She did what she liked with them; indeed, the awed, penitential Spanish murmur they carried on in her actual presence was almost always amused, loyal, and admiring, as Gregory knew, if she did not.

During the convulsed period immediately following her arrival at the ranch, when all sorts of radical interior changes—papering, plastering, plumbing—had been carried on, she had become familiar with all of Gregory's affairs, and she made a sort of game of them, chattering while she wrote checks and compared invoices, busy, amused, almost maternal in manner.

The pandemonium of the first few days, when Charteris had been helpless under a fierce attack of pain and weakness, little Audrey tearful and bewildered, and the old lady angry and unhappy, had established, once and for all, an intimacy and confidence between Gregory and Pamela. Their problems had been vital, incessant, and innumerable. They had consulted in agitated asides over every phase of Mrs. Chard's dissatisfaction, Robert Charteris's illness, the little girl's plans, the rebellion kitchenward, the plastering and gardening and papering, the steady and depressing rain, the mud in the patio, the draughts and musty odours of the long-neglected house.

And as order gradually shaped itself from chaos, they had not grown less companionable. Rooms had been aired and swept and added to the occupied area of the old hacienda; trays had been somehow made more and more acceptable to the old lady; Audrey, in the charge of her old school teacher, had departed for Santa Barbara; and more than all, and affecting everything and everybody profoundly, the glorious sunshine had come out, the fogs and clouds had evaporated over the green rancho, lilacs had rustled their green tents in warm shade, and fruit blossoms had come drifting on perfumed little gusts of soft air, across the discovered flags of the patio.

The five o'clock tea, the puppy and the parrot, the first letters from a small girl happy in school, the evening games of halma and poker-patience, had taken form too, now—had composed themselves into a routine that quite absorbed and satisfied Mrs. Chard. She usually kept Gregory chatting for some twenty minutes over her breakfast tray, then bathed and dressed at nine, appearing regally at about half-past ten, to be bright and conversational until early afternoon, when she went ponderously upstairs for a nap. She even began, as May deepened and sweetened and ripened toward the perfection of June, to defend her new home truculently.

"In Devonshire you don't get days like these until July, let me tell you! This climate is the most beautiful in the world, and this place is the loveliest place! I'd forgotten just how beautiful it was," she confessed one day. "It had sorrowful associations for me, I suppose—poor Chard's death; we hadn't been married but seven years. And then, twenty-five years later, to be getting ready to come out here and join poor Tony—your father, Gregory—and to get the cable that he was gone, too."

She was querulous, dictatorial, impatient, unreasonable by turns, but there were intervening times when she could be as brightly kind, as helpfully pleasant a companion as anyone could ask. And she was never old mentally, although physically her régime was simple and restful, as became her eighty-four years. All her interests, her viewpoint, her suggestions were as young and fresh and vital, and infinitely wiser, than any from Pamela or Gregory.

On the fifth night, as Pamela had spread an extra coverlid over her for her nap, the firm old hand had drawn her down.

"Look here, little Carter—you knew I knew your grandfather, didn't you?"

"You told me so yesterday, Mrs. Chard."

"And you and I like each other, don't we?"

A pause, while Pamela, her hand still captive, had laughed in embarrassment.

"If *you* like *me,* we do," she had said, with her sea-gray eyes, strangely luminous, gazing down at the magnificent form that was comfortable in the pillows and covers.

And since that moment, the old woman's affection for the young one had been evinced in a sudden, "I declare I like that girl!" often repeated, always spoken as if against her will.

She and Charteris had indeed made up a match between Gregory and Pamela, confident that two young things could hardly experience their intimacy and discover their congeniality without that outcome. To find that Pamela had interests elsewhere was a real disappointment to the old lady, but with characteristic vigour she had diverted herself to the question of Carterbridge's social claims. Only her older grandson knew what inspired the malicious, mischievous twinkle in her dark bright eyes during those days when preparations for the garden party were in the making.

Pamela was so entirely in the dark that she could express quite innocent surprise to Gregory at the instantaneous response to the cards of invitation.

"Everybody's coming, apparently, Greg."

He looked up at her, surprised.

"You sound as if you didn't expect that they would," he said bluntly.

"Well—knowing Carterbridge, I would suppose that some of them would make excuses! After all, it's nine miles."

"I'll bet you've missed them—all your old crowd—awfully," he suggested, struck by a sudden thought.

"Yes, I have. Sometimes," the girl answered, smiling and blinking.

"I'll bet you have," he repeated thoughtfully. "Well, when my grandmother goes back to England, or down south, or anywhere, you'll go back to them," he consoled her, challenging her to express regret.

"I suppose so." Pamela had not thought of him at all. Her thoughts went to Carterbridge, and she wondered what her next job would be; wondered if, perhaps, she might be married in a few months.

Chester's letters—the five weeks had brought her many of them—were not entirely satisfactory. And yet they *were* letters, indisputable evidence that he thought of her, and that was enough. She kept them in their envelopes, in order, and knew without taking them out exactly what each one said, knew just where to look for some phrase she wanted to reread.

She had a small, white-plastered room next to Mrs. Chard's on the upper floor; both rooms were connected with the narrow-poled balcony that ran up on the three sides of the patio, and had deep-silled windows on the other side of the house, the garden side, as well. Pamela's had once been a dressing room; it was as plain and white and orderly as a cell.

In the early morning, when opal light was beginning to creep in through the drowsing garden and over the silent patio, she loved to lie there, in her small, narrow iron bed, under the plain coverlet that her slim long body raised into a white hill—lie there with Chester's letters under her pillow, and her arms locked under her head, and her thoughts roving idly over the day ahead, and on and on into the future.

Her first days in the hacienda had been wretched; she had had this same cot in a corner of old Mrs. Chard's room, and had shared not only the old woman's apartment, but her bureau, her smoky lamp, and her washstand, pitcher, and basin as well.

But on the third day after her arrival electric lights from insulated wires crudely concealed by wooden cleats—for there was no use trying to pierce the solid adobe of the walls—had bloomed suddenly all over the hacienda, and on the eleventh day Pamela and Gregory, in excusable excitement, had kneeled to wash the tightly pasted label from a new bathtub, and had established soap and towels, racks and mirrors in the enormous bedroom that had been sacrificed for the much-needed bathroom.

Mrs. Chard's trunks, at first eternally bumping Pamela's elbows and catching at her ankles, were emptied at last; one troublesome task after another was relegated to the past, and presently Pamela could take possession of this little chamber and fit it up as suited herself.

She had a blue rug on the floor, one chair, one chest, and the narrow bed. A magnolia looked in upon her from the garden side, and sometimes gulls came up from the patio at dawn and walked busily about on her windowsills, jerking their little bodies like pigeons in the sunlight.

At seven she could always hear a stir beginning

down at the cabins, the cowboys laughing, the women's
shrill voices, dogs, and the lowing of cattle. And Pamela would touch Chester's letters, and dream, and
stare at the creamy-white ceiling and the plain walls,
her soul at peace.

"Dear Pamela——" That was the way they all began. They were not love letters, exactly. But their
words, although much younger and cruder somehow
than Chester's speech, curiously brought the vision of
him before her——his handsome mouth, his fine figure in
white flannels, his sleek black hair. Chester!

It seems queer not seeing you—there is not much doing—there
is no more fun like last year—will you ever forget Rodeo Week?
You and I never will forget it, will we? Every time I go into the
Arms I think about you. Four days after we got back from the
camping tour my uncle sent me to S. F. for two nights—I wrote
you that. I saw two fellows I used to know in coll. and we went
to shows every night. Hope everything goes well in darkest
Africa—it must seem queer to you to be out there, the old lady
sounds like a character all right. I meant to come down Sunday,
but don't know whether you want callers or not, please be sure
to write me, and tell me if I could take you off for a show or
something if I came. Maisie told me to write you that nothing
was half as much fun without you.

This was the gist of them all, with slight variations.
But each had its own personal note, too. There was one
in which Maisie was quoted again, this time as saying
that she supposed Gregory Chard was in love with
Pamela by this time, to which Chester added "but we
know better than that, don't we, Pam?" There was
another that had a "darling," casually included, and
a third that said:

I meant every word I ever said to you, and I am working hard,
and hope for a break soon.

Best of all was the very first, although even in her own heart Pamela would not admit that. She read it and reread it, until the paper was limp and rubbed with handling, and she kept hoping that one of the others, the next, or the one after that, would say something as thrilling.

You seem to me still too beautiful and too sweet for any man to win, Pam, and I'll make you so happy some day that you'll forget all this last winter—when you've been worrying so.

That hadn't come until she had been five terrible days at the rancho; it had marked the beginning of better times.

Everything had bettered; not suddenly, not sensationally—even now Pamela could not feel that any one thing in her life was quite righted, was quite what it should be—but at least everything was not wholly wrong, nowadays.

M'ma was still at Mrs. Pettys's, and Mrs. Pettys's was unchanged. The change had been in M'ma. Or perhaps it was not a change; perhaps M'ma had always had within her a capacity for boarding-house existence.

Not that M'ma was happy in words; her occasional letters were gentle little jeremiads still. But Pamela had gone into town with Gregory one day, and had had an hour with M'ma. And M'ma was undeniably content. She would talk of nothing but affairs at Mrs. Pettys's; they interested her—they seemed worth while to her.

Of Pamela's friends she knew nothing. She had not returned Mrs. Broome's call, she had seen nobody. Pamela had known, on this occasion, that Chester was in San Francisco. She had tried to telephone Maisie, but

Maisie had not been at home; finally Pamela had had a rather unsatisfactory chat with Sue Rose.

At Gregory's side on the front seat, she had returned to the rancho rather silently. It was satisfying, certainly, to know that Carter had a job in a radio store in Bakersfield and that M'ma was not suffering acutely in her humble surroundings, but it was rather baffling, too.

Then had come the thrill of her first month's salary, following the thrill of doing her first real work in the world and discovering that she really did have some executive capacity—some talent for affairs. Pamela had wondered with what awkwardness and self-consciousness Gregory would pay her. Perhaps he would put her check in an envelope at her place at the table. Perhaps he would ask Colonel Charteris to give it to her. He was so *gauche* at the best of times. . . .

But he had handed it to her quite simply, after a casual, "Wait a minute—this is the tenth, I owe you some money!" and it had been Pamela who was flushed and uncomfortable during the few minutes of taking it. One hundred dollars. She said to herself that she had spent many hundreds in her life, but she had never really seemed to sense what a hundred dollars was, before.

One hundred dollars' worth of homesickness. One hundred dollars' worth of hard work, nervous work, work for which she would have supposed herself to be absolutely unfitted. One hundred dollars to compensate her for those nights when she had cried herself to sleep, picturing Chester and Maisie and the Billingses all happy—all together—without her; those nights when her back had ached from climbing stairs and carrying oddly assorted armfuls of china and, linen and clothing to and fro; those nights when her surroundings had seemed so strange, so disheartening, that she had felt she could not bear the loneliness, the strangeness of it all, even until morning.

There had been times, in those four weeks, when she would have given the whole hundred to be speeding toward Carterbridge, just for a few days—a few hours!—of that old life under the trees in the Carter garden, with Maisie just around the corner, and Carol so near, and laughter and gossip and companionship again. One soda in Murphy's drug store, one idle hour looking at the hats at Elaine's, or the frocks at Mockby's, one evening of dancing at the Arms would have seemed worth a hundred million dollars then. Youth—Pamela would sob, burying her face in the stiff new sheets that still had their blue and gold labels pasted to them—youth was so short, and the days at the rancho were so lonely and so long!

She had sent three quarters of her first salary to her mother, and Mrs. Raleigh, in a very gush of love and gratitude, had immediately bought Pamela a sixty-dollar dress, all gold lace and small yellow rosebuds, and had telephoned Gregory that he must come get it and take it down to the ranch.

This action on her mother's part had caused Pamela actual despair, and between laughter and tears she had displayed the frock to Mrs. Chard and asked the advice of the family in general.

"If you don't want it, turn it in and get the credit," Gregory had suggested, in his practical way.

"She probably got it at Mockby's, and we owe—I don't know what!—there already," Pamela said, discouraged.

"Well, that's just as good a way to make a payment on the bill as any," Charteris reminded her.

"I'll do it," she had said, suddenly satisfied. "Because I have no use for a dress like that!" she told Gregory later. "Imagine an evening dress of gold lace down here at Molino!"

"You—you won't be here always," he reminded her, clearing his throat. "Or if you did stay, you could go to parties—you could give parties here, you know."

"If ever we gave a regular party here, Greg," she said, suddenly fired, "wouldn't it be fun to have it a real ranch party—I mean dress in Spanish costumes, and hoopskirts, and have horses for everyone to ride——"

"That'd be easy," he agreed, considering it.

"And you'd have to grow those little sideburns, you know, Greg, like your grandfather's portrait, and we'd have a bullfight——"

"You can't have bullfights." He was, as always with her, clumsy and dull, and Pamela was, as always, impatient at his slower-moving wits.

"You could have what the boys have every Sunday, couldn't you—down at the old ring? They tie a dollar bill to a bull's horns, and then they turn him loose in the ring, and about a dozen of them try to get it."

"Oh, yes," he said, with his confused air of taking his attention from the speaker to consider the words, his face brightening. "You could do that!"

"You could have a *wonderful* party!" Pamela mused, her eyes shining.

It was the morning of the tea party, and they were down in a little wooded cañon, gathering great branches of beautiful young live-oak leaves, pale green, furry white, and coral pink, and the bushy delicate leaves of the huckleberry, with which to decorate the hacienda for the festivity. Pamela had been in the kitchen from eight until eleven, trying to impress upon Anita and Maria the rudiments of formal service, and mixing with her own swift hands the fillings for sandwiches. Gregory had heard her laughing out there when he came down to the patio before breakfast, and had gone out to find her captured in drifts of steam and smoke and the beams of sunlight that struck through the small, high, wide-silled windows. The slender, young, fair thing had looked like a beam of light herself among the dark Latin women who were all laughing and curious about her, in her blue apron, with her blue bowl.

She had extended toward Gregory the tip of a mixing knife loaded with some delicious mixture, and he had said fervently, upon testing it,

"My gosh, that's good! What's in it?"

"Oh—green olives and boiled eggs and mustard and chives and cheese." And with a triumphant laugh she had dipped up another sample from another bowl, again directing him with childish despotism, "Now taste *that.*"

Heavenly—heavenly quarter of an hour in the blackened, wide old kitchen, with one door opened upon the spring sunshine of the patio and another upon the shadows of the storeroom and pantries, with the Mexican girls in such high spirits and the day at morning—sweet and dewy and full of promise! And above all, heavenly to find Pamela in this mood, laughing, eager, beautiful—she had always been sweet and helpful, in his knowledge of her, but she had not often shown this enchanting gaiety, since her arrival at the ranch.

Now, hours later, down in the cañon, he told himself with contempt that it had been because of the tea party that her spirits had risen so suddenly; it was because her own group, her beloved and indispensable intimates, were coming down to the rancho this afternoon. She had missed them, poor kid; her quiet manner, her serious eyes, and the little sighs that he had heard from her now and then in the troublesome weeks of getting his cousins and grandmother settled had all been tributes to her loyalty and her homesickness.

To have her belong here, happy here—often in the kitchen, as she had been this morning, with the maids about her, the sunshine slanting in upon blackened walls and blackened pots and upon the babies and cats and dogs that were indispensable adjuncts to all Latin cooking—no, that would be too much felicity—that would be more than any man on earth could expect of life.

He walked along beside her, his arms, as her arms were, filled with the young branches, the warm sunshine pouring down through a roof of leaves overhead, the air sweet and perfumed, with not a breath stirring, and the sea, at the little cañon's end, where the woods opened out into marshy strips and pebbly shale, singing its eternal surging song of loneliness, and change, and far ports, and vast and endless silences.

"Isn't it pretty?" the girl asked, as they emerged from the trees, and mounted to the cliffs, and could see the long line of ranch buildings and the trees that towered above the hacienda lying before them. The pink-tiled roof of the house was gracious in warm lead shadows; the windmills, the cattle, and hay barns, and the straggling line of the bunkhouses and cabins were all dappled with light and shadow, all silent and sleepy in a dreaming noontide. Gregory's prize Hereford breathed a little whine of protest through his wet muzzle, pawing the ground with one dangerous, sharp hoof; calves blatted in pens, immediately forgetting their troubles to spring about their small prisons ecstatically, infected, as all the world was infected, with the wine and glory of the day.

"You like Molino, don't you?" Gregory asked, his heart beginning to beat fast. He had not meant to say it.

Pamela looked up at the broad, squarely built form and the olive face, with its Latin flash of white, white teeth, and smiled.

"Gregory, who wouldn't!"

"But I mean—more than you did when you came down?"

"Oh, when I first came here? Well, I was sunk, then," admitted Pamela frankly. "I was heartbroken —everything was going wrong—I wouldn't have wanted to go to heaven itself, then!"

"Money troubles, huh? And living at that boarding house?"

"Oh, yes, and other things. People," said Pamela.

She laughed up at him, a laugh of sheer excitement. Her thoughts were far away from Gregory, striding along beside her in his faded khaki and high-laced boots and disreputable sombrero. She told herself that this afternoon she would see Chester—Jessy Stokes had been invited to Mrs. Chard's tea, as a matter of course, and Pamela had written Chester that he was invited, too, and he must bring her down. Chester! And he would see her, Pamela, in her batiste dress; it was not a new dress, but always fine and delicate and transparent over the little white slip. He would

see Pamela in the exquisite setting of the patio, with
the green parrot and the magnificent old lady and the
romantically invalided English officer to lend ad-
ditional colour. Yes, and Greg, too, for Gregory was
undeniably handsome and effective; and it might sur-
pise Mr. Chester Hilliard to see how brotherly and
affectionate! Gregory beside her, helping her enter-
tain the very cream of Carterbridge's society . . .

Thinking these things, she laughed up at Gregory
excitedly over the furry jade-white leaves of oak, and
Gregory lost his head completely, and said thickly, excitedly, in his turn:

"I don't suppose—I guess you know what I mean—
I don't suppose you'd stay here?"

Instantly she sobered, and her face grew warm. She
had thought of this, but not to-day. Laughing as
awkwardly as he did, she answered uncomfortably:

"I hoped—I hoped you wouldn't say that, Greg."

"I never will again!" he promised quickly, fervently,
chilled and ashamed. "I sort of knew you wouldn't,"
he added, aware that he had taken her at a disadvan-
tage and anxious to spare her. "It—it wouldn't be
much of a life for you!"

"What?" she asked, regaining her poise. "To be
mistress of the hacienda? It'd be wonderful; don't be
foolish, Greg. It's the most beautiful place in the
world, and you're—" her nod indicated the other
occupants of the hacienda, as well as himself—"you're
the kindest people! But—but you see I'm not free,
Greg. You see I'm—" She laughed, confidential,
rosy, all the small, endearing sister—"you see, I'm in
love!" she confessd.

He cleared his throat; his face was a deep red.

"I see. With—with some feller in Carterbridge?" He was talking to help get control of himself.

"With—" she hesitated, but it was delicious to say it; she had to go on—"with Chester Hilliard," she said.

There was a silence.

"I know who you mean—he's in the bank with old Bob," Gregory said then, slowly. "Slim, dark feller, with smooth hair."

It brought the vision of Chester before her, and her voice sang.

"That's he."

"And it's an engagement, is it?" the man asked, still with some little difficulty in his speech.

The enormity of it scared her a little, and she ran to cover.

"Oh, not quite that. Well—almost, I guess. That is —it's an understanding."

It made her happy, saying it. Everything seemed to be so right and simple and natural on this singing early summer morning.

"Why hasn't he——" Gregory began, almost truculently. He changed the form of his question, his voice softer. "Why haven't you asked him down here?"

"I should have, I suppose." It did sound an obvious oversight. Chester wouldn't come without an invitation —that was it. "But you see the roads have been out of order, after the rains—and then it *was* wet, you know, for ten solid days, and then he was away—he went away twice. To San Francisco, for one thing. And then everything had been so awful—I've told you of the smash, our old house being sold, and no money, you know, and—I don't know, everything came at once!

And this was my first job. I suppose, perhaps, Chester didn't know how it would go, or whether he *ought* to come down here."

"I see," Gregory said, again speaking slowly, his eyes upon her flushed and eager face.

"But I've had letters from him every week, and of course he'll be here this afternoon," Pamela said, her gray eyes starry.

"And how soon—were you going to get married?" His own heartbreak, his own agony meant nothing to her, and he could see it. The experiment at the rancho had been merely a bridge across a time of waiting; she felt that the probational weeks were almost over now, summer was upon them, Chester was coming down to the rancho, M'ma was comfortable, debts were being paid—anything might happen. Happiness sang in her soul again, and Gregory knew that she was scarcely conscious of his presence, that he might have been anybody or nobody for all that she knew or cared.

His question scared her a little, and she caught her breath childishly and laughed.

"Oh, we haven't talked at all of marriage! You see, Chester only came out here a year ago."

She had to hesitate, for a second of exquisite recollection. It was twilight, summer twilight, in the tea room of the Arms again, and Pamela Raleigh, the most popular girl in town, was dancing her first dance with Jessy Hilliard's handsome cousin, a college graduate from the East.

"He only came out here a year ago," she went on, "and for a while old Mr. Hilliard kept him simply dangling, not knowing whether he would take him into the bank or not. And then—you see—they all got

down on me——" Pamela said, stumbling, her innocent eyes upon Gregory's face.

"You told me. And this Hilliard was the fellow
whose gas gave out?"

It was nice of him to condense the whole wretched
incident to that. Pamela felt a little rush of sisterly
affection for Gregory.

"He was the man. And then, you see, I was simply—" she searched for a word, had to revert to her
former phrase—"I was simply *sunk,*" she confessed,
laughing. "It appeared that M'ma had been letting
her affairs run into the ground, we'd been borrowing
and charging and scrambling along in a manner that
was—well, nothing more nor less than unscrupulous,"
she said. "Chester went over our affairs with me. . . ."

Another arresting vision of the fine hands and the
smooth dark head beside her own in the dilapidated
and collapsing kitchen of the old house. Pamela had
to give it a few seconds, before she went on:

"My brother Carter wasn't working, we owed
nearly two thousand dollars, Chester's position wasn't
settled—it was all—*awful!*" Pamela said, her eyes
round and childish as they appealed to his for sympathy.

"And the rancho was—any port in a storm?" he
said, taking a queer satisfaction in turning the knife.

"I was just despairing. I cried myself to sleep the
first three nights here; I've never done that before in
my *life.*" And then with a sudden recollection of her
manners, she laughed apologetically. "You know what
I mean, Gregory?"

So sisterly, so dear, so utterly desirable, with her
bared head, and her arms full of leaves.

"Sure, I know what you mean!" he answered, with

a gruff little laugh. And then, arresting her in the very arch of the patio doorway, "Pamela, if things are still unsettled—I mean if you and Hilliard have to wait awhile longer—for any reason—don't be afraid I'll ever—bother you again."

"Gregory—I'm only so sorry——" she stammered, stricken and ashamed.

"Oh, that's all right!" he said.

"And if it weren't—" her happy colour rushed up again—"if it weren't for Chester," she explained, "I can't think of any life—any home—and you're so good and kind, too, Greg—and it'd be more—well, more than I deserved, to be down here! But—you see—I can't!" She smiled up at him, and he smiled back, and they went into the patio with their leaves.

The afternoon rushed upon them; it was time to help Mrs. Chard into plum-coloured silk and lace; it was time for Pamela to run upstairs for a last ruffle of her tawny hair; it was time to watch for first-comers.

Then, suddenly, they were all about her; Maisie, laughing and loving as ever, Carol, and Sam; the voices and the presences for which she had hungered for two endless months—hungered indeed for far longer than that.

For the clock seemed to have been turned back a whole year, and she was old Pamela again, the queen of them all. There were kisses and confidences and all the happy gossip that had once been her very breath.

"Pam—*what* do you think of Maisie here?"

"But, my dear—is it announced?"

"Rather! And we're giving her showers! And Mrs. Broome is going to give her a regular dance when it's cooler."

"And listen, Pam——" This was Maisie, with her arm about Pamela, in their old happy fashion. "Listen, you've got to come in and stay with me that night!"

"You knew Harry Beaver'd broken his collar bone?"

"You knew about the Junior Auxiliary?"

"Heavenly sandwiches—you made these, Pam. Nobody ever made them like yours!"

"And isn't old Mrs. Chard a darling?"

"And isn't Gregory nice—in his own home? He seems so much thinner, somehow—or older. Or maybe it's younger?"

The sun shone down, and the high branches above the patio waved softly, and more black cars, like labouring beetles, crossed the green fields below the hacienda, and more beautiful frocks and bright hats, like inverted moving flowers, came through the adobe arches, and there was more laughter, and more identifications, that were like royal recognitions, by the old lady. The Broomes, and the Catherwoods, and the Stokeses, and the Beavers—after fifty years!

"It was long before you were born, my dear—I left there in '78," Mrs. Chard would say, her keen old eyes reading the younger faces. Everybody made a charming little excitement over meeting her; there was a flattering stir all afternoon long about her chair. Fancy—an old, old resident, a real pioneer of Carterbridge coming back, after half a century! Did she know that old Mr. Hilliard and Judge Beaver's father —who was nearly ninety!—and several of the other real pioneers were coming out to see her? And dear old Colonel Troutt, who was in the Odd Fellows' Home, had said that if she'd fix the day he'd be driven

over for an hour of reminiscence with young Mrs.
Charteris—for that was what her name was when *he*
knew her!

Chester Hilliard had dutifully remained at the
office and would drive out with his uncle at about five,
it was explained. But Jessy was here, most cordial to
Pamela—the one to suggest indeed that Pamela
mustn't forget the Cinderellas next winter, even if she
only came in to one dance!—and looking charming in
a dress that hardly showed it at all. And Sue Rose
looked charming, looked almost pretty, and, as usual,
had something really important to say to Pamela; and
must take Pamela off into the blue shadow of the north
arcades, and drive Harry away, and drive Sam away,
and put a hand on Pamela's shoulder as she said:

"Pam, Mother told me to get this over to you—
and I know she talked about it to Mrs. Broome—you
know they have confabs about everything. She said to
assure you that that—you know, that thing that happened to you and Chester Hilliard last summer had
nothing—*nothing* to do with your membership in the
Cinderellas being suspended—do you see?"

Pamela's face had flushed, but she was smiling; she
was sympathetic. This ugly little bit of ground must be
got over—it must be endured. This explanation must
be made, of course, and then it would be all forgotten,
and the future would be all roses, and the past the past.

"Mother said that it was *because* she liked you so
much—and we all did!" Sue Rose rushed on; "and because, through Jack Stokes at the bank, you know, and
Judge Beaver and everything, she and Mrs. Broome
knew exactly how bad your mother's affairs were. And
then, besides—we all *had* been going it pretty fast, you
know?" Sue Rose ended, on a questioning note, with a

little compunctious laugh, "and they had just determined to stop it. But—but you will be back, *sometimes,* in Carterbridge, this coming winter, won't you, Pam?" Sue Rose pleaded, forgetting, in the importance of "Mother's" message, that Pamela had been waiting, neglected and heartsick, and only a square or two away, all through last winter's dreary months, for just these words.

Pamela, however, was in heaven to-day, and she could afford to forget it, too. Her voice broke on a little excited laugh, as she said generously:

"Oh, I know I will! I may *have* to, in fact."

"You mean if old Mrs. Chard goes back to England?"

"Yes. Or—oh, anything!" Marriage, for instance; a simple little morning wedding, on an autumn day, in —well, it would have to be the Hilliard house, probably. M'ma in dark blue silk . . .

"And you're coming in for Maisie's party?"

"Maisie asked me to."

"Oh, Pam, it'll be such fun to have you with us all again!" And Sue Rose gave one of her chummy, affected little wriggles to which it was so hard to respond, somehow, even though it meant only affection and a desire to be demonstrative.

They went back to the others, and Sue Rose asked about Carter so sweetly, so interestedly and circumstantially that Pamela was encouraged to dream a sudden mad dream of Carter and Sue Rose uniting two of the oldest families of Carterbridge. After all, why not? Her twin was only a matter of a few months younger than Sue Rose.

"You know, or I don't know if you do, that I always liked Carter enormously," said Sue Rose, laughing.

"And he always liked *you,*" Pamela said, in duty bound.

Six o'clock; she could hear the angelus ringing faithfully down by the little crossroads settlement of Madroña Vista; as it had rung since the days of the *padres*—since *El Rancho del Molino Solitario* had been built. The sound of it came sweetly across the fields and the fresh green trees to the hacienda, where gulls walked on the roof and eucalyptus tassels of cream and pink fringe moved gently in a late afternoon breeze. And all Carterbridge sat having tea with old lady Chard.

Everything was going well so far—everything was wonderful so far. Anita brought the cake, and Maria passed the sandwiches, and there was a sweetness, a clear translucence about the dying day in the old garden that seemed to make the social occasion strangely fitting; the crumpled napkins, the voices, the moving, brightly clad forms, the pleasant laughter.

A great snowball bush, a very fountain of round blooms, tumbled to the grass beside the old lady's chair; climbing salmon roses on the roof were transparent in straight lances of sinking light; bees whizzed by like low-flying projectiles between the bells of the lilies. The air was sweet with lilac, and trampled, wilting grass, and delicate tea, and cigarettes. Pamela, seeing that she was not particularly needed anywhere, took a cushion at Mrs. Chard's feet.

Dr. Broome and Mrs. Broome, Mrs. Billings, Jessy Stokes, and Mrs. Catherwood were all there, talking and drinking tea; about Colonel Charteris's long chair, a dozen feet away, there was a younger group. Pamela discovered that among the elders a rather curious conversation was going on.

She reached for a sandwich, smiled at Anita, and listened idly. The old lady, behind her and above her, put down a friendly, stout old hand, and patted her cheek. It was some seconds before Pamela appreciated that there was a certain constraint in this familiar circle.

Mrs. Broome looked flushed, Jessy Hilliard Stokes was rather pale. There was an uneasy light in Mrs. Catherwood's eyes.

"Whatever happened to that old lawsuit of Jim Hilliard's, Dr. Broome?" asked Mrs. Chard. "You remember—about the property down there toward San Jacinto?"

"I don't remember," said the old doctor. "My father was the lawyer, I know, but I was only a child."

"The Paulsons—they were mixed into that some way," mused the old lady. Pamela, looking about the circle merely for sympathetic, indulgent interest in an old lady's wanderings, was amazed to see Mrs. Broome stiffen nervously. She remembered suddenly that Paulson had been Mrs. Broome's family name. "Well, you remember the scandal at the Golden West House, Doctor?" resumed Mrs. Chard briskly. "You remember the girl—somebody—who was it?—who married the coloured man there? He was the only coloured man in town for a while, and old Colonel Carter—this child's grandfather—was simply his idol. He was never so happy as when he could do something for the colonel—drive his bays, or burn rubbish, or wait on table. He was only a half-black, a handsome, big fellow. And he—unless my memory fails me—married——"

Pamela's cheerfully wandering gaze was arrested at Mrs. Catherwood's face. It was never a really pretty face, any more than Sue Rose's was; their nose flanges were a little wide, their cheek bones a little high, and although both mother and daughter had curly, dark-brown hair and fine brown eyes, somehow the effect they made was never that of beauty. But Pamela had never seen her look as ghastly as she looked now. The whites of her eyes showed oddly, and her face had an ugly, strange pallor; she was breathing hard, and the girl could see tiny beads of moisture on her upper lip.

"We don't have things like that, people like that, nowadays," Mrs. Chard, without finishing her last sentence, said innocently. "I've got it all in my notes— I've got the whole file of the *Pioneer*. That was the little newspaper poor Bob Charteris amused himself with during the last years of his life. He ran it for about two years, and afterward it went on for about another year. I don't know that even the public library would have a file of that little old paper—the *Star* was started in '76, and after that the other never had a chance. It was hand printed; we had a little press—I daresay the copies I've got are the only ones in existence!"

Dr. Broome cleared his throat.

"I never heard of it," he said. "We had a big fire here in '89 that destroyed almost all our records—the little library we had then was wiped out. But it would seem—no more, thank you, delicious!—it would seem just as well sometimes not to disturb all the old memories," he suggested mildly. "Did you—did you bring that little old newspaper out with you?"

Pamela, only partly in the dark now, wondered if she saw, or only imagined that she saw, Mrs. Broome's eyes go hungrily at this point to the upper windows of the hacienda, as if she thought of these documents securely hidden away in some old trunk. It was turning into a strange tea party; somehow, none of these dignified and middle-aged persons was expressing in manner or words the simple pleasure of having a chat with an old, old lady who had known most of their fathers and grandfathers before them.

"How long are you to be here in Carterbridge, Mrs. Chard?" Mrs. Catherwood asked pleasantly, after a few minutes. And again it seemed to Pamela that they all waited for the reply.

"I wasn't going to stay as long as this," the old lady responded. "But my grandson—and this child here! —have made us so comfortable, and Colonel Charteris is so much better—better than he's been in ten years—that I'd stay some time, if I could be sure that this girl"—again her hand touched Pamela's cheek gently—"this girl would occasionally have a good time with her old friends, as a girl ought to have!" she said.

Pamela did not quite know why, it was no extraordinary wish for an old lady, who could be kindly enough when she chose, to express, but at the words and touch tears suddenly stood in her eyes, and the lovely panorama of the patio blurred into blots and streaks of green and gold light. It was as if a champion —the father she could barely remember, or what her mother might have been—stood suddenly between her and the rough wind of life that had blown so harshly across her for almost a long year. She gulped, and smiled and tightened her own fingers about Mrs. Chard's hand.

"Maisie is hoping to have her overnight, very soon," said Mrs. Broome promptly, cordially.

"Yes, you must let us see more of you, Pamela, now

that things here have settled down so nicely," Mrs. Catherwood said.

They were all so kind! They were all so friendly again. It was like the old days, when she had stayed overnight with Sue Rose and Maisie and Carol quite as simply as in her own home. Pamela's face glowed with pleasure, and she told herself that she had misjudged them all, her sensitiveness and morbidness had built this wall between her and all her old associations.

"Pamela is going to be my amanuensis," said Mrs. Chard. "I shall dictate to her—a little at a time, with quotations from the *Pioneer*."

"Pamela will have to deal gently with all of her old friends," said Dr. Broome, in a dead silence.

"A great many things go on in a young community that naturally could not possibly go on in after years," Mrs. Catherwood added, in a challenging tone.

Pamela heard neither. One more car had come chugging out across the flat road that wound between the meadows of the Molino rancho, and its occupants were coming into the garden. An old man, stately and impressive—Robert Hilliard of the Carterbridge Bank—and a young man, slim and dark, his figure faultless in striped trousers and dark blue coat, his dark eyes seeking the corners of the patio eagerly, threading the groups, oblivious of the smiles that greeted him. Chester!

CHAPTER XIV

THE colour left Pamela's face, and as she walked toward him she was very pale and looked taller and even slenderer than usual—with a strange light in her gray eyes. She gave her right hand to his uncle, but at the same time her left went to Chester, and he gripped it, and when the old man went on to Mrs. Chard's chair, Pamela's fingers did not loosen their hold.

"Well, hello, Pamela!"

"Hello, Chester."

He nodded, smiled here and there in response to casual greetings. Then they escaped the moving groups somehow, and were beside the old fountain, sheltered from the rest of the patio by the great flowery mound of a neglected rose tree.

Pamela, half sitting, leaned against the stone rim of the fountain; their hands were linked, at arm's length, and they stood laughing at each other.

"Well, Pamela! And lovelier than ever!"

"But, Chester—Chester—it's so good to see you again!"

"You've missed me, then?"

She wouldn't answer this. She said:

"I hope I wasn't rude—carrying you off this way.
But I *had* to see you!"

He smiled down at her, and his smile was as wonderful as the memory of it had been, and his voice as
haunting.

"I don't think you were rude. But as I wasn't in the
least conscious of anyone else, they may have all been
speechless with wrath, for all I saw!"

There it was again—the smooth, polished, half-
laughing, and wholly enchanting manner! She had so
hungered for it.

"You look simply radiant, dear."

"Ah, well, why not—*now?*"

And they both laughed again, excitedly and youthfully.

"But, Pam, what a beautiful place, and what a
pretty party!"

"Isn't it? Molino's the most beautiful place in the
world, I think. You should see it in the early morning."

"Do you mean that you're an early riser, at last?"

Delicious—delicious to be talking to Chester again.
She could hardly think of what she said.

"I was. When I first came here, you know, it was
wet and cold and uncomfortable, and there was—well,
just everything to do! You never saw such a jumble
of new things, and old things, and crates to unpack,
and trunks; and Colonel Charteris—he's Gregory's
cousin——"

"You wrote me. Is he nice?"

"He's just—adorable!"

"I see. And in love with Pam?"

"Oh, no, nothing like that!" She laughed exultingly.
"He's nearly forty, you know, twice as old as I am,
and he idolized his wife—and besides, he's ill. But,

Chester, would you be just a little jealous if I liked him?"

"Oh, more than that," the man said seriously. He smiled a little constrainedly. "You and I weathered some pretty bad times last winter, didn't we? And the friendship we formed then is one of the most precious things in my life."

Pamela looked at him, surprised and uneasy. There was a change in his manner: his gaiety, his nonsense, his air of well-being and of satisfaction with the world seemed suddenly to have vanished; he was grave, affectionate, exquisitely polite, but—but somehow he wasn't Chester!

"Chester, everything's all right?" she asked in alarm.

"What could possibly not be all right, to-day, here?" he countered, smiling. And then suddenly, deliberately: "But tell me about yourself. Do you know that I haven't seen you for eight weeks? What have you been doing, and how are you? It's so lovely to find you in a place like this, looking so well. It hasn't been too horrible, has it?"

"Oh, no. Not after the first. But lonely!"

"Chard isn't exactly what you'd call thrilling, eh?"

"Gregory? Oh, yes—he's really fine!" she defended him quickly. "And he's—he's the *kindest* person—and handsome, too, when he rides round with his cowboys, don't you think?—Spanishy looking. And he's funny, too; you've no idea how he makes us laugh sometimes. That isn't stupidity, Chester, that queer look, when he half shuts his eyes—it's partly shyness, and partly pride. He can be bold enough when he wants to be! But——"

Chester laughed, as she passed, and Pamela, red-cheeked, very earnest, suddenly broke and laughed, too.

"But——?" the man teased her.

"But—well, he's not you, Chester!" she said simply.

"Well, I'm glad he's so nice," Chester said, with unexpected generosity. "He has all kinds, hasn't he?"

"Oh, yes, he's enormously rich," Pamela answered indifferently, rightly interpreting the rather cryptic phrase as referring to money.

Chester gave her an odd look.

"If I hadn't come along, just when I did, Pam, you'd have fallen for him and been fixed for life!"

She answered with a look of reproach.

"I *am* fixed for life!"

"I'm fixed for—I don't know what!" Chester said vexedly, taking advantage of the word to rush into confidences. "I'm in the deuce of a lot of trouble!"

"Oh, Chester, how?" Her tone was stricken, yet happy in being his confidante.

"Oh, I've just got mixed into some funny business!"

"With the bank?"

"No. Yes, partly. I'll get out of it all right," said Chester. "And I made up my mind I wouldn't tell you about it—and here I go blabbing it the first thing!"

"Well, of course. Much wiser to tell me. You don't know—I might help you out?"

"No—it's nothing, really. It's just—well, my own fault entirely. I can thank myself! But it just—it makes me mad to think I'm such a fool!" Chester said youthfully.

"Well, but tell me, anyway!"

"Nothing to tell. It was just that Jack Stokes and my uncle asked me to help them with a client—in—in San Francisco—managing an estate——"

"You've been playing the races!" Her eyes were dancing; she could not be serious to-day.

"Lord, if it was as simple as that!"

"Well, go on, tell me! You know you'll tell me sooner or later!"

He deliberately evaded the subject.

"Tell me what you do with yourself all day."

"Oh—everything. You get interested, you know, in the cattle and the Mexicans. And Colonel Charteris is a wonderful person—always getting books by the crate. He tells me what to read; we read a lot. And then we talk—and play games—card games. Lately, it hasn't been so bad. At first I felt horribly! No, but go on now, Chester," the girl coaxed, the fragrance and sweetness of her very close to him. "Tell me. Wh..t's worrying you?"

"Well, it's this woman!" he burst out, vexed, ashamed, penitential, half whimsical.

"Woman?" Her eyes were amazed.

"The woman whose estate I'm runni..g, I tell you!"

"Oh——?" Enlightenment and mirth struggled together in Pamela's eyes. "I see," she said slowly, reading his face. "She's fallen in love with you?"

Chester was scarlet with annoyance and a sort of unwilling pride.

"Something like that."

"Oh, Chester—how awful!" But there was nothing but laughter in her voice. "Is she terrible? What is she —a widow? An old maid?"

"No, she's very nice. She's not married. My uncle has been running her affairs for years, and he handed it over to me, and I consulted Jack at the bank, and— of course, I had to see her——"

"Well, of course! And she really has a case?"

Pamela said musingly. Presently the brightness faded from her face. "I'm not sure I like avaricious spinsters falling in love with you, Chester," she said slowly.

"It's the deuce of a mix-up," the man admitted gloomily.

"Of course—hurt her feelings and you lose the case," Pamela reflected aloud. "That wouldn't do. Couldn't you get Jack? He's married, after all." She paused. "She doesn't think you're going to ask her to *marry* you, Chester?" she demanded flatly.

"I don't know what she thinks!" he answered bitterly. And then, with a little effort, "Yes, I suppose she does. I don't suppose she sees any reason why I shouldn't."

Pamela's gaiety suffered a sudden check. Across her face went the expressions that spoke as clearly as words could have done: he has let her think he admires her, he has made love to her, he has been at least as much to blame as she!

To hold a client—well, men did queer things in the name of business. Perhaps this unmarried woman was lonely; it was a foregone conclusion, her attraction to the handsome and magnetic man of business.

"Well, I fell in love with you when you were running my business, Chester," the girl admitted, with a little rueful laugh. "You're too fascinating, that's all!"

"You can josh about it!" he said. "But I've kind of let myself into it—and now I don't know what to do!"

"That was what took you to San Francisco!" Pamela pieced it together.

"What was?" he roused himself from despondent musing to ask.

"Why, to confer with your new lady-love!"

"Oh, yes. Oh, yes. Darn it!" he said.

"Is she terribly rich, Chester?"

"Yes—she has a pot of money."

Pamela studied him a minute, all love and sympathy and tenderness in her beautiful eyes. From the other side of the garden they could hear the babble of voices and laughter—Sam's shout of mirth, Maisie's voice suddenly raised. But here, beside the dry old fountain, close to the peaceful arcades of the hacienda that were filling with sunset light now, there was peace.

"Why, my dear," Pamela said presently, in her motherly voice, "you mustn't let this worry you! There's only one thing to do: tell her the truth honestly—tell her that you had a girl long before you went up to San Francisco. Tell her, if you like, that you like her—you do like her!—but that you aren't free."

His face did not brighten. One of his hands played with the delicate linen of her blouse, folding and refolding the transparent batiste with nervous fingers, his eyes following his hand.

"I refuse to set you free!" Pamela said cheerfully. "Tell her that."

"You'd be an awful fool—— This isn't what I meant to say to-day, but I think it, and I might as well say it!" Chester said, in a low, troubled tone, without raising his eyes. "You'd be an awful fool to wait for me!"

Pamela stared at him, puzzled and uneasy.

"*Wait* for you! But Chester—" she tried to speak as if he had been joking—"but Chester, what else *should* I do?"

He was silent a minute, his fingers still pleating the white gown.

"Marry Chard, I suppose!" he said then with an uncomfortable laugh.

Pamela was hurt. She stepped back, turning toward the group at the other end of the patio.

"Come on, we must go back, Chester. People are going, and I ought to be there!"

He followed her a few steps quickly, caught at her unwilling hands, turned her about in the shelter of the wild, overgrown rose bush.

"Pamela, I'm sorry! Just believe that I—I'm miserable about it! Give me another month—four weeks —and I'll come down here and tell you that the whole thing is a dream. My *darling*——"

One arm was tight across her shoulders, her head was tipped backward until a sharp pain ran through her throat, Chester's lips were on hers, pressing down, drinking deep of the purity and sweetness of her own.

"You glorious—you glorious—you beautiful thing —the most beautiful God ever made!" he muttered. And against her own breast, she could feel his heart beating hard and fast.

"Pamela—I'm sorry——" a voice said behind her. She turned about, dizzied and bewildered, coming down from heaven with blinded senses, putting her hand instinctively to her tumbled hair, panting, laughing, trying to keep her feet steady on the ground. The patio, and the arcades shadowy in purple twilight, and the soft sunless light on the fountain, and the blossoming rose tree . . .

"Yes, I know, Gregory! I'm coming."

"No rush," Gregory said, turning away.

Chester, at her side, had time for only one more word in Pamela's ear.

"You'll trust me, won't you? I'll come down and tell you all about it—I'll get out of it, I swear I will, and without hurting anyone, either. It'll take me a few weeks—tapering off—but you'll not be angry, Pamela?"

His kiss still burning her mouth, her eyes filled with the remembered charm of him, her ears with his voice, she could not be angry.

"No, no. But, *come!* Don't keep me wondering—waiting—again! Any day, to tea, or any time. And write me, Chester!"

"I'll write you every night!" he promised fervently. "Seeing you to-day—well, I know now that there's nobody else!"

They were close to the others.

"Then you'd forgotten that?" Pamela could say significantly, cheerfully.

Chester made no attempt to hide his chagrin and self-contempt.

"I'm an ass! But it was all mixed up—it was all—no, it was all my own fault!" he said.

Then Pamela was surrounded, and there was a bustle of good-byes and departures. The Archers and the Beavers and the Lees and the other Archers and the Billingses were going, and it had been *so* lovely, *so* charming, *so* sweet to have the old rancho really opened again—and Pam must telephone, any day—and there must be a lunch at the club—and she must see the new card room. . . .

Pamela stood at the patio arch, and Maria ran for wraps, and the big cars, parked in a circle about the outer garden, sputtered and roared and wheeled away, one by one, leaving the oil-stained and wheel-crushed young grass in their wake. It was twilight in the patio, but out here a clear light lingered over the sea, and little red clots of sunshine hung high up in the oaks and eucalyptus. There was a smell of sweet Indian grass and tarweed, and of the first dews on the dry dust.

From the gateway arch Pamela could see the long descending line of the barns meeting the long level line of the quiet sea; smoke was rising from the cabins, and men and dogs and babies were idling before the dark little doorways, fed and weary and content, enjoying the last hour of the summer day.

There came to the girl's heart one of those moments of utter felicity that are rare even in the happiest lifetime. The world seemed to smile at her, and her own soul to be reconciled and lifted into the eternal beauty that is always close to the earthly beauty of a spring sunset.

Had she analyzed her emotions, she might have said that she was glad to have the social occasion that had given her so much concern successfully ended, that it was pleasant to be young and fairly comely, standing in the glory of an old adobe doorway, looking down at a gracious June sea. She might have said that the praise and the friendship and the quiet evening ahead, were all good things upon which to muse. And above all she might have said that to have Chester back in her life again—nearer and dearer than before, seeking her out for his confidences, sharing with her his troubles, catching her to his heart for his almost angry kisses—that this was the crown of her happiness and the underlying secret of it all.

But she did not analyze to-night; she merely felt. She felt the atmosphere of affection and harmony about her, and she breathed, for a few minutes, the very air of paradise.

Happiness shone in her face; Sam, Harry, Dick, Kent, saying their good-byes, told her that she was prettier than ever. Chester who, with the Cather-woods, was the last to go, did not have to say it aloud; his eyes said it.

He escorted his old uncle carefully to the car; there was time merely for his "I'll write to-night!" and Pamela's nod, before Sue Rose and her mother came to say good-bye, last of all.

The patio was deserted now; the guests had drifted away. There was left only Gregory, who was lying on the grass talking to a still alert and untired grand-mother, and Charteris, who lay with closed eyes, a half-smile on his lips. Napkins and teacups were strewn about on chairs and ledges, the grass between the flags was trampled flat, and the basket chairs had been scattered at every angle. Pamela thought, with a little prick of mirth, that as soon as the Catherwoods were gone, now that the tea party was over, the family would have some tea.

Sue Rose, departing with enthusiastic praises, kissed her; and Sue Rose's mother, which was the more amaz-ing, kissed her too. It was an agreeable change in atti-tude, the wiser and older Pamela reflected, but puz-zling. They repeated that she was positively coming in to spend the night next week—any night, any time?

Sue Rose was in lemon organdy, with more lemon organdy underneath it and little violet ribbons trailing from a great violet silk chrysanthemum on her shoul-der; her hat was lemon straw, with another chrysan-themum on it and more little twisted velvet ribbons straggling across its transparent gauze brim. Pamela

could see the whole outfit in Elaine Mulligan's show
window, and could hear Sue Rose deciding, "Oh, I
want that. I think it's the most adorable thing I ever
saw!"

Mrs. Catherwood was in tan: silk gown, silk coat,
silk hat, gloves, and stockings, all the same shade of
coffee and cream. The Catherwoods, mother and
daughter, had no other interest in life as vital as that
of their clothes.

Pamela, weary, happy, accepted their farewells.

"Oh, thank you! Oh, wasn't it? And isn't she amaz-
ing? Eighty-four, you know. Gregory's father—or no,
it's Colonel Charteris's father—would be sixty, if he
were living."

"She's wonderful," said Mrs. Catherwood. "But
there's just one thing, Gregory," she said to her host,
who was with Pamela at the gate; "your grandmother
hasn't lived in America for so long—she may not appreciate that we have—well, we've left a good deal of
our pioneer days behind us!"

"You mean that book of hers—her memoirs?"
Gregory asked, with his sudden flash of charming and
sophisticated and Spanish smile.

"Yes, I do mean that," Mrs. Catherwood assented,
maternal and warning. "It's a dangerous thing to do,
you know—and perhaps she doesn't realize that
memory isn't a very safe guide. . . ."

"Oh, she has all the old files of that newspaper!"
Pamela said innocently. "I've not seen them, but they
—they'd be definite, wouldn't they?"

"I don't know whether they would be or not," Mrs.
Catherwood, who seemed inexplicably disturbed, said
shortly. "It seems to me that I'd—I'd go very slowly
with it, Gregory."

"Well, she hasn't started yet," Gregory said, with the veiled expression that made him look so foreign. "She says she's going to get into it with Pamela, in a week or two. It ought to be darned interesting!" he added ingenuously.

"Yes, it might be——" Mrs. Catherwood agreed, in an absent-minded, rather hard-lipped manner. "But after all, one has to think of people's *feelings!*" she added, in a dissatisfied voice.

Sue Rose, demure, mischievous, frightened, irresolute, and tremendously determined, by turns, was meanwhile looking at Pamela. Now she said impulsively, daringly:

"Mother, mayn't I tell just Pam?"

Mrs. Catherwood immediately brought a reproachful and protestant glance to rest upon her daughter, pursed her lips, shook her head, and elevated her eyebrows as if she were shocked.

"No, indeed you may not, you naughty girl!"

"Oh, please, Mother!" Sue Rose begged childishly.

"No, of course not! We said New Year's. Is this New Year's?" demanded the mother inflexibly. But she was smiling.

"Mother! Just Pam?"

"No, dear! There's somebody else we have to consult, you madcap," Mrs. Catherwood said, in a fond undertone.

"Oh, I know, Mother! But *he* wouldn't care!" Sue Rose, the timidest and most self-conscious and sensitive of mortals, had always liked, in moments of high spirits, the delusion that she was a reckless dealer in hearts. Now she tossed her head and grasped Pamela's shoulders, and Pamela, with her face all roses, said eagerly:

"Oh, Sue Rose *Catherwood!* You're engaged!"

"No, no, now—this won't do!" Mrs. Catherwood interposed with real concern. "She had no business to say a word about it, Pamela. It is only an understanding, and she promised me—she *promised* me that she wouldn't breathe it to anyone until New Year's Day! Now, I really am vexed with you, darling, I am indeed —this is very naughty," she said warmly.

Sue Rose laughed, unabashed. Her voice was high with mischief.

"But, Mother, these things will out! They're in the air."

"In the air or not in the air," Mrs. Catherwood said disapprovingly, "you've said too much not to go on, now. Tell Pamela—did you ever see such a crazy girl, Pam!—and then promise me that not another soul shall know!"

"I promise!" Sue Rose, scarlet and stammering, blurted out the name. It seemed to scream itself through the air.

Pamela's soul left her body for a few seconds, returned to it jarred and blind and suffocating. She was all right, she struggled to say, deep within her. She was all right. This was the patio gateway, and these persons—who were they?—were going away.

The sweat came out on her hands and forehead, and her head ached as if it had been hit with a mallet; her throat was very dry. She groped—groped for consciousness—she had her arms about someone, was kissing Sue Rose. She heard herself say, "Well, Sue *Rose!*"

The patio garden and the rocking arcade settled down into place, and she was all right. Quite all right. Only she could not look at her companions' faces,

somehow, and she was breathing hard. But nothing had
been noticeable—no one had seen anything amiss. Sue
Rose—announcing her engagement to—to Chester
Hilliard.

"I should say I *did!*" This was Pamela Raleigh, in
answer to Sue Rose's arch, "You ought to sympathize
with me, because you had a regular crush on him yourself last summer, didn't you, Pam?"

"I should say I *did!*" And then Sue Rose, all giggles
and shy pride again.

"Oo-oo-oo, and wasn't I the jealous!"

Pamela's head ached fiercely, blindingly. Someone
was beside her. Had he been there throughout? Had
he heard? Gregory, of course.

"Pam, I'm sorry," Gregory said smoothly. "But
Anita's burned her hand in the kitchen—it looks awful
bad——"

"And we must run—it's disgraceful!" This was
Mrs. Catherwood.

Pamela did not see them go; she did not know how
she got to the kitchen. In the big, darkening room the
maids, still in holiday spirits, were lazily attacking the
heaped tea dishes.

Nobody had been burned. Their dark, curious eyes
searched her strangely pale face, with the oddly glittering eyes, amusedly. Nobody had been burned,
señorita.

Then Gregory must have heard. Not that it mattered.

She said something vaguely, absently, not knowing
what she said, and went on into the shadows of the
dining room. Gregory was standing by the stairway
door.

"Everything all right?" he said. The girl stared at

him a second, wondering what was changed in him. He looked older—thinner—oddly fierce, somehow.

"No one was burned," she said lifelessly.

"I thought they said something about Anita being burned. They were all jabbering like parrots," he said curtly. "You had better go upstairs and lie down, Pamela. You're all in!"

"Oh, no—I'm all right," she stammered, surprised at his manner.

She put her hand on the white china knob that opened the door upon the stairs, wavered, and turned toward the garden.

"That—Miss Catherwood is going to marry Mr. Hilliard," she said.

"I heard her say so," Gregory said briefly.

Pamela raised her dark-rimmed eyes; she looked pathetically shrunken and small and helpless somehow.

"I feel as if there must be some mistake!" she faltered, with a little desperate laugh. "I told you—this morning—only this morning——"

Again the quick and positive manner; he seemed ten years older than the boy he had been only this morning.

"Anything you've told me I've forgotten, of course," he said briefly, almost coldly, as if he were annoyed.

"I don't—understand it!" Pamela whispered.

Gregory shrugged. His face, almost as bronzed and dark as an Indian's, was expressionless—it was as if he was not interested. He had put on white flannels for the tea. Pamela wondered if it was the strange costume that made the man look so unfamiliar.

"There may be some explanation," he offered, with a curious effect of lifelessness, with an impersonal steady look into her eyes.

"Explanation!" Her voice broke upon a breathless, scornful laugh, and the hand on the old china door knob shook.

But to whom was she talking? This squarely built, dark-skinned, polished and inscrutable Spaniard in his white flannels was surely not the awkward and blundering American boy who had gathered leaves with her in the woods this morning—this was not the young rustic who always laughed noisily and became clumsily incoherent when she was about? Pamela, shaken by her own utter bewilderment of spirit on Chester's account, was additionally confused by the discovery of another identity in Gregory. She had only had glimpses of this man before; the cowboys' "señor," lord of some forty big cattlemen and some four thousand widespread acres, half-Latin, all self-possession and easy Spanish poise.

She peered at him, in the low-ceiled, dark old dining room. Who was this man, anyway?

"Gregory, has something happened? Are you cross at me?"

"Why should I be cross at you?" The white teeth flashed in the dark face. "No, but I will be, if you don't go upstairs and rest," he said, not urgently, not dictatorially, still with the detached air of advising a wearied child for its own good. "Go upstairs and lie down, Pamela. You look ill!"

She stared pathetically for a minute or two into the inscrutable face. Then she went upstairs. She must think of Gregory—how funny he had been—how unlike the man she had known for all these weeks.

She *would* think of Gregory, while she bathed her face and ran a deep comb through her tawny mane— Gregory—Gregory . . .

She sat down on the edge of her bed. And the words formed themselves like iron chains in her soul, and dragged her down—dragged her down. . . .

Sue Rose Catherwood and Chester—to be married. Chester in love with Sue Rose.

Her throat thickened and her temples throbbed, and she felt her hands wet against each other. But of course it wasn't true!

Chester kissing Sue Rose—Chester saying, "When we are married," to Sue Rose! But of course it wasn't true.

"I mustn't think about it. Whatever's happened—or going to happen—won't be altered by my thinking about it. I'll just go mad—thinking. Chester! Chester! I've got to go downstairs, and act as if nothing had happened—I wish I didn't feel so sick. I feel as if I'd been ill—months and months. I wonder if Bob felt like this when his wife died. Oh, my God——!"

She knelt down by the bed, and buried her face in her hands, and clutched her hair with tensed fingers as if she would tear it out. She knelt there a long time.

After a while she walked to the window, and looked out. The garden was dusky now; she could hardly distinguish, from the general shadow, the outlines of the old fountain and the great tumbled mass of the rose bush and the winding paths of the mellowed old flags.

A tangle of lilies, over by the patio wall, shone with the opaque lustre of mother-of-pearl in the gloom. From the kitchen doorway, through the arches, came tunnels of soft golden light across the dusk. And on the cooling air the scent of roses and trampled grass and wallflowers and heliotrope rose to the window, and a cool evening breeze touched her hot cheek.

No use to stand here and think. No use to try to

think! She went downstairs. The old lady was in her chair, and Charteris in his, reading lazily, desultorily aloud; Gregory was not in the room. The lamps were lighted; a drop light over Charteris's shoulder, and a great standing lamp, with a shade that bloomed like a little green umbrella. But nobody could see her face, and nobody seemed to suspect that anything was wrong. The room was confined and close after the sweet airiness out of doors, even though all the windows were open and the great shutters folded back.

Charteris did not stop reading when she came downstairs, nor did the old woman look up. Pamela could sink into a shadowed chair and recover what calm she might, unnoted.

"Doesn't anyone want any dinner?" she asked, when Charteris closed the book.

"I do," he said. "Maria's getting it. I believe it's an artichoke, toast, and a baked apple."

"I'm having the toast and the apple and a glass of hot milk," said Mrs. Chard.

"And where's Greg? It's after seven."

"I believe," Charteris said blandly, "I believe that Greg has gone out to look at the moon. Well! Didn't you think that, on the whole, we had a rather filling afternoon? My grandmother here is sitting meditating upon her sins—she blackmailed the whole community, as nearly as I can find out."

"I did not!" said the old lady, with a sinister deep chuckle. "Anyway, blackmail on a large scale is respectable, like everything else on a large scale."

They discussed the tea idly. Pamela, from her seclusion, could identify this caller and that for them; she was surprised, she said, that the mention of this old file of Carterbridge papers could interest them so.

"You wouldn't think they could remember things so long ago."

"Oh, they have very good memories indeed," said Mrs. Chard. "What worries them is the refreshing of other people's memories!"

Pamela's head ached; she was glad to sit still. She felt numbed and exhausted—too tired, too dazed even to think. Gregory came in and began to talk, a brisk and stern and authoritative Spanish gentleman.

"I don't know why you remind me of your great-grandfather to-night, Gregory," said Mrs. Chard. "I mean Don Aindini. He was a great ladies' man, that one," she added reminiscently.

"What's happened to you?" Charteris asked wonderingly, in the first pause.

"Nothing at all," Gregory answered unsmilingly, almost with an easy insolence. "Come on, Pamela, we have to eat!" he said.

She went with him to the table, but she could eat nothing. Gregory made her drink some tea, her first that day.

"My head aches," she explained simply, "and I feel tired."

"You ought to be!" Gregory said. "That Catherwood girl impresses me as a liar," he added, with apparent irrelevance. Pamela could manage a forlorn laugh.

"I don't think she was lying," she said briefly, quietly.

"Maybe not!" Gregory agreed indifferently. Looking up, in the dimly lighted room, she saw that his dark eyes, glinting in his Indian brown face, were fixed upon her. A match and a cigarette were held between her face and his, but his hands were arrested for the moment; he was watching her.

She took her bursting heart into the sitting room, and there was a pretense at cards. But the old lady was tired out with the excitement and conversation, and Charteris was never sorry to be helped upstairs early to bed. At ten o'clock the entire hacienda was in darkness, a tangle of inky shadows and white stretches of roof and flagging and spreading fences, under the moon.

It was almost midnight when Pamela crept downstairs. She came by the outer stairway from the narrow piazza, a loose Chinese wrapper over her pajamas, her feet in straw slippers, her head bare.

She made no sound on the soft old adobe flooring of the dark arcade, the patio was as bright as day, the patterns of grape and passion flower lying like delicate lace on the flags.

She went to Charteris's chair and sat down on the foot of it, and locked her arms about her knees and stared straight ahead of her.

"If that is the way it is to be, then that is the way it is to be," she said, half aloud. "And I must face it."

Before her was the gate in the patio wall, the place where Sue Rose had told her. It seemed years and years ago that those words had been said. She seemed to have been tossing in that hot upstairs bedroom, watching the moonlight rise on the wall, for endless hours.

"Oh, my God!" she said in a whisper, "what am I going to do?"

Her soul felt sick, there was a sort of vertigo upon her; she was an older woman now than the Pamela who had faced her first troubles a year ago, and she had lived to laugh at much that had frightened her then. But this she could not face.

Sue Rose a bride—the church all roses and smilax —congratulations—a new establishment somewhere for the young Chester Hilliards—no, no, no, she couldn't bear it! They said Sue Rose's father had left her a million dollars—a thousand dollars a week. A thousand dollars a week—that meant travel and hospitality and beauty. . . .

Pamela writhed and put her head down on her knees. "Oh, what shall I do? I can't go through with it all—I can't face it—I can't pretend——

"Maybe he's there now, at the Catherwoods'. Talking plans——

"And in the bank. 'You have to sign this, dear. . . .'

"Oh, my God, if I could get away!"

Suddenly, with a strangling and choking pain that almost tore her in two, she was sobbing. For a few minutes she fought the rising storm; she got to her feet, flinging back her head, and walked to the patio doorway, beating her hands noiselessly together, gulping, breathing deep.

But it was no use. The flood was upon her; she flung herself at length in Charteris's chair, and drew his pillow against her face, and sobbed heartbrokenly, unresistingly, for a long, long time.

"It wasn't my fault that I loved him!" she said to herself after a while, drying her eyes. But immediately the tears came again and she succumbed again, hugging the pillow against her face, stretched face downward in the steamer chair, in all the dappled silver and black, the sweet mysterious silence and flower fragrance of the garden.

Presently she sat up, and brought her feet to the ground, and wiped her eyes with a soaked hard ball of handkerchief. She remained staring blindly ahead of her, exhausted, not thinking, her mind a blank.

Her childhood passed before some strangely lucid inner vision. Little Pam Raleigh—one of the Raleigh twins, living romantically in the old Carter house. The most important persons in town, of course.

Little Pam Raleigh learning that the Beavers and the Catherwoods and the Broomes and the Billingses had plenty of money, servants and motor cars and expensive clothes, and that the Raleighs didn't have anything. But what mattered it! Pam Raleigh was the most popular girl in town, just the same. She could make a joke of money.

And then, gradually, Maisie being engaged, and Sue Rose engaged, and happiness and excitement for these other girls—plainer girls, much less popular girls—and Pamela was squeezed out, ignored, the girl who could be snubbed with impunity. . . .

But why? Why? Pamela wanted, like everyone else, to believe that life was fair—that everyone had an even chance. But why should some girls, like Maisie and Sue Rose and Jessy, have everything and other girls nothing? Why should it be Pamela's mother, rather than theirs, who must live at Mrs. Pettys's and Pamela, rather than either of them, who must work for her livelihood?

If old Mrs. Chard died Pamela must go into the Woman's Exchange, or perhaps become a mother's helper somewhere—no more fun, no more freedom and youth for her! She would go, shabby and admiring, to Maisie's wedding and Sue Rose's wedding. . . .

How long she sat staring at the moonlit patio she

did not know. The night was warm and soft; there was no movement in the dark masses of foliage high above her head that were pepper trees and widespread oaks. The beat and swell and enveloping rush of the sea came steadily to her ears. There was a scent of night, mysterious and penetrating and exquisite, in the black and silver patio.

Suddenly, suffocatingly, tears were upon her again. And again Pamela jumped to her feet, and flung back her head, and walked to and fro—to and fro—to master them.

It was then that she heard a voice, close to her, quiet.

"Pamela!"

"Chester!" she said in a whisper. But immediately she saw that the squarely built, easily moving figure that came toward her across a patch of clear light was Gregory.

He had awakened, it appeared, and felt restless, and had come downstairs for a smoke and some fresh air.

"Lord, these old rooms do hold the heat!"

"Bu—bu—but I love the hacienda!" Pamela said thickly.

"Some night!" He looked at the unearthly beauty of the old arcaded, tiled hacienda and the trees, and the moon, sailing now across an open sky, and, sitting against the lip of the old fountain as she had sat earlier in the day, he folded his big arms on his chest and yawned frankly. Pamela wound her little wrapper tightly about her and looked at the stars, too—the fluttered long scarf of the Milky Way seeming so much lower than the others, so close above her bare head.

"Some day I mean to travel," Gregory said unexpectedly. "But it will be only to come back to Molino. There's no place like it! I don't think there is any place in the world like it."

"I don't think there is," Pamela said in a low voice, but steadily, and with returning self-control. "Were you born here, Gregory?"

"No, I was born down at Mazatlan—in Mexico. We've—I've a place there. You think this is savage—you ought to see that!"

"I don't think this is savage, now." It was simple enough, as conversation. But somehow she couldn't feel as if she were talking to Gregory, who had discussed window curtains and bathroom rugs with her a few weeks ago, who had seemed to be so awkward—loutish—undeveloped. The man who was smoking in the shadows might have been a complete stranger, a young Spanish don, smooth of voice and manner, quite at his ease with a woman in a moonlit garden in June.

"Gregory, you seem so different to-night. Perhaps it was that tea party to-day; perhaps it was that I'd never seen you with so many people—as a host—entertaining in your own house, before."

"I think perhaps—" he blew a long plume of smoke from his cigarette—"I think perhaps I had been wanting something I couldn't have," he said lightly. "And now I know I cannot have it, and my mind is at rest about it—and—and that's over."

His tone told her to what he referred, and with a little sympathy for his trouble, in the midst of her own, she said deprecatingly:

"You see how it is, Gregory?"

"Oh, I see how it is!"

"You're not—you're not cross at me?"

"Cross! No. You mustn't—you mustn't take these things too seriously!" he reminded her.

"I think—things had gone a good deal further with me than with you," Pamela said, feeling ashamed and cowardly, yet longing for comfort in spite of herself.

"Perhaps so," he said. "You know I'm part Spanish."

"I know you are! But you've always seemed all American, like one of the cowboys," Pamela said frankly.

"Oh, but I'm not. Are you going in? If you can't sleep," Gregory said, flinging away his cigarette, "let me tell you something to do. Get up before dawn—that's about half-past three, now, and walk down by the shore and see the sun rise."

"Do you do that sometimes, Gregory?" the girl said, surprised.

"I have done it. It may be some time," Gregory answered as they entered the dark, stuffy house, "it may be some time before I do it again!"

CHAPTER XV

D R. and Mrs. Lawrence Benjamin Broome having bidden all Carterbridge to "Hazelawn," for the wedding of their daughter, Yolanda Joan, to Mr. Prentiss Samuel Billings, on the eleventh of August, Pamela Raleigh came in from *El Rancho del Molino Solitario* to be maid of honour for Maisie.

She had not been in Carterbridge for many weeks; she did not want to come now. Her mother, after a long day's visit at the rancho, had gone to Bakersfield to be with Carter, upon whose twenty-year-old charms a certain widow of thirty was supposed to have designs. Pamela felt that she, herself, had no tie with the town her grandfather had founded, now, and she was willing to forget it and let it forget her.

But to Maisie, on this tremendously exciting and thrilling occasion, she could send no excuse. Maisie, in her affectionate old fashion, had been making it a habit to come down to the ranch occasionally, and had shown in a thousand charming ways her pleasure in the restoration of the old friendship, and Pamela could not hurt Maisie. Maisie had sat at tea in the patio on summer afternoons, gossiping in her innocent, innocuous fashion with Charteris and the old lady; Maisie had confided to Pamela every detail of her affair with

Sam, and what Sam had said, and what the financial adjustment had been. For Maisie's coming of age, and her heiress-ship, and her marriage were all to fall upon this one autumn day, and Maisie was as excited as a fairy-tale princess and a bride in one.

Gregory was busy getting a shipment of cattle ready, but one of the cowboys, chewing tobacco, dangling a long superfluous leg out of the car as he drove, escorted Pamela to Carterbridge, and as they threaded the familiar old streets she felt like a girl in a dream— like a disembodied spirit returning to the scenes it once had known.

The familiar corners, the familiar trees dropping yellowed leaves through still, crystal, hot autumn air, the smell of dreamy leaf fires, the charm of homes and gardens and shops and sidewalks, the excitement of nodding occasionally to some woman who was watering a red-and-gold autumn garden, or of identifying some forgotten landmark, all filled her heart with a sweet sort of wringing pain; she touched her charioteer on the arm.

"Not too fast, Frank. I've not seen it for so long!"

"They're puttin' up a big apartment house there— Pimmerton's father-in-law's goin' to have the drug store in it."

"The Carter Arms," she read, from a big, stretched cloth sign painted in bright red. "Carterbridge's Most Exclusive Apartment Homes. Open Fires—Breakfast Ingles—Sommers Wall Beds."

"That's where our old house used to stand, Frank."

"That's right. I remember that, too. Trees all cut down, huh?"

"Trees all cut down!"

Pamela fell silent, her heart beating fast. The Bill-

ings house, and a new house starting in an ugly muddle
of cement mixers and planks, and the library, and the
Arms . . .

And here was the Broome house, all uproar and
confusion and laughter and delight. Mrs. Broome, en-
veloped in a big apron, with her head tied up securely,
was checking china plates, and held both dirty hands
well behind her as she kissed Pamela.

"My dear—how lovely you look! You'll find our
bride upstairs! Some boxes—shut that door, Annie!
Answer the telephone, Flops. Just put those down
there, Spratsy darling—some boxes just came, Pamela,
and our bride carried them upstairs! Yes, you can go
in Sissy's room, Baby dear. Only ask Sissy first. Go
right up, Pam. You'll find everything simply frantic!"

"I'll come down and help you," Pamela promised.
She wondered, as she saw the pleased, faintly surprised
expression on her hostess's face, if she would have
made that offer a year ago. Had she been such an
oblivious young egotist?

She went upstairs. Men were carrying palms into
the hallway; maids were moving catalogues and medi-
cal instruments away from the doctor's study and pil-
ing them into the skates-and-rubbers closet, under the
stairs; someone was tuning the piano; sweet autumn
airs, scented with damp leaves, and bonfires, and the
acrid odours of chrysanthemums and cosmos, floated
through wide-open doors and windows everywhere.

Maisie was in ecstasies over Pam's arrival; this was
the audience she wanted. Pamela took off her hat and
the old white coat, that still was smarter, as Pamela
Raleigh wore it, than any of the other girls' new coats,
and she and Maisie looked at cups together—scores of
small, delicate cups with the senders' cards tied with

white ribbon to their handles—and looked at silver spoons and bowls and salt shakers, and at plates and glass, and at Maisie's lovely clothes. "Everything—everything!" Maisie kept saying happily. "If I thought for an hour I couldn't think of anything else!"

Then Maisie's mother came upstairs and said that Maisie must write just this one note and then lie down. So Maisie wrote to old Mrs. Trowbridge, who had just sent her a most unexpected silver vegetable dish, and said that by some wretched accident Mrs. Trowbridge's invitation to the wedding had been slipped under a blotter, and would Mrs. Trowbridge forgive her, and come anyway, affectionately . . .

Then she lay flat on her bed, jumping up every other minute to drag something out of her closet, write something down, or answer the telephone, but still nominally resting, and Pamela sat in a deep rocker, enjoying the nearness of the neighbouring houses and the stir of the town after the lonely rancho.

"Pamela, you look lovely. But older and quieter and —different!" Maisie said affectionately.

Pamela smiled. And it was a wiser and an older smile than her face had ever known a year ago. But she did not speak.

"Now tell me," Maisie said, with that happy little air of being loved and spoiled that became her so well, "is Gregory Chard coming in to my wedding, day after to-morrow?"

"Positively—yes. He's smothered—buried—in Herefords, just at the moment," Pamela said, laughing. "But he said to tell you to wait for him, if he wasn't here on the stroke of eight, for he was coming!"

"Herefords! He's kind of a rough-neck—kind of a

dumb-bell—isn't he?" Maisie asked, stretched luxuri-
ously flat, her hands locked behind her head.

"Gregory? No—quite the contrary. He does rather
give that impression," Pamela said, "but I assure
you——"

She paused, thinking of the silent, curt, preoccupied
man, handsome and dark in his loose leather jacket
and shabby sombrero, galloping about the rancho, chattering in rapid Spanish to the cowboys. Odd, curiously
youthful and American, curiously old and Latin,
Gregory Chard. But not a rough-neck, not a dumb-
bell, by any means.

"And is he in love with you, Pam?" Maisie asked
slyly.

"He is not. Just because you're in love, Maisie, the
whole world isn't holding hands, you know!"

"I know—I know." Maisie laughed delightedly.
"Sam and I have to keep reminding each other of
that!" she said. "But seriously, Pam, do you like
Gregory?"

"Very much. In every way! And there was a time
this summer," Pamela said in a matter-of-fact tone,
"when he had a sort of case—for a while, anyway. But
just because persons live in the same house doesn't
mean that they fall in love with each other, Maisie—
almost the contrary, it seems to me. Look at boarding
houses!"

Maisie laughed again. Her world was all laughter
now. But she looked at the beautiful woman sitting idly
and dreamily in the rocker; at Pamela's thin crossed
ankles, at the slim figure outlined rather than concealed
by the plain white dress—the rise of the breast, the
long slender line of the arms, the clean-cut chin and

black-lashed gray eyes—and at the close cap of lustre-less tawny waves that framed Pamela's head. And she had her doubts.

"I'm convinced," she said, "that I'd never have got Sam if you'd been in town."

Pamela smiled and spoke absent-mindedly, without bringing her dreaming eyes back from far spaces.

"My dear, Sam was never a beau of mine!"

It was then that Maisie said, in a little self-conscious rush, with her cheeks suddenly hot:

"Pam. Did you know about—Sue Rose?"

"And Chester? Yes, she told me," Pamela answered, in a voice that was also a trifle strained.

"Who? Sue Rose?"

"Yes. That day this summer when Mrs. Chard had her tea."

"You never told me!" Maisie said accusingly.

"No. I know. We didn't speak of it."

"You mean," Maisie burst forth almost belliger-ently, "that Sue Rose Catherwood told you *that* long ago?"

"Yes. In May—in June, it was."

"Well, I call *that* disgraceful!" Maisie exclaimed.

"Disgraceful?" Pamela echoed mildly, and was still.

"Pamela, do you want me to tell you what I think about it?" the other girl demanded suddenly.

There was a slight pause. Pamela's eyes were far away.

"You can imagine that I'm—interested, Maisie," she said then, simply.

"Well, listen," Maisie began. "I've just been dying to talk to you about this, Pam, but I almost never see you alone—and I don't know, I was afraid, I guess.

But you know last June, just after you'd gone down to Molino? You remember that we all went camping up by the lake? Well, it was on that party that it happened, only it *didn't* happen!" Maisie sputtered. "You know that big room up there? Well, we were all getting our bags in and everything, and Sue Rose and Chester happened to be standing by the hearth, and she said—she was fooling, and she sort of put her arm in Chester's, and she said—'Mr. Hilliard and I are so glad you could come!' And we all laughed about it. And then later the Japanese cook's little baby came toddling into the room, and Chester said—you know the way people fool!—he said, 'Ah, here's our darling; isn't she the image of Sue Rose?' And then, when we were all breaking up at night, they said something about, 'Come on, dear, I'm sleepy!'—you know the sort of thing we always say—and Mrs. Catherwood got up—I give you my word, Pam, it was as raw as this!—and she walked over to Chester and kissed him, and she kissed Sue Rose—he had his arm sort of round her—and she said solemnly to the rest of us, 'Children, not one word of this! I don't want it talked about, and I don't want it even thought about. But,' she said to Chester, 'I am going to say this, my dear boy: I am very glad!' "

Pamela's eyes continued to stare into far spaces; her lower lip was slightly caught in her teeth.

"It couldn't have been *quite* as raw as that, Maisie!"

"Oh, it was. I tell you it was *raw*," Maisie persisted eagerly. "We all simply looked at each other aghast—you know, we think Sue Rose is shy—well, she's about as shy as a carthorse!" Maisie interpolated vigorously. "They simply put it over, that's what they did!"

"Chester's not deaf and dumb, you know," Pamela

said quietly, significantly, after a silence during which neither her position nor expression had changed.

"Yes, but what could Chester do? He looked sort of bewildered, and he laughed and said, 'We'll give you all the surprise of your lives some day, won't we, Susan?'—He calls her Susan," Maisie threw in parenthetically—"So—anyway," she rushed on, "the next day Mrs. Catherwood and Chester were walking up and down beside the lake a long time, and from what he told Sam afterward she just took the whole thing for granted, and he said—he told Sam this—that he liked Sue Rose immensely, and all that, but that he couldn't—he didn't know about his job, and so on, and Mrs. Catherwood said—and this I got from Sue Rose herself!—that they didn't know each other well enough to make up their own minds and that things must just go on as they were for months and months, but that on account of all Sue Rose's money she *would* be glad to have her marry young; 'and,' she said, 'if on New Year's Day you and Sue Rose still feel sure of yourselves, why then we'll see about a definite engagement!' And Sue Rose told me," Maisie said, "that she wanted Chester to be perfectly sure—you know—that she didn't want him to have any—well, you know, regret——"

She floundered and was still.

"Sue Rose said that?" Pamela asked levelly, in a silence.

"She did say that!"

"Meaning——" there was a cold pride, like a knife, cutting through the words—"meaning me, I suppose?" Pamela asked.

Maisie trembled.

"I suppose so!" she stammered. "You—you know we all thought you liked him, Pam."

"Didn't you think more than—liked?" Pamela asked, with a swift searching glance and a bitter little laugh.

Her eyes were idly resting upon what she saw in Maisie's mirror, across the spacious, airy bedroom. A girl—no, it was a woman now; a slender, tawny-headed woman, in a white gown, with wisdom looking out of her gray eyes, and hard-won knowledge shaping her red, red mouth.

"You—I suppose you—loved him, didn't you?" Maisie said uneasily, shyly.

"The tense is wrong," Pamela answered briefly, and Maisie was silent before a passion that made her own engagement cups and embroidered lingerie the mere froth on the boiling pot. "I made a fool of myself about him," Pamela said, in a low tone, as if she talked to herself; "they had to ask me, down at the rancho, not to mope about, making them all miserable, because of my disappointment in love! I dragged myself through the depths—for him; I wrote him, begging him to leave her and come back to me!"

"Pamela, I knew it was bad! But I never dreamed that!" Maisie said in a whisper. "What—he's one of the ushers!—what'll you do when you meet him?"

Pamela looked at her bridesmaid's costume, displayed on a hanger across the room; creamy taffeta cunningly piped in cherry red, with cherries on the shoulder, and cherries on the quaint scoop bonnet.

"I'll tell you what I'm going to do—I'm going to get him back!" she said.

CHAPTER XVI

THE whole bridal party had assembled at Sue
Rose's house for a dinner party when Maisie and
Sam and Pamela Raleigh arrived. Pamela's eyes found
Chester's tall, slender figure and dark head before the
big door had fairly been opened upon the wide, lighted
hallway and the blazing open fire and the cheerful
group.

She had a Spanish shawl of old Mrs. Chard's
wrapped tightly about her; she stood tall and slender
and silent for a minute, still wound about with the
gorgeous splashes of carmine and black and yellow,
smiling at her old friends.

"Pamela!" everybody said ecstatically. They all
swarmed through the wide drawing-room arch and surrounded her, and she turned this way and that, her
exquisite tawny mop never still, as she was kissed and
embraced, her slim hand ready for their greetings.
Chester was almost the last to address her.

He came up, quite naturally and simply, and her
gray eyes looked up at him, and suddenly she was quite
unsmiling, and a little chill seemed to blow like a
breeze over the group.

"Chester——" her voice said slowly, in a silence.

The man cleared his throat. He wanted to say, simply, "Hello, Pamela," of course. They all knew that. But he seemed unable to say anything, and they stood still there for a second, their eyes riveted together, Chester looking pale and dark in his evening clothes, and Pamela, with her fair head and the glowing folds and long fringes of the shawl slipping down her beautiful long body, as radiant as a flower. But his colour had fluctuated a little, too.

Maisie, who was full of graciousness and sweetness to all the world in these days, came swiftly forward, and put an arm about Pamela, and said affectionately:

"Isn't it fun to have her back again for my wedding?" And in the general assent and sudden release of laughter and voices the moment passed. But everyone had seen it.

The dinner was extraordinarily successful for one of Sue Rose's affairs. Usually the entertainments in this house were rich, and dull, and handsome; to-night there was electricity in the air. Maisie's approaching wedding was an obvious reason for the excitement, but Maisie had nothing to do with the real cause of it, except indirectly, as Pamela's hostess. Pamela, eating her dinner, raising her gray eyes to laugh, raising her memorable voice to retort to Sam's or Dick's or Billy's gallantries, was the centre of the scene rather than either hostess or guest of honour.

Halfway through the meal, in a silence, Pamela said quite audibly to the man at her right, a new man in the group who had come down from San Francisco to be Sam's best man:

"Mr. Hotchkiss, I've made a hit with you, haven't I?"

"Oh, help!" said Mr. Hotchkiss simply.

"You wouldn't say that you were in love with me, would you?" Pamela pursued.

"Well, yes, Miss Raleigh," the young man said, "I think I would."

Pamela considered him, thoughtful eyes moving over his face; she was quite unsmiling, in a general gale of laughter.

"That's too bad," she said; "that complicates. I was going to ask you to change seats with Mr. Hilliard for a few minutes; there's something I want to say to Mr. Hilliard. But no matter—I'll have an opportunity to-morrow!"

However, when with some laughter and a gracious permission from Sue Rose Chester came to the seat beside her, Pamela appeared to have changed her mind. She hardly glanced at him, answered him in monosyllables, and addressed him not at all.

Afterward they all walked warm autumn moonlight to St. Luke's and rehearsed day-after-to-morrow's ceremony. It was Pamela who walked up the aisle, with a saintly and rapt expression, to give the organist his time, and who met Walter Hotchkiss there at the altar and breathed an ecstatic "Darling!" as they sank gracefully to their knees on the satin pillows.

"Pam, you are disgraceful!" Maisie said, laughing with the rest.

"Walter and I have been keeping this pretty secret until now, haven't we?" Pamela said lovingly.

"Say, listen—listen——" protested Mr. Hotchkiss, who was completely subjugated by this time and expending all the conversation that he did not direct to Pamela in agitated queries aside, as to where this girl had come from, and who she was, and who was in love with her, anyway.

An hour later they were all dancing, at the Arms, and Pamela once more was in Chester's arms, and the dreamy, swaying music was wrapping them about. Even now she hardly spoke to him. Bending his handsome dark head close to hers, he asked her if she had forgiven him, and Pamela looked straight up at him and said, "Forgiven you—what?"

"For being a skunk," he muttered.

"Entirely," she said dreamily, her slippered feet moving beside his own, her silk-clad form close to his heart, her beautiful, fragrant mop of loose tawny waves almost touching his cheek. "You were—probably—quite right," she said, after a while.

"My God!" was Chester's only answer. "There never—there never," he presently began again, hoarsely, "has been anyone but you!"

It was as easy as that. It was as easy as that, after all. She had needed only the gown, and the courage, and the opportunity. She sat at the table in the dancing room, and looked dreamily off across the hot, filled space, with its monkeys and palms, lanterns and lattices, bared shoulders and bobbed heads, its perspiring musicians and hurrying waiters; all crossed and walled with slowly moving lines of gray tobacco smoke. She twisted her ginger-ale glass slowly, and brought her gaze to Chester's slowly, and looked away again, speaking almost not at all.

The next day he came to the Broome house, and he and Maisie and Sam and Pamela put jars of autumn flowers about, and climbed ladders to hang white ribbons and silver bells. They all lunched together on scrambled eggs and canned asparagus on one end of the dining-room table, and then Sue Rose, who had been having a permanent wave, came in, and they talked wedding, and went up and down through the homely, comfortable house on a thousand errands full of excitement and charm. Chester leaped into his car to run down to the express office for one more box, and Pamela went too, to see if she could get half a yard of green felt to put on the piano under a vase; and when they had the felt and the box, they parked the car under a great oak down near the station, and sat in it, talking, talking, talking—Pamela's slender body turned toward his, Chester's hand gently moving the accelerator to and fro on the idle wheel.

Her starry beauty, the beauty of black-lashed gray eyes and soft fair hair, of wide, chiselled mouth and the flash of white teeth, smote him with a sort of agony, so that whatever he said to her, or she to him, seemed unimportant; merely being together was life again, and more than life. The intimacy between them deepened and strengthened from minute to minute. He hated to lose sight of the swift, eager, slender figure when she went upstairs with Maisie, and the interval in which he did not see her, between tea time and supper, was one of dreamy absent-mindedness, ringing, as the air might ring after a deafening noise, with the one clear note—Pamela, Pamela, Pamela.

They dined at the Arms to-night, a formal dinner to the bridal party given by old Porter Hilliard, and afterward, when the seniors went home, the younger group remained again, to dance. And by this time everyone knew what was happening between Chester Hilliard and Pamela Raleigh—and poor strained, pale little Sue Rose, too.

Chester was making no secret of what he felt, and Pamela appeared to be like a woman in a trance, deaf and dumb and blind to everything but the one voice, the one pair of eyes, the one beloved presence.

They danced very little to-night; Chester danced once with Sue Rose, and Pamela with somebody—with young Hotchkiss, she rather thought—and then Chester said he had a headache, and pla ed himself close beside Pamela at the table, his head a little dropped, her hands linked idly before her, their eyes and words only for each other. It might have been the beginning of their friendship instead of this strange recrudescence of it after so many wasted months.

It was as if Chester's eyes made Pamela conscious of her own beauty to-night, and his low voice taught her her power. She seemed to herself intoxicated with the heady wine of it, the ecstasy of knowing that this man was hers, to be controlled by the laziest lift of her heavy lashes, or the faintest intonation in her voice. She breathed the perfume of herself, she saw the whiteness of her hands, the curve of her round white breast under the satin gown, she knew that the smile on her faintly parted lips was raising him to un-suspected heavens, and that the touch of her warm, white, powdered shoulder, as she leaned suddenly against him, was simply madness.

"You Beautiful!" he whispered.

"Am I?" she murmured back.

"The most beautiful woman in the world," he said.

The old faces, the old music, the old cabaret, the pony girls in Pierrette costumes to-night, the Russian woman with her red and black zither, Yvette in rags, with a beret and bare feet, slashing at her violin . . .

"I know you never can feel to me again—that way," Chester said. "But I can't—I can't give you up!"

Pamela was silent a long time, her face almost devoid of expression, her eyes following the dancers.

"Not even for Sue Rose?" she said presently.

"Not for anybody!"

"My dear Chester, you can't talk this way to me. You're engaged to Sue Rose."

He was silent. Then, "Nothing is announced," he said reluctantly, shamefacedly, between his teeth.

"Why, it's all over town. She told me months ago!"

Again he was silent. There was an expression of real suffering in his handsome face.

"The trouble is, Chester," Pamela began idly. She picked up Carol Billings's fan, and furled and unfurled it carelessly as she spoke. "The trouble is that you are too fascinating!"

He had crossed his arms on the table before him. The expression on his face was one of grim and forced endurance.

"I suppose so," he said briefly, bitterly.

"You say that I never can feel what I did feel for you, again," Pamela presently resumed. "I shall take pretty—good—care that I shan't feel that way again."

The old emotion, a hundred times accentuated, trembled between them in the long silence that followed.

The dancers came back to the table, and panted, and drank, and smoked, the girls reddening their lips, in the unchanged way. Maisie had to go home early to-night; they were all going home early. To-morrow was the big day. She said, "Pamela, did you see Gregory Chard?"

"Here?" Pamela looked toward the door.

"He wasn't dressed. He just stood in the doorway for a few minutes. Sam and I went over to talk to him, and I asked him if he wanted to dance," Maisie said, pressing her bobbed hair against her temples with one tense hand and holding a small mirror in the palm of the other. "He is the divinest dancer—I danced with him once at Mardi Gras. Spanish, I suppose. But he said he was going back to Molino to-night."

"I didn't see him," Pamela said. "I didn't know he was coming to town."

"Well, Pam," Sue Rose asked gallantly, "have you and Chester been having a wonderful talk? I looked at you now and then, and your heads were close together, and you seemed *absorbed!*"

"We settled the entire universe," Pamela said, smiling, raising her eyes, lowering her look and the long dark lashes, while her gaze idly followed the movements of the fan that lay beneath her fingers. "And now," she added, suddenly stirring, "we've got to go home, Cinderella. I promised your mother, you know."

"We'll take you," Chester offered. Sue Rose pursed her lips slightly, smiled a second time rather forcedly. After all, it was her car.

"Oh, no," Pamela declined it. "Sam's taking us home. Or rather, he's taking me home, and we don't mind having poor Maisie along, do we, Sam?"

"Not a bit," Sam agreed, with his wide, foolish smile. "I rather like the little thing!"

"Oh, Sam, don't say that, you crush me," Pamela protested.

"Now, look here—look here!" Maisie exclaimed. "You leave *my* man be!"

The faint significant emphasis on the possessive pronoun gave a moment's pause to the laughter, and the colour crept up into Pamela's clear skin, and Maisie turned scarlet.

"What did I say that for—what a bonehead!" Maisie repeated over and over an hour later, when she was undressing, and Pamela, who had been half an hour in bed, lay with her hands locked under her head, discussing with her hostess the events of the crowded day.

"It didn't matter in the least," Pamela reassured her. "Everyone knew I was vamping him!"

Maisie, in her thin silk undergarments, doubled over while she loosened garters, looked up, smiling, anxious.

"Just—just for fun, of course?" she said uncertainly.

"How do you mean just for fun?"

"Well, I mean, that you—you weren't in earnest, Pam?"

Pamela reflected for a moment.

"Why not?"

Maisie, in her nightgown now, came to sit at the foot of Pamela's bed. Her expression was one of fright.

"Oh, my goodness!" she whispered, under her breath.

"He was mine before he ever was hers," Pamela said, in a queer, defensive tone.

"Oh, but, Pam—she'd kill herself!"

"Nobody—" Pamela paused—"nobody cared whether or not *I* killed myself," she offered, after a silence. But there was no particular conviction in her tone.

"But you're infinitely superior to Sue Rose!" Maisie stated warmly. Pamela laughed.

"That's cute of you," she said simply.

"If he would make love to Sue Rose and let every-one think that they were going to be married and then turn right around and flirt with you—" Maisie said indignantly, as if she were merely thinking aloud— "well, Sam would never speak to him again, I know that! But—why, he can't."

"Can't?" Pamela laughed again, lightly. "Maisie, will you keep it absolutely a secret if I tell you some-thing?" she asked, after a minute.

"Oh, I won't even think of it!" Maisie exclaimed, thrilled and fervent.

"Well—of course, you can tell Sam," Pamela inter-polated.

"No, I won't even tell Sam!"

"My dear—" Pamela smiled, and looked at her bunched finger tips, and back at Maisie's face—"by this time to-morrow night you'll have told Sam Bill-ings everything you ever knew!" she predicted.

The thought of that complete surrender brought April colours to Maisie's confused and radiant face, and she said faintly, "Oh, don't!"

"No, you can tell Sam," Pamela conceded. "It's this. Chester wants me to run away with him—get out of Carterbridge, go East, make a fresh start. He says he doesn't care if his uncle fires him—he doesn't care about anything——"

Her voice dwindled away and she lay staring at the ceiling, with a faint smile touching the corners of her mouth.

Maisie was stricken dumb.

"Would you think I was terrible to do that, Maisie?" Pamela asked.

There was an insolence, a consciousness of power

about her youth and beauty and slimness as she lay there, that wrought upon Maisie as it always had wrought.

"Oh, no, Pam—oh, oh, Pam—" she said breathlessly—"if—if it's as big as that, why, of course—of course—you couldn't say anything," floundered Maisie, meaning that she couldn't, at any rate. "I'd —I'd always forgive you for whatever you did. Only —only I didn't know it would be as—as bad as this!" she ended, awestruck.

"Then he doesn't love Sue Rose?" she presently added blankly, as Pamela continued to regard her thoughtfully, without speaking.

The other girl roused herself a little and sighed, as if the business of getting the whole matter straightened out, even in her own thoughts, was wearisome.

"Yes. Yes, I think he does, in a way," she said. "But —but in a different way. He's—he's extremely unhappy about the whole thing. We had been talking, there at the table, you know, when you all came up. He knows perfectly well that I—cared, cared horribly——"

"But, Pamela, you don't now!" Maisie said eagerly.

"I don't know about that. But, anyway, we were interrupted. And a few minutes later, when you were all getting your coats—I had my shawl with me— and we were standing in the foyer there, alone again, and he said suddenly—what I just told you, about going East and getting married quickly—immediately. He says he's been in hell since he saw me last June."

Maisie remained silent, words failing her in this crisis.

"Pam, it seems so terrible!" she said, after a while.

"It does seem terrible!"

"It'll kill Sue Rose!"

"I wonder——" Pamela mused. The other girl sat staring at her in troubled amazement; Pamela, whatever she felt, betrayed nothing. They had not spoken again when Mrs. Broome came, whispering and affectionate, to their room, pointing out that it was almost two—and this darling girlie needed every ounce of rest she could get, for to-morrow. . . .

Maisie went to sleep, after some whispered communications regarding the morning and Sam, but Pamela lay awake all night long.

She lay quietly, flat on her back, with her wide-open eyes fixed upon the dim ceiling. Across it lights flashed in wide fans and arcs, when a late motor car went by; from the street below the window came a faint dull light.

It was just enough to show, in blocked forms and shadows upon deeper shadows, the varied chairs and tables in the room, the bureau with its pool of dark glass, mirroring only shadows and dimness, Maisie's wedding dress, spreading its petals like an inverted peony, its ivory satin gleaming faintly in the dark, and Maisie's veil, hung delicately on an electric light fixture, and floating to and fro, wraithlike and pure.

In the corners were stacked jeweller's boxes filled with wedding presents, and crates that held linens and china and books. Maisie's new suitcase, with the startling "Y. J. B." that stood for Yolanda Joan Billings stencilled upon it, was wide open upon a chair. Maisie had stood distracted and enthralled to-day watching Pamela and her mother pack it, even while Miss Yates fitted Maisie's new flannel sport skirt; all four women had enjoyed the thrills of selecting the linen, the frocks, the cosmetics and brushes and powders that should first be used by the bride.

Pamela thought of these things carelessly; she thought of marriage, the sweetness of home and family, the romance of a girl, given by father and mother to the new custody. Queer thing, marriage, and, like everything else, important or unimportant in a life, exactly as one made it.

She thought of Chester; it excited and thrilled her to think of him. There was some shame and some amazement at herself when she went over their words together, when she remembered the merciless swiftness with which she had drawn him to her side.

Two days—much less than two days—had accomplished all that she had dreamed, and more than she had dared to dream, in all these lonely months. She had held tight to her courage, she had not lost her nerve, and now Chester was hers again—as she had known he would be!

Her heart thumped, thumped, as she recalled his words and his glances. A brief, scornful little laugh broke from her in the darkness.

How petty it was—two girls wanting one man! Silly. She wondered how many women, after ten years of marriage, liked to remember the fears and jealousies and little meannesses of courtship days.

Gregory had been in town, had he? Funny. He had said nothing about it yesterday. Pamela was diverted from the thought of him by surprise that all this had actually happened since yesterday. Chester. Men wanting girls to marry them.

"I'm in love with Chester. I suppose I am, anyway," she thought irresolutely. "But not the way I've always wanted to be in love. Or else something's happened to him in these weeks I haven't seen him. He's changed or I've changed. Maybe the rancho has changed me."

And suddenly a pang of homesickness smote her like a pain so poignant that for a few minutes she felt that she must arise and slip off toward Molino even now, in the middle of the night. She *must* go back. It was incredible that they had had two tea hours without her in the patio, two evenings of solitaire and poker-patience. An agony of longing for her cell-like room in the old hacienda seized her, twisted her heart as if with violent hands. The arcades, the fountain, the parrot, the puppy—she wanted them all, with the longing of a despairing and helpless child.

"If Chester wants me, let him come after me!" she thought feverishly, jerking the pillow higher under her shoulders, sighing in the dark. "I don't want to go East—I don't want to take him away from this chance here! Perhaps I only wanted to see if I could. . . ."

She got up and went to the bureau and noiselessly turned up a small petticoated light that stood between Maisie's tortoise-shell topped brushes and bottles. Pamela sat down on the little bench and put her elbows on the glass shield, and studied her own beautiful face with its haggard eyes and its pale cheeks and dishevelled, lustreless tawny hair.

Her head felt heavy and dull; she put out the light and went to the window and knelt on the sill.

The cool air came in, infinitely refreshing, and touched her jaded cheeks and forehead kindly; pouring over the garden slowly, like rising waters, was the strange awkward grayness of dawn. The stars were gone, and the sky dark; it was only by a queer taking shape of trees and fences and garage wall that Pamela knew that day was coming, rather than deeper night.

Suddenly she put her face in her hands and began to pray.

"I don't want to do anything silly," she whispered, deep in her soul. "I seem to have done enough silly things for one life! What'll I do now? I can't say one thing to-day and another to-morrow—he says he's going to tell Sue Rose immediately after the wedding that it's all over. Help me! Help me! I don't know what to do.

"I don't know that I want to marry Chester or anyone," she said aloud.

"I suppose I do—I suppose I'm just tired out and blue to-night, and that's what's the matter with me. He and I couldn't stay here—that's positive. I wonder what makes you fall in love with a man?

"Because what could he do here if his uncle put him out of the bank? And I suppose his uncle would. What a mess! Why couldn't we just have fallen simply and quietly in love when he first came here, more than a year ago, and have saved all this fuss? I would have married him in a minute, then. . . .

"No, I can't see us getting married here, with Sue Rose and her mother making all the trouble they could. Poor Sue Rose—if she *is* the richest girl in town, she doesn't have much fun!

"Oh, please——" She had supposed herself to be a believer; she had supposed herself to have prayed before. But to-night's formless supplications, addressed vaguely to forces and powers far beyond her comprehension, were her first real prayers. "Oh, please help me! I don't want to make a lot more mistakes!"

Not at all conscious that she had prayed, and yet

comforted, she turned away from the window. There was dull light in the room now, like a strange dusk. Maisie's little figure, humped under the gay satin comforter, was still lost to the world. Pamela felt cold and weary and mentally exhausted, and yet miserably wide awake.

"I must be a stupid woman," she thought. "I don't believe other women get into such corners! I suppose if I married Chester it might be the best thing to do —to go away—only I don't want to go away. I don't want to leave the ranch; I've never been so happy anywhere as there. He'll talk to Sue Rose to-morrow, if I don't stop him. I'll have to see him before the wedding, and at the wedding, and then afterward at that supper party. I'm not supposed to go home for two more days. I don't know what to do!

"Nothing will interfere with all this wedding fuss, and the kissing and talking and running around—and I'm in for it all, and I just can't go through with it!"

She straightened her cold bed, and looked at it irresolutely in the strengthening light that was still not even dusk in the room. And beside the bed she suddenly knelt again and buried her face in her hands and said the same formless prayer.

"Help me. Help me!"

Afterward she jumped in between covers, and she and Maisie had to be awakened by Maisie's excited and thrilled little sisters late in the morning of the wedding day.

CHAPTER XVII

PAMELA saw Chester many times in the next four hours, but the wedding was over and the bride and groom gone away before he and she were alone together and she could talk to him.

He looked rather strained and pale, and very handsome in his usher's costume—striped gray trousers, cutaway coat, gray tie, and white gardenia. She herself was a vision—somewhat pale, somewhat weary, but exquisitely lovely in her little dark silk frock again. She had taken off the big poke bonnet and her maid of honour's regalia of white taffeta piped in cherry red, and laid them aside with the wilted bouquet of scarlet and white sweet peas. Chester and she had the parlour of the Broome house to themselves in the late afternoon.

Everyone had discussed the wedding exhaustively; the beauty of it, the suitability of it, the smoothness with which everything had been managed, the sweet little trusting look Maisie had given her husband, the fine, protecting smile Sam had given her in return. Now the guests had vanished and the caterer's men were gone; the flowers were drooping in the autumn afternoon and everything was over. There was a clatter kitchenward, where some dishwashing still persisted, and Elinor Broome could be heard far upstairs, weepingly practising her scales, with her flower-girl costume put back in the closet and her old blue middy blouse reassumed. Mrs. Broome was supposedly dozing, with Flopsy, now the daughter of the house, installed on the couch in her room. The doctor had gone off for late calls.

"Did you take Sue Rose home?" Pamela asked.

"I did. And I told her."

She winced and paled a little.

"Oh, I'm sorry you told her. Did she—was she broken up?"

"No; she said she expected it."

This should have been a moment of triumph; Pamela felt it only rather cold and flat.

"I asked you not to."

"I know you did. But it wouldn't make any difference what you did, now, Pamela; it would have to be this way."

Life seemed suddenly flat and gray. Pamela did not smile.

"I'm ashamed of myself," she said.

"Why should you be?" Chester said quickly.

"Oh, to make so much of my emotions!" Pamela said impatiently, distressedly.

He shrugged, not much happier than she.

"We couldn't help it," he offered uncomfortably.

"No. Or if we might have, months ago, we can't now," Pamela said. "So perhaps the best thing is to forget the past and hope that Sue Rose will fall in love with somebody else."

"Sure she will!" Chester said, as Pamela paused.

They were standing in the ugly bay window, looking out at an ugly stretch of porch painted an ugly gray, trimmed rose bushes cramped and ugly in a garden whitened with some sort of autumn fertilizer, a gray fence shutting out a gray street. There was a heavy fog on Maisie's wedding day; the streets were softly fuming and filling with it; passers-by and motor cars were merely gray shapes on paler gray mist.

Pamela looked sidewise at her companion, standing handsome and silent and impeccable in wedding raiment beside her. Chester Hilliard. She wondered why a determined, an almost violent effort at concentration couldn't somehow make him seem real. It was as if she were discussing a dream affair with a dream man. So much fine pale skin and sleek black hair and courteous voice and adoring eyes—but it meant nothing. She was bewildered by a constant impulse to shake herself awake, hurt herself, feel something acutely and uncomfortably again.

"Isn't it a pity!" she said suddenly.

"Yes, it's a great pity. I've acted like a boob," Chester admitted.

"No—it's all been a mess. Sue Rose—probably—" she was thinking of Maisie's revelations a few days ago—"probably took a good deal for granted," she suggested, a faint interrogation in her tone as she glanced at him.

"Oh, well——" He would not betray Sue Rose, and Pamela liked him for it. She tried to appreciate the wonderful moment. Chester Hilliard and she were reunited, and going to be married, and talking about it.

But if she could only wake up! It all seemed so unreal. She had thought this would be a very pinnacle of happiness; she could not find in it an emotion of any kind. It was all gray, vague, dreary, like the fog that had swallowed up Carterbridge.

"The important thing," Chester said, with a new decisive gravity that was infinitely becoming to him, at least in Pamela's eyes, "is that we have straightened this out before it is too late. I'll have to see my uncle about it, right away, and, of course, he may be angry."

"He oughtn't to be. It's none of his business, after all, whom you marry!"

"No, but he expects me to marry——" Chester jerked his dark head in the direction of the Catherwood house and left the sentence unfinished.

"If he *does* suggest your leaving the bank——" Pamela began courageously. She had a puzzled feeling that she ought to say something.

"Oh, that won't make any difference!" Chester said quickly. "He wouldn't do that, probably," he added, reflecting. "He'd just hold me down—an under clerk —indefinitely." He put his arm lightly about her, so that when she turned to look up at him over her shoulder their faces were close together. "This is all that matters!" he said, in a low, tender voice.

It should have thrilled her—it should have thrilled her. But she could feel nothing at all, because she was in a dream.

"You wouldn't mind taking one of those little new apartments down on State Street, Pam? Beginning at the very bottom, I mean. We'd have only my two thousand—for I couldn't very well go on with the Catherwood estate—I'd have to hand that back to Jack Stokes," he went on, with a rueful laugh.

"I'd love one of those apartments on State Street," Pamela said unconvincingly, trying to think what these unfamiliar words meant anyway, trying to shake herself inwardly, shake herself into some sort of sensibility.

"Or," he said, "we could go East. My mother and stepfather are there—I'd get into something better than anything here, most likely. But the main thing— the main thing—" he tightened his arm—"is that whatever we do, it's together now, forever. Isn't it, Pam?"

"Forever," she echoed, looking at his face strangely.

"Does it thrill you?"

"Of course it does! What is this all about?" she said to herself dazedly. Eyes, teeth, hair, smile, and voice—all this was Chester Hilliard, madly in love with Pamela Raleigh, mad enough to throw over Sue Rose Catherwood with her million and his prospects of a position in his uncle's bank and his uncle's will. Chester Hilliard—half the girls in town were crazy about him!

Only Pamela—only Pamela felt oddly dull and insincere as he bent to kiss her and she felt his cheek against her own. What was the matter with her?

"Oh, dear, oh, dear, I will have to run away!" her thoughts said, panic-stricken. Aloud she said, "Let's —let's go very slowly, on account of Sue Rose."

"Oh, we'll have to!" he said, instantly serious.

"Isn't it too bad, Chester?"

"Yes, it is too bad. Too bad that we have to have all these complications."

Pamela looked at the gray street, the gray, pulsing fog, the gray-painted wooden balustrades on the porch. Then she turned back to the room and crossed to the

grate, where a gas log was realistically burning in a
setting of fringes and tassels, painted satin drapes and
marble clock, vases and cushions and leather-bound
gift books.

No help there. Pamela settled herself in a big chair,
and Chester sat opposite, bending forward on his own
low seat, linking his hands together between his knees.
They smiled at each other.

"Tired to-day, aren't you, Pam?"

"I must be. I feel so—blank."

"This is distressing you, isn't it?"

They were talking like strangers. "Perhaps if he
took me in his arms, made love to me," the girl thought
bewilderedly, "it might seem all natural and right
again!" But instantly she knew that she did not want
that, and her mind recommenced its distressed churning, milling, twisting. Perhaps, she said to herself, it
was only the courtship that was thrilling and irrational
and perfect; engagements were definite, human relationships, and all human relationships had their flaws.
Poor Maisie—she had had fuss enough with the Billingses' stuffy old relatives to-day, and with the Bishop,
who wanted her to be married in her own old
church! . . .

"You aren't listening to me!" Chester said, smiling.

She roused herself with a start. "I think I'm half
asleep."

"I'll go away and let you get some rest," he said
fondly. "I'll come for you at seven."

"Oh, but, Chester, I ought to go back to the ranch
to-night."

"That's nonsense," he said. "Did you telephone?"

"No, I didn't. Because I really ought to go back!"

Suddenly she was alive again; she wanted, with

every straining fibre of her being, to go back to Molino. She *must* go back. Everything else faded into
insignificance. It was heavenly to feel even these pangs
of homesickness.

"But aren't we all half-dated with Carol?"

"Yes, I know we were. But I don't suppose Sue
Rose'll go now?"

"No, I don't suppose she will. And I know you and
I won't. Because I'm taking you somewhere to dinner,
all by ourselves!"

This was too swift. She drew back in her chair,
shook her head.

"Oh, Chester, no. Not so soon I couldn't—knowing
that she is all broken up about it."

"I know how you feel," he said. "And I agree with
you. But this is an exceptional case, Pam. You'll be off
to the ranch in a day or two, anyway, and then—unless I can slip away down there occasionally, which I
don't much enjoy—we'll have nothing at all. You see,
I hate those people! I loathe that grinning, lazy-
voiced Englishman who thinks he's so damn superior,
and Jessy says the old lady is nothing but a mischief-
maker—says she's stirred up enough mud—or says
she will!—to ruin the town."

Pamela was staring at him, her head up, her cheeks
scarlet.

"You don't mean Colonel Charteris and Mrs.
Chard?" she interrupted him to demand, aghast.

"Yes, my dear! Don't look so shocked!" Chester
said, amused at her excitement.

"But—but, Chester, you don't know them! Why,
they're *darlings*," the girl said, hurt and amazed.
"They've been simply angels to me—my heart would

have broken if it hadn't been for them—I'm devoted to the Colonel——"

Chester came over to a hassock at her knee and sat there, mirth in his eyes, his fine hands holding her own.

"No, you aren't, my dear," he said, unimpressed. "You were down and out when you went there, you slaved yourself to death for them, and they're grateful. But it's over. I'd be glad, myself, if you never had to go back there again. But since you do, don't be in any rush. Let 'em wait for you! I told Sue Rose," Chester continued, "that I wanted to talk to her mother to-morrow morning. I told her frankly that you and I had been deeply in love, and that we had thought separation," he smiled, "would cure us, and that it simply hadn't—that's all. I told her that there wouldn't be anything sudden or sensational about it, but that in these marvellous days—God! what days they have been!—we'd found out the truth."

"It's romantic, but of course it isn't true," Pamela heard herself, to her own amazement, saying disagreeably.

Chester looked at her quickly, and she saw his jaw stiffen a little.

"How do you mean not true, you bad girl?" he asked lightly.

"I mean that you and I *needn't* have separated—as a matter of fact we *didn't,* until I felt that you—didn't care," she said steadily, yet with difficulty. "Not that we really can tell people the truth!" she added, after a moment. She felt as cold, as remote, as a drifting glacier.

He dropped her hands, his faintly frowning forehead a little puzzled.

"I didn't expect this from the girl who was half ready to run away with me last night," he said reproachfully.

"No, and I didn't expect it either!" she answered. Suddenly she got to her feet and walked to the window again. "I don't know what's the matter with me!" she whispered, as if to herself.

"I think you're tired, and I think it's my fault for tiring you," Chester said, following her.

"No, no, it's not your fault, Chester; it's entirely mine!" she answered, with an effect of feverishness, of breathlessness, that made him frown bewilderedly again. "You must forgive me—I'm sorry." She turned about, trying to laugh, distressed, two spots of colour burning in her cheeks. She put her hands on his shoulders. "I just don't feel—that way, any more," she said. "It's all dead—inside me here. I like you—I even like the thought of marrying somebody, and starting life in one of those flats in State Street—but it's all over —the real thing, the excitement."

Chester, looking down at her, regarded her in stupefaction for perhaps a long half-minute.

"What do you mean?" he said then, expressionlessly.

"Oh, Chester, I'm sorry! I've liked it all as much as you, since day before yesterday—the dancing, the talks—but it isn't real to me any more! It's pretending, now, and I can't—my dear, I can't go on with it. Go back to Sue Rose——"

Chester's face was white; his eyes flashed.

"What are you talking about?" he asked angrily. Pamela's heart quailed.

"It's just come to me—I didn't sleep all night, worrying about it—but it's clear now! It's just—" she took her hands from his shoulders and made her favourite little spreading gesture of freedom—"it's just over," she said simply.

The man's mouth was firmly closed; the flanges of his nostrils moved on his stormy breath.

"That's Charteris," he presently said briefly, when he and Pamela had stood regarding each other for a long space of silence.

"Colonel Charteris! He must be almost forty!" the girl said with a cool, scornful laugh.

"He's thirty-seven, that's all. I asked Chard last summer. And believe me," Chester said fiercely, "he's in love with you—any fool can see that!"

"*You* must be a fool to imagine it!" Pamela said warmly. She stood, struck with the utter novelty of the thought, considering it for a minute. "He just— likes me," she said uncertainly.

"I'll say he just likes you!" Chester agreed satirically.

But Pamela's confused thoughts were too absorbed to leave her free to notice him. She caught her lower lip in her teeth and stared absent-mindedly into space, thinking, pondering.

"That's nonsense!" she said presently, as if she were relieved. "He's hopelessly crippled—he never thought of such a thing. And I simply don't want to marry anyone—that's all. That's all it is, Chester, and I'm sorry."

"Then yesterday down at the station, when we talked in the car, and last night at the Arms—that was just flirting?" he asked, with an air of cornering her.

The scarlet colour dyed her cheeks again, but she looked bravely into his eyes.

"I guess so."

Chester was silent for a few minutes, staring out of the window into the thickening dusk and fog.

"You've made it nice for me," he said bitterly when Pamela, unable to bear the silence any longer, had gone back to her chair and sighed so deeply, so profoundly, that the sound of it reached him at the window.

"Oh, I know it!" she said wearily.

"You mean—" he was back on the hassock, he had her hands again in his—"you mean that you don't love me, dear?" he said, his mood changing to gentleness and entreaty.

"Not—not that way," she answered slowly.

"And don't you know that that only makes me love you more, Pam? Don't you know that I can make you love me again, as you did in those first days of the Rodeo, when we were so happy together?"

"Chester, it may be all the trouble I went through last spring—I don't know what it is. But— I just don't feel that way any more!"

He meditated this in a silence, his eyes upon her face.

"You *did* feel that way, day before yesterday, when you came into town for Maisie's wedding and we all went to Sue Rose's for supper?" he said.

"I think I only thought I did!" Pamela answered, after thought, and with a conscious feeling for words.

"My dear, aren't you tired now, aren't you just overexcited, and perhaps worried about Sue Rose? Isn't that all it is?" Chester asked anxiously, indulgently, as he might have spoken to a child. "Pam, you needn't have that on your mind. Sue Rose is the best little sport in the world; she'll understand. Talking to her this morning I said, 'You'd rather have me say this

now than afterward, wouldn't you?' and she was absolutely game—— What's the matter?" Chester interrupted himself, to ask suspiciously. For Pamela, whose
face had been close to his own, leaned forward suddenly and laid her cheek against his, and she was
laughing.

"Laughing because you're so—so delicious!" she
said, not attempting to check herself.

The man was hurt. He drew back, staring at her in
displeasure.

"Delicious in what way?"

"Oh, because it's all so funny, Chester!" Pamela
said. "Sue Rose and I both wanting you, and the scale
going up and down, and all of us so solemn and important about it! It suddenly—" Pamela wiped her eyes,
grew sober, and pulled herself together—"it suddenly
struck me as funny, that was all," she repeated, her
voice fainting into unwilling laughter again as she
stopped. She got up. "Jenny and Al Scarlett are taking
me back to the ranch at five," she said, "and it's four
now." She stood close beside him, still somewhat
shaken by her recent laughter, infinitely dear, infinitely inaccessible. "I didn't mean to hurt your feelings,
Chester," she said, "but I agree with you and Sue
Rose. It's much wiser to have these conversations before marriage than after. I like you very much, we've
had some wonderful times together, and what you did
for me last winter—well, saved me! But I'll never
marry you or anyone, my dear. Marriage doesn't interest me. I want to work, and read books, and learn
French. I sound mean, Chester," Pamela interrupted
herself to add in a more feeling voice, "but I don't
mean it. I'm only trying to say what you told Sue Rose

this morning—that I've made a mistake in my feelings. That will happen now and again, won't it?"

He caught her wrist.

"What are you trying to get away with?" he asked.
Pamela was a little frightened at his voice. She laid a
placating hand on his arm.

"It would be a mistake, Chester. You were my first
real beau; I don't know how our lives would have gone
if we'd married then—it might have been all right.
But since then I've been so tossed about, I've made up
my mind so often and changed it so often that I—well,
I'm just sick at myself! But this I do know, that whatever *was* between you and me——" She stopped, her
coaxing, beautiful face appealingly raised to his own,
eyebrows and smile eloquent when her words failed.

Chester laughed mirthlessly.

"And you think it can be settled like that?"

Pamela's heart gave another little twist of fear.

"*Mustn't* it be? You don't want me on any other
terms, do you?" she asked.

"I want you on any terms," he said huskily.

"Oh, no, Chester," she pleaded. "Just now you do,
perhaps, when we've been flirting for forty-eight hours
—I blame myself for that. But seriously—reasonably——"

His arms were about her. And all the passion and
fury for which she had ever longed were there at last,
in his face.

"I love you, you cruel, wonderful thing!" he said.
"I'll kill you and myself before Charteris gets you, and
think nothing of it! I'll have you, Pamela, if it takes
me ten years to win you back again. You *did* love me—
in those days last winter when we wrote down the lists
of 'Liabilities' and 'Assets'—in the old house."

"Oh, don't!" she said, near tears at the memory of that despairing girl, who had longed so for this man's love, and lain awake through bitter nights of pain, hoping for it.

"You see!" he said triumphantly, seeing that he had stirred her. "Why, these are my eyes, this is my darling head of curls, you are my girl! Do you think I'll ever let you go? No—never! Kiss me—kiss me——"

But she kept her lips stubbornly closed against the almost angry pressure of his own, and tried to divert his kisses from her mouth to the head she bent and turned away.

"No, no, no," she kept saying. "It's no use. You mustn't—you mustn't——"

He let her go after a while, and stood looking at her, angry and humiliated.

"I'll come down to Molino; that won't stop me!" he said in an odd breathless voice.

"It—" she was angry, too—"it won't do you any good!"

"We'll see. Pamela!" He was all softness, all entreaty again. "Don't be unkind to me," he whispered, taking her hands. "I've got it—I'm sick with love for ..—I tell you I can't stand it! I only want to touch you—to hear you—I can't have you go away from me! Marry me to-morrow—marry me now, to-night, and let all the rest take care of itself—you beautiful, beautiful——"

She was frightened now, ashamed and sorry and puzzled. And with it all she felt a certain pity for him, a certain regret that she could not even feel thrilled by all this—that she was as cool and quiet now as when the scene began.

"What can I do?" she asked, in a whisper.

"You don't have to do anything," Chester said eagerly. "Let me do it! Let me see Sue Rose—let me manage everything; only—only be my little girl, as you used to be!"

Her head, with its tawny waves of hair, shook relentlessly.

"But I tell you it's no *use*," she persisted. "You're making me feel terribly—I'm sorry. . . ."

The man remained standing for a full minute, looking at her.

"And you mean that you're going back to the ranch to-night?"

"Yes—now, in a few minutes, as soon as I can say good-bye."

He continued to stand, stubbornly staring at her.

"This is Thursday. Can I come down Saturday afternoon?"

Pamela shrugged, her face full of distress.

"What *good* would it do?"

"I didn't ask you that. Can I come?"

She met his tenacity with her own.

"I'd rather you wouldn't."

At this, after a full look into her eyes, he half turned toward the window, crossed his arms on his chest, and stood looking out into the damp and foggy dusk.

"My God—my God—my God!" she heard him whisper.

Pamela bore the silence as long as she could, and then burst out remorsefully:

"I wish I hadn't come to Maisie's wedding! If I hadn't—all this wouldn't have happened! I don't know what to do. Why, how—*how,*" she said forcefully, going to him and turning him toward her with an imperative hand on his arm, "could I say now that I'd marry you—just to make you happy? I tell you—I've only just discovered this for myself, Chester—I tell you I don't love you!"

It sounded youthful, school-girlish, as she said it. "But what else can I say? It's true," Pamela said in her heart.

He caught her shoulders, his face haggard.

"Well, then—let that go. Will you marry me? I'll do the rest, I'll make you love me—once you're mine! You've given me a glimpse of heaven, in these two days. Don't turn me down now. It's too late for Sue Rose—it never would have worked, anyway, with you alive in the world. All this might have happened at my wedding, instead of Maisie's, Pam, and then where would we all have been?"

"We're sensible persons," she said, so far from being stirred that she could even wish herself in this moment of the storm a little more impressionable, a little weaker. "Sue Rose cares for you—oh, terribly, Chester. She'll forgive you—she'll be willing to be the one who loves most, for a while."

"Just a moment." He had turned away, now he faced her again. "You would have a man marry one woman, loving another?"

"I say that Sue Rose feels for you what you feel for me, Chester, and you're willing to risk it—with me. Why not with her? We can't *all* be happy," Pamela protested, so confused and tired and excited that she was conscious only of wishing the conversation at an end. Oh, if Mrs. Broome would come downstairs! Or Angela, or Flops, who were always prying about when they were not wanted.

"You *want* me to marry Sue Rose?" he demanded at white heat.

"Well—I want you to do what would make you happy, and make her happy, that's all. I just want you to understand that—well, that I'm sorry I was so—so crazy, these last few days," Pamela floundered.

"I see." Chester was white. "I marry Sue Rose, and Sue Rose marries me, and what do you do? Go down there and study French with Charteris—is that it?"

"I like very much studying French with Colonel Charteris," Pamela said hotly, angered in turn. "I'm not in the least anxious to marry him, as you seem to think, or anyone else! I simply—s-s-simply want to live my own life, and mind my own affairs. I've m-m-mixed things up enough——"

To her horror she felt her eyes sting and her throat thicken; she dropped upon the broad arm of a chair and put her elbows on the table and began to cry.

"I don't know what to do," she sobbed. "I've doubled-crossed Sue Rose and you and myself and everybody, and I want to go home!"

The sound of tears brought Angela Broome, eighteen and pretty, and deeply impressed by the older girl's affair, into the room. And while Pamela dried her eyes and spoke of the wedding excitement and the wakeful night and dear old Maisie gone and other good reasons for emotion, Chester slipped away.

CHAPTER XVIII

A L SCARLETT drove his mud-spattered open car
slowly, with a rattling accompaniment that threatened its dissolution at any second. Jenny, his wife, who
rode, raced, ate, slept, worked, and played close beside
him, was asleep, with her head on his shoulder. They
had been to a Rodeo "up State," and the *Rancho del
Molino* horses and bulls had won more blue ribbons,
and Jenny more trophies, and they were happy and
weary and silent on the drive home.

Pamela sat alone in the back seat, watching the fog
drift away in the twilight and the last leaden strips of
light vanish across the Western ocean. The water
looked as if it had been patted level with hands. The
surf, breaking almost on the low dripping road, was
low, and gulls cried and peeped on the strand.

It was almost dark when they turned in at the ranch
gates; there was a smell of wood fires and aromatic
sea bushes in the cool, darkening air. The windmill
was creaking and creaking over the long line of the hacienda; Pamela could see the lumbering shapes of cows

sheering away from the feeble red lights of Al Scarlett's car. . . .

It was heavenly to find the family in the sitting
room, tea things still in evidence, but dusk in full possession, and lamps lighted; heavenly to slip upstairs to
her cool, plain little room and bathe her flushed, jaded
face, and brush her hair, and be home again. She put
her head out at the opened shutter and saw angles and
shapes that were peppers and adobe walls in the patio;
she heard the sea murmuring its eternal song, and the
hiss of frying and chatter of girls in the kitchen. The
parrot croaked from his perch in the arcade, and a
wandering little night breeze turned the windmill
again with a splash of water.

When she went down the Scarletts, husband and
wife, were relating their adventures, and Gregory and
Charteris and the old lady were attentive and amused
listeners.

"Have her leg fixed up?" Gregory was asking of
some mare.

"Oh, yes, señor, sure," Scarlett said.

"She'll go lame, huh?"

" 'Twasn't nothing but a scratch, Greg," said Mrs.
Scarlett, a rouged, hard-faced little person, with sloe-
black hair in a club on her neck. "We left Buster there
to come down with the cattle," she added, "and I
yelled all night without my baby, didn't I, Al?"

"I says I bet anybody'd think he was fourteen days
instead of years," recounted Al, pleased with his *bon
mot*.

"I'll bet he's having fun. I remember taking some
cattle up to the Oregon Rodeo when I was about his
age," Gregory said, with a reminiscent smile. Pamela
thought that he was always very nice with the men.

She slipped into a big chair, smiling at Colonel Charteris and the old woman, and was silent until the Scarletts had gone away.

Then they asked her about the wedding, and she tumbled it all out topsy-turvy, Charteris watching her with
a smile, Mrs. Chard briskly interrogatory, Gregory
silent, his eyes on the fire. But he was listening, too,
Pamela knew, for his brown hand, playing with the
poker, would halt now and then, and he would glance
over his shoulder at her with a speculative sort of
expression, as if he were putting his own interpretation
on what she said, above her own.

"You didn't come, Gregory?"

"Oh, yes, I was at the church. I stayed in the back
and came home as soon as I was sure they'd seen me,"
Gregory said. "Well, and did all this make you want
to get married?" he asked idly.

"Isn't that rather a leading question?" Colonel
Charteris said, with his nice British laugh.

"You don't have to answer it, Pamela," said Gregory, not looking at her.

"It made me want to do anything—*everything* else,
first!" Pamela said, with a fervour as unexpected to
herself as to them.

"Hello!" said Charteris. "The wind's in that quarter? What was the matter? Wouldn't she say obey?"

"Oh, no—no, it was a lovely wedding. But the whole
thing seemed sort of silly," the girl said. "It was probably in me—the trouble," she added, floundering.

She drew back into her chair in a shadowy, kind
lamplight, and put her slender feet to the fire, and
locked her hands behind her head. There was a silence.

Gregory continued to play with the poker; he did
not look up.

"I gather," Charteris said presently, "that we are not to know what this trouble is?"

"Oh, I'll probably tell *you* the whole thing, as soon as we are alone together!" Pamela said, with an excited, rueful little laugh. And as her eyes bent to his, she remembered Chester's absurd suspicions, and the colour crept into her face, until there was the blaze of satin red poppies under the wide-open, smiling gray eyes and the thatch of tawny hair.

Their look clung together, and she thought that he was conscious, too; thought that she saw his bronzed, hard skin darken. Apparently Gregory did not see anything; he had not stirred; and the old lady was half asleep.

"W-what?" Pamela stammered then.

"I said, 'Any time you say,'" Charteris repeated it smiling.

Her heart began to beat hard and fast. Why—why —he had always seemed more like a father. Why— why—he was twenty—or no, it was only sixteen or seventeen years older than she. But Robert Charteris was of another generation, and in experience and culture and character and position she had always felt him far, far above her.

"Someone making love to you, was that the trouble?" Gregory said unexpectedly, in his new, easy, half-amused and half-scornful manner.

She sent a glance toward Charteris.

"You're a good guesser," she said. "An old beau of mine."

Gregory said nothing for a while. Then he drawled, in the smooth, silky, Latin voice he occasionally used:

"I thought girls liked that. I didn't know that would be called 'trouble,' exactly."

It was Charteris she was trying to amuse; he loved to hear her half-earnest, half-whimsical confidences. But she had not meant to go quite so far. Some odd impulse pushed her on against her own will.

"Not when you don't want to marry a person," she said, "and have told him so many times, and are afraid —you *will!*"

Gregory glanced up now, and she saw the dark eyes in the dark face, and the flash of teeth.

"Oh, I didn't know," he said mildly, returning to the fire.

"And did he—this admirer—worry you, Pamela?" Charteris said affectionately, indulgently, after a while.

"Oh, yes—he made me cry," she answered, in her honest little-girl mood. "You don't know how I wanted to get home to-night!"

"Home?" Gregory said with a quick glance, taken unawares.

"Here," she explained.

"And nice to have you, little girl," Charteris said. "We've missed you. I'm glad the fleshpots weren't quite so charming as you thought they would be."

"A man," Gregory said conversationally, lazily, in a pause, "should never ask one woman twice. I should imagine that that would be the quickest way to lose her respect, and his. If he wants her and can't have her, let him try somewhere else. There are always plenty of pretty, sweet, good girls to raise his children and manage his house and love him, and what more does he want?"

"Exactly!" Pamela said, with a nervous little laugh.

"Most women are exactly alike, anyway," Gregory pursued, busy with the fire.

"But most women are not like that one," Charteris

thought, looking at the slender wearied girl in the armchair, her slim white figure and bright head lighted fitfully by fire and lamplight, her slim ankles crossed, her cheeks poppy pink, her long-lashed gray eyes on the fire.

"When you say that, Gregory, it only proves that you have never been in love!" Pamela said.

"Love is a much better thing than being in love," Gregory argued casually. "And a man may love many women—love all fine, pure, good women—yes, and some of the other kind, too!" he added under his breath.

"You sound like a sultan or a Mormon or something!" Pamela said disgustedly. "He doesn't know anything about it, does he, Colonel?" And then suddenly she lowered her arms, and buried her face in her hands, and gave a child's deep sigh of content. "Oh, but it's so good to be home!" she breathed.

Later that night, after the tired and early breaking-up of the circle, Pamela, descending for a hotter hot-water bottle for old Mrs. Chard, was startled to discover Gregory still musing by the fire in a room that was lighted only by the sleepy embers.

He got up, and lighted a lamp to guide her, and accompanied her into the big, dim, warm, odorous kitchen that was scented deliciously with sour Spanish bread and apples and sweet butter. Pamela poured the boiling water from the kettle slowly, spilling some of it on the hot range with a great rising of steam.

When they went back to the sitting room, Gregory, about to return to his chair, delayed her a moment.

"Did you know I was going down to the Mexico place?" he asked carelessly. "Some time soon—in a few weeks."

"Oh, no! I'm sorry. For how long, Greg?"

"Indefinitely, I guess."

"Indefinitely!"

"I guess so. I may come up now and then. I'll probably," he said deliberately, "get married down there."

Pamela's amazed eyes shone at him like star sapphires in the lamplight.

"To whom?" she demanded.

"I'll write you all about it," he assured her, yawning. And in parting, he added, "Too bad that—that the old beau, who made love to you, wasn't the right one."

She turned back.

"How do you mean the right one?"

"Well—you told me——" he blundered. "Hilliard, I mean!" he said, almost with an effect of anger in his embarrassment.

Pamela turned toward the stairs again. "How do you know he wasn't?" she demanded, in level tones.

"Well, because—because naturally, *that* wouldn't have been 'trouble'!" Gregory said simply.

The girl was still, her back half turned toward him in the dim, shadowy room.

"No, of course not," she said.

"Well, good-night," Gregory said.

"Good-night, Gregory." She closed the door behind her, and after a few minutes he could hear the murmur of her voice and his grandmother's voice, upstairs.

After a while the voices stopped, and there was utter silence in the hacienda. Gregory knew that Pamela must be sleeping the sleep of exhausted infancy, after the excitement of the town visit and the wedding and the white night to which she had confessed.

For himself, he felt that he would never sleep again. He was gone early in the morning and had his breakfast down at the branding corral with the cowboys, three miles from the house. The cattle were soon to be turned out to range for the winter, and the year's crop of calves had to be marked.

"That'll do for an excuse," he had thought, leaving this message with Aña when he came downstairs at six o'clock. And immediately he had added, in his own soul, "Why should I worry about excuses? It's none of *her* business!"

He returned late for dinner to find Pamela playing a double solitaire with Colonel Charteris, and after that, for some days, things went on as usual. The autumn weather was clear and sweet, warm in the daytime with blue sunlight sparkling on the Pacific, and gloriously red at six o'clock, when the sun went down and the crimson light lingered in the little lanes between the cabins and dropped slowly, in blots of fire, through the branches of the eucalyptus. And the ink-black nights were chilly, with a sharp reminder of winter in the tick   oises falling leaves made on the wooden roofs of the piazzas, a film of pearly frost on the corn shocks, and the cattle's breath rising visibly into the morning airs.

Every day or two young Hilliard drove down from town to see Pamela. He drove a small runabout and parked it outside the patio door, beside the palings of the old gardens, and even if he stayed but a few minutes, he always saw her alone for at least half of them. Gregory was civil to him, Charteris and Mrs. Chard only a little more. Exactly what Pamela felt none of them was able to discern.

She walked with Chester along the beach and up across the meadows, where a line of willows marked the course of the creek. Charteris thought she always seemed a little relieved when her caller went away, and drooped a little and grew quieter when he came; the old lady expressed a crisp wish that the girl could make up her mind; Gregory made no comment whatsoever.

Chester's manner was serious and determined; he seemed to Pamela a different person from the gallant Eastern youth in the becoming sports clothes who had made the Rodeo so memorable to her only eighteen months before.

He *was,* in fact, a different person: grim, stubborn, and bitter. And she was no longer the girl who had dreamed away her ignorant childhood in the old Carter house, innocently teasing her mother for the hats and frocks and pleasures that alone would have accounted for the entire Raleigh income, innocently exultant over a new admirer.

"I do my best," she said in a troubled confidence to Charteris.

"To like Hilliard, you mean?"

"To feel—*something,* for him. I walk about with him," said Pamela, "I look at him—he's handsome, you know."

"Very," said Charteris gravely.

"I try to remember how I felt about him less than a year ago; I tell myself," Pamela pursued soberly, "that he's just what he was—he's more than I deserve! His uncle's failing, it seems, and they really need him at the bank; there's no talk of his being dropped, any more. He's going to have a raise. And Miss Catherwood—the girl whose business he managed, the girl who was so crazy about him—has forgiven him—her mother hasn't, but that doesn't signify!—and there's *no* reason he shouldn't go right

ahead, and why we shouldn't get married, some time
next year, except—except——"

"Well, go on. Except what?"

"Except simply that I don't want to, Colonel. You
know," Pamela elucidated, "when you're madly, desperately in love with a person, there's no explaining it,
and when you're not in love—well, it's simply a blank,
and there's no explaining that either. I *want* to be in
love with Chester Hilliard, if only for my own self-
respect. I say that I *will* be in love with him—and I
can't."

"Then I wouldn't let him come down here, Pam.
You can see that the poor fellow is unhappy. I'd not
encourage that, at least."

"Encourage it!" Her face was crimson. "Why, I
beg him—I order him not to come down here again!"
she said quickly, sensitively.

"And he pays no attention?"

"He says I don't know my own mind!" She drooped
and looked at her companion doubtfully, and Charteris laughed. "Oh, it's not funny," Pamela said shamefacedly. "He's quite right. Just think of the way I've
blown hot and cold—and what it's cost me, and what
poor Sue Rose has been through!"

"But I thought she was in love with this Don Juan
anyway—from the very beginning!"

"Well, yes; she told Maisie she was."

"Then I wouldn't worry. She would have lost him
anyway," Charteris said comfortably.

"But I don't *want* her to lose him!" the girl said
anxiously, ruefully.

"You mean that you expect this man who comes
glooming down here, and never takes his eyes off you,
and changes colour every time you speak, to marry

some other woman?" Charteris demanded, studying her face curiously.

"Not—not immediately," Pamela said stoutly. "But after a while. Only—I don't know how to stop his coming, and as long as he comes . . ." She spread her slender hands eloquently.

"Can't he take 'no' for an answer?" the man asked.

"Take no? He can't take a thousand 'noes'!" the girl fretted.

Charteris mused. "I don't think you ought to have to put up with that," he said. "I rather thought you were trying to make up your own mind—I don't mean to marry him—for I thought you cared for him and would do that anyway. But to take the step, everything considered—I mean this other girl, and the uncle, and the whole situation generally."

"Oh, no—*no!*" she answered fervently, hopeful eyes on his face.

"Oh, well, there ought to be some way to stop *that,*" the man said temperately. "Would it do any good for me to speak to him—as a big brother?" he asked.

Pamela was assorting hose, matching them, rolling them, jerking them into shapely little folded oblongs. She had on a blue cotton dress and a white sweater; the late September sunlight fell shining and soft on her bright hair. Charteris noticed the flawless curve of her clean-cut jaw and throat, the busy slender fingers, and the lowered thick lashes.

She looked up, and he saw April colour flickering in her face, and an odd, abashed smile in her eyes.

"Chester's insane with jealousy as it is," she observed.

"Of Gregory?" he asked quietly.

"Gregory! Heavens, no! Nobody ever seems to

count Gregory in at all. Gregory says he's going to
marry immediately, anyway," she added lightly. "Do
you suppose he will?"

"I shouldn't wonder," Charteris said idly, watching
her closely.

She breathed oddly for a moment, looked down at
her work, looked up again.

"Oh, I hope he won't! It's none of my business,"
Pamela said. "But I think it would be a mistake to
jump into marriage with—just anyone. You can't do
that. You have to be in love!"

"I don't see Gregory falling in love, somehow,"
Charteris said, with a faintly interrogative inflection.

"No. And yet he wants to get married," Pamela submitted doubtfully. "He despises *me*," she added, with
apparent irrelevance.

"Oh, I don't think so," Charteris protested mildly.

"But he *does*," the girl persisted. "I think he thinks
I'm vacillating and school-girly—and, of course, I
am!" she added ashamedly. "He talks to me so scornfully, he never listens to me when I say anything, and
he doesn't—honestly—seem to like me."

"Perhaps he thinks of you as Hilliard's property;
he hasn't had any special reason to know exactly how
things stand," Charteris suggested.

"When I get out of this," Pamela said, after a silence, "I'm done. I may marry ten years from now,
when I'm thirty. They say marriages at thirty are
often the happiest. I'm going to let men *alone* for ten
years! I don't know what gets into me. I feel sorry for
Chester, and then I'm too nice to him, and to make
him realize that there really isn't any use in it I'm
mean to him again. And with Gregory I'm a perfect
fool. If ever I'm going to do some absolutely bone-

headed thing, it always seems to be when he's around!
I'd just told him that I was practically engaged to
Chester, last summer, when Sue Rose told me of her
engagement to him, and then Chester kissed me—or
sort of kissed me—by the fountain here, and it had to
be Gregory who came to find me, and saw it, and then
he came into Carterbridge the night before the wedding and was looking on at the dancing at the Arms,
and by bad luck I didn't see him at all; I was at the
table, talking to Chester as if my life depended upon
it! And now, of course, Gregory thinks I'm madly in
love with Chester, seeing him down here all the time,
and if I suddenly came out with the news that it's *all*
over—well, I suppose Greg's right about women. A
man ought to pick a wife just to have children, and
take care of him, and raise flowers, and all this talk
about being in love is just nonsense!"

"But it interests me to hear that Hilliard is jealous,"
said Charteris dreamily, when the hosiery was all
arranged and Pamela had put the basket on the sunshiny flagging beside her chair and was engaged with
the parrot.

"Hello, Polly—come on, come on, Polly," she
crooned, as the big bird walked up her arm and sidled
against her cheek. "Don't bite me, darling," said Pamela. She stood looking down at Charteris, a confused
and bashful and wholly enchanting smile on her face.
"No, Chester's jealous of *you*," she said, with her own
air of little-girl daring.

"Me?" the man echoed stupidly. And Pamela saw
the deep red colour creep up into the bronzed face and
a look at once embarrassed, amused, and annoyed
come into the gray, keen English eyes.

"You."

"Oh, for Heaven's sake!" Charteris said, with a brief laugh.

"He thinks you and I—with our French and games and books and afternoon tea——" Pamela began gaily. But suddenly some odd psychic change came over her, and her throat grew dry, and her face red. She kept her eyes bravely on his, her lip bitten and her head hanging a little, like those of an ashamed little girl.

For a long moment there was silence in the patio while they looked at each other. Then Charteris said in a low voice:

"Come here. I can't go to you."

Pamela, not moving her eyes from the man's face, tossed the parrot to his perch, and went to take a wicker hassock at Charteris's knee, and put her hands in his.

"There might be sillier things to do than that, Pamela," he said, not quite steadily. "I like you an awful lot, you know. You like me better than you do Hilliard, don't you?"

She was very pale.

"Oh, a thousand, thousand times!" she whispered.

"And that would end his visits, Pamela, once and for all."

"Yes, but—'Lisa——" she faltered.

"My wife? Of course. But, after all, I'm a broken man who isn't going to be separated from 'Lisa for much longer; it wouldn't rob *her* of anything," Charteris said.

"But, Colonel—Colonel—you'll think I'm just a plain fool," stammered Pamela. "Only—about being in love, you know?"

"You mean you're not in love with me?" he said quietly, amusedly, almost teasingly.

"But I love you!" she said quickly.

"And haven't we just decided that loving is better than being in love?" He still held her hands fast. Pamela had drawn herself away, full arm's length on the hassock; her face was still pale and her eyes dazed. "Why not?" Charteris went on. "No hurry about it, but think it over! It would mean an end to other men's attentions, wouldn't it? And it would mean that you had an established position when I died, or my grandmother died, and enough income to do what you liked with. It would mean that Audrey had a stepmother that she adored—and who'd lose anything?

"On the other hand, you're only twenty and I'm past thirty-seven," Charteris pursued, as Pamela, staring at him with wide gray eyes, did not speak. "I might live forty years, I suppose, and then you'd get the worst of it. Greg may bring this imaginary wife of his in here any day, and then we'd have to get out."

"Oh, yes, we'd have to get out then!" Pamela said, speaking as if to herself, in a relieved, barely audible breath.

"And then, of course, in the sense of pure romance," Charteris said, in a lower tone, "it wouldn't be like any other marriage. You know that, of course? No new ties——"

She could answer this, it was at least definite and comprehensible.

"Oh, yes—yes, I know that!"

"It would be, strictly, a *mariage de convenance,*" said Charteris, smiling. "But you would have a very adoring husband, my dear, who would truly try—with all his heart and soul—to make you happy!"

She slipped to her knees on the flags beside him and put her shamed and laughing and puzzled face impulsively against his cool, long hand. And he felt that the thick lashes that framed her innocent gray eyes were wet. He bent over and kissed the top of the tawny head, and caught the fragrance of her, sweet and young, wet cheeks blazing with colour, neck white as daisy petal against the dark blue gown, warm firm hands holding his own.

"Who was that?" she said, suddenly on her feet, brushing her cheeks childishly with the back of her hand, looking toward the patio arch.

"Nobody. Only Greg. He didn't see anything, or if he did, it doesn't matter!" Charteris assured her. "Well, did that scare you? Will you think it over?"

She was thinking it over now.

"Could it be a secret?" she asked youthfully.

"Of course it could!"

"And it wouldn't have to be for a long time," she stipulated quite innocently.

"A long time, or a short time, any way you liked it," he assured her generously.

"I could write it to Chester to-night!" Pamela said eagerly.

"Now, if you liked!"

Her eyes were fairly blazing with excitement. Suddenly she checked herself, and came to the hassock, and sat down again, reproachful and grateful eyes on his face.

"Colonel, are you doing this just to get me out of a scrape?" she asked.

"Watch me carry it through, if you'll have me!" the man answered gallantly. "Men don't do these things for fun, you know."

Pamela, unconvinced, studied his pain-tortured, finely aristocratic face at close range.

"If we—if we *do*," she said, flushing deliciously, "I'll—I'll make it up to you!"

"I know you will. Oh, Greg!" Charteris called over her shoulder. "Come here a minute!"

Pamela whirled about. She had not known that Gregory, in sombrero and riding boots, with his old leather jacket, was descending the narrow wooden stairs from the narrow upper balcony.

He came toward them. He looked distraught.

"Anything wrong?" Pamela asked, alarmed by his expression.

"Not at all," he said briefly. "What was it, Bob?" he asked his cousin, with an air of cold patience.

"Are you going into Carterbridge?" Charteris countered.

"No. I'm going down to the lower ranch. I'll be there a couple of days," Gregory said darkly.

"Oh, well, then, I needn't have called you back!" Charteris apologized. "Pam had an important letter she wanted to mail, and I thought perhaps—— But that's all right, go on your way!"

"Not going to be here for lunch, Greg?" Pamela asked blankly. "Why, you said to have steaks. And Goldie made a special trip for them, because Tony wasn't going into town!"

Gregory looked at her, breathing hard, trembling.

"Steaks!" he almost shouted, with a loud laugh. "My *God!*"

Pamela sent Charteris a significant look. "You see?" it said. "He hates me!"

"Could you get back for supper, Greg? We'd keep them until then," she suggested.

"Certainly," he said insolently. "I could drive three hundred miles easily, see about the cattle, and drive home again. It's only eleven now—I could take that letter into town before I start, too!"

"Well," said Pamela, with spirit, "it was only because you *asked* for the steaks that I mentioned it—it doesn't seem fair to Anita or Aña to have them go to all the fuss of a hickory fire—and then walk out as coolly as if——"

"Good-bye!" Gregory said rudely, as her earnest, troubled little-girl voice hesitated. And over his shoulder he flung a Parthian shot at Charteris, with his flashing white grin in a copper-brown face. "Can you beat it? Married stuff, Bob. I have to be here on account of the steaks! It's going to be very different here! What was it?"

He halted in the patio doorway, his wide sombrero already shading his black eyes, arrested by some involuntary word from Pamela.

"What did you say?" he asked, coming back to her.

"I said that—it doesn't matter what I said!" Pamela said, vexed and confused and close to tears.

"Pamela said not to forget the perfect wife you are going to bring back with you, Greg," Charteris said.

"All right, I'll remember!" Gregory said coldly, with a final parting bow. His big figure shut out the vista of green garden and blue sea for a minute, and was gone.

"You see, he hates me!" Pamela said, in a sort of furious and excited triumph, when she and Charteris were alone again. She had taken a few steps in the direction of the patio doorway; now she turned about, fingers linked and resting on her chest, eyes bewildered and dark with pain, and breath coming unevenly. She sat down on the hassock again.